A SEMBLANCE OF JUSTICE

BASED ON TRUE HOLOCAUST EXPERIENCES

WOLF HOLLES

ISBN 9789493322646 (ebook)

ISBN 9789493322639 (paperback)

ISBN 9789493322653 (hardcover)

Publisher: Amsterdam Publishers, The Netherlands

info@amsterdampublishers.com

A Semblance of Justice is part of the series WWII Historical Fiction

Copyright © Wolf Holles 2024

All Rights Reserved. No part of this publication may be reproduced or transmitted in any form or by any means, electronic or mechanical, including photocopy, recording or any other information storage and retrieval system, without prior permission in writing from the publisher.

CONTENTS

Special note	v

PART I
RECOGNITION

Chapter 1	3
Chapter 2	7
Chapter 3	16
Chapter 4	24
Chapter 5	28
Chapter 6	32

PART II
REMEMBRANCES

Chapter 7	37
Chapter 8	118
Chapter 9	123

PART III
RETRIBUTION

Chapter 10	183
Chapter 11	186
Chapter 12	190
Chapter 13	193
Chapter 14	197
Chapter 15	211
Chapter 16	216
Chapter 17	222
Chapter 18	229

Memoir by Wolf Holles	235
Amsterdam Publishers Holocaust Library	237

SPECIAL NOTE

Scenes and locations described in Nazi concentration camps and in the prewar area are real and are based on a true story.

However, this is a work of fiction. Any resemblance of the characters in the work to real persons, living or dead, is purely coincidental.

PART I
RECOGNITION

1

The Courtyard by Marriot Orlando was an unpretentious, five-story beige brick hotel with a spacious lobby, filled with tourists. Two clerks were working behind the reception desk when William Wingort, an elderly guest in his early seventies, walked through the lobby to breakfast. He was tall and white-haired. A cautious and perceptive man with intense, sad deep-brown eyes.

William sat down at a corner table in the breakfast restaurant. There were about 30 people in the long room, most of them business people. Some guests stood lined up at the expansive breakfast buffet. There was the sound of clinking glasses and the soft hum of voices in the room. The waiter came to William's table. "Would you like to order, sir?"

"I'll take something from the buffet. Thank you."

William filled his plate with scrambled eggs, pancakes, and a cup of coffee, and sat back down. As he glanced around the room, he saw old people like himself enjoying their vacation. Matt, his only son, was right to get him to take a vacation. Away from New York. Away from his memories. He was enjoying the warm weather and relaxing. After 50 years in business and the death of his beloved wife, it felt great just doing nothing. It was a nice distraction. He sighed. He thought about his beloved Megan and how she would have enjoyed this trip.

As he enjoyed his meal, his gaze fell on two people sitting a few tables away. One was an elderly, distinguished-looking man and the other was an attractive, chicly dressed 30-ish woman. He sat sipping coffee and was talking to her. They looked like business people.

He watched as the waiter went to their table to check if they needed anything. The man rudely waved him away then, glancing around, probably unintentionally, he turned to stare across at William for several seconds before his eyes turned back to the woman. William put down his fork and frowned. *No need for him to treat the waiter that way*, he thought. *Mean, dismissive.* He watched as the man turned toward him briefly. He saw that the man's face was scarred. It was unusual, yet there was something familiar about it. Where had he seen it before? Who is he? He searched his memory. *Hey, maybe...* No, no. William didn't finish the thought. No, no. He could feel the blood rush to his head. Could it be? No. It couldn't be him. Too many years had passed. *You're just imagining things*, he told himself. Not that sick SS guard Pavlenko. No, not him. Not Pavlenko. Definitely not here in the US. That sadistic Lukas Pavlenko who had tormented him and his family in the camps during the war had to be dead by now. It's the damn memoir he finished before leaving on his trip. The images of that Nazi bastard were fresh in his mind. *Forget it*, he told himself. Whew! He took a deep breath. With relief he watched the man and woman get up from the table and walk out the door. Looking down at his hand, William noticed it was shaking. He lost his appetite. He pushed his plate away and got up to follow them. He had to be sure.

They were standing outside the hotel, waiting for a car. William stood behind them, near enough to listen to them. His ears pricked up. They were chattering away in German about some business deal. His German was rusty after all these years, but he could understand them. William held his breath. He felt his body tense. He turned to look more closely. *My God!* he thought then, *it's him, it's him!*

Yes, features change. His face was wrinkled and his black hair had turned white. But that scar running from the man's left eye down to his chin. It was burnt in his memory even after six decades. The slightly bent posture, the sharp features, the raspy, husky voice – it all fit.

Chills flooded over him like watching a coiled poisonous snake slithering through the grass towards him. They had stood four feet away. On an impulse, his hands trembling, William reached for his cell phone. Without being seen, he snapped a picture of the couple.

Moments later, the couple got into a Mercedes and drove away. He checked his phone. The photo was clear. *Perfect*, he thought. He went to the business office and had the clerk help him print out the photo. Then he returned to the lobby and walked over to the concierge of the hotel seated at a desk.

The man glanced up. "How may I help you, sir?"

"I have a favor to ask of you."

"Sure. I'd be happy to help if I can."

William held up the photo. "Do you know this man?"

The man studied the picture for a moment and nodded. "Oh yes," he said. "I've seen him at the restaurant often."

"Do you know his name?"

"I am sorry," the man said, looking at him blankly. "We are not allowed to give out personal information about our guests."

"I understand," William said, taking a 100-dollar bill out of his pocket and placing it on the desk. "It is very important to me."

The man looked around quickly and took the money. "He is Bruno Stettler," he said. "Mr. Stettler is the owner of Hulot & Associates in Orlando. He comes here for business meetings."

William returned to his room and stared at the photo. The bastard had escaped to America, changed his name, and prospered. Where was the justice? He'd tortured and killed so many Jews in the camp. William had been just a boy then, a frightened prisoner, unable to stop the monster. But now? He was not afraid anymore. He couldn't hurt him anymore. Fate has brought him here and perhaps now he could finally see justice done.

He looked up Hulot & Associates on his phone. It wasn't far

from the hotel in downtown Orlando. *I have to know if he is the same man*, William thought. I have to. He cancelled his planned events for the next day and resolved to confront the man at his office.

That night, lying in his bed fighting against sleep, his brain filled with nightmares; frightening visions of his friends with their fear-haunted eyes and his two brothers, Eli and Josef, each with hollow-eyed faces turning to him, smiling sadly before more close-ups moved on to his weeping mother and his father waving goodbye to him; vivid images of the starved nude corpses, their mouths hanging open, piled up like cords of wood on trailers dumped like trash in ditches, or the inmates with emaciated faces and with their heads shaved standing outside at roll call in all weathers to be counted and be recounted ... and Pavlenko barking insults and orders at them.

He had survived the ravages of the Holocaust, but had seen the misery of thousands. He watched as his mother was tortured, his father sickened and dead. The memories were burned into his soul. He would never forget what that bastard Pavlenko and his cohorts did.

Now he must make him pay.

2

After breakfast the following morning, he took a cab to the offices of Hulot & Associates. He approached the receptionist. "My name is William Wingort. I'd like to speak to Mr. Stettler, please."

She looked up. "Do you have an appointment?"

"No, but–"

"What's it about please?"

"I have some information," William said, "of a personal nature for him."

"I see. You need to make an appointment."

There was a pause. "Okay. When is he available?"

"You'll need to contact his office directly."

"Then, could I just leave him a message?"

"Certainly."

William reached in his pocket, took out a notebook he'd gotten at the hotel, tore out a blank page, and wrote something down. He folded it and handed her the paper.

"I'll be sure he gets the message, Mr. Wingort," she said smiling.

After he left, the young woman called Carol Best, saying she had a message from some old man for Mr. Stettler.

"Mr. Stettler is in a meeting. I'll come out to get it. Thanks, Liz."

After his meeting ended, someone knocked on the door.

"Come in," Stettler said.

Carol Best, his vice president in charge of communication and operations, walked into the office. In her thirties, she was tall, attractive and impeccably dressed. She'd worked with him for years, moving up the ranks to become one of his most trusted people.

"Sir," she said, "we just received this message from an elderly man at the front desk. He said he knew you."

Stettler shot her a frown. "Well, what is it?"

Carol handed him the sheet of paper.

Stettler stared at the message: *I KNOW WHO YOU REALLY ARE. I KNOW ALL ABOUT YOU. I KNOW WHAT YOU HAVE DONE. WILLIAM WINGORT.*

He stared at the note for a long moment. His mouth tightened and his eyes hardened menacingly. He looked up at Carol. "Who was this man?"

"Just an old man," she said dismissively. "Dressed like a tourist with a European accent."

Stettler grunted. "I never heard the name. Probably some small business looking for a handout."

"Yes, probably," Carol said, and rose. "Should I try to find out more information about him?"

He tried to remain calm. "If you have time. But first, we need that report about the Smithson deal."

After Carol left, Stettler got up and walked over to the bar. He poured himself a gin and vermouth and lit a cigar, and sat back down behind his desk. He felt a deep sense of pride. He glanced around his plush office and let his mind wander back to the days he had started from scratch, creating the company.

Born Lukas Pavlenko, he grew up in a working-class family in Lithuania. His father was German, an electrician. His mother was a Lithuanian nurse at the hospital. His parents and his brother Vladas, were content with their lives. But not Lukas. Lukas kept looking for something else. He was waiting for the opportunity to escape boring, working-class life.

When Lukas turned 18, Hitler had come to power in Germany. He would sit at a friend's house, listening to Hitler's political, inspiring speeches on the radio. The Führer promised the Third Reich would conquer the world and reshape it for future generations. With his parents' blessing, he moved to Berlin and joined the Hitler Youth. The strikingly, handsome teenager with Germanic features was cheerily welcomed by the new regime.

On September 1, 1939, World War II began. Young Pavlenko joined the elite storm troopers of the Waffen SS. Pavlenko progressed through the ranks, gaining the attention of his superiors for his dedication and ruthless adherence to order. In 1943, Lukas was promoted and transferred to Bergen-Belsen, the detention camp for Jews and other undesirables. Anxious to make his mark, he masterminded special ways and methods to make the real agenda of the extermination of the prisoners more efficient and brutal.

However, in 1945, hearing the reports that the war was going badly and the Reich near collapse, Pavlenko joined many of his fellow SS officers and fled the camp a few days before Bergen-Belsen fell into British hands. He traveled through Europe, acquired a new name and credentials, then eventually immigrated to America where he became a citizen. He took a series of manufacturing positions, using his management skills to take control of Hulot & Associates. He turned it into a multinational corporation with divisions in munitions manufacturing and financial institutions.

Now, seated in his chair in his luxurious office, Stettler took a long sip, looking out of the window at the lovely summer day. *I'm a respectable citizen today,* he thought. *I'm an important businessman. A rich man.* No one knows about his true past and he had to keep it that way. Stettler's eyes narrowed and he sat back.

Stettler thought about the note again. I KNOW WHAT YOU HAVE DONE.

The man's trying to destroy everything I've worked for, he thought. *What would he know? What if he knows something?*

A witness, he thought then. He shook his head. *Can you believe this? A witness. The last thing I need right now is a witness bringing charges against me.* His jaw tightened. *I must take care of this problem right away.* And then he thought, *Not to worry, my men will deal with it. I'll teach him what happens to people who try to destroy my life.*

Later that day, Best shared what she had found about Wingort.

"He's a retired jeweler from New York. Born in Frankfurt in 1923, he emigrated to New York after the war, where he married and started a business. Recently widowed. He has one son, a journalist. Nothing else important to note."

Stettler narrowed his eyes. "Is he Jewish?"

Best looked down at her notes. "Yes. He's a member of a small temple in New York."

Stettler thought a moment. "What about his parents?"

"His father was killed in one of the Nazi concentration camps. During the war."

A frown appeared on Stettler's brow. "I wonder what he thinks he knows."

"It's unclear," Best said. "Sounds like a troublemaker, looking for some kind of payoff. We've dealt with them before."

"Yes, find out what he wants."

"Understood, sir." Best got to her feet. "I'll see to it."

That afternoon, William received a call at the hotel. He was in his room, getting ready for dinner.

"William Wingort?" a male voice said. "My name is Clyde

Taylor. I'm an agent with the US Department of the Treasury Office of the Inspector General."

There was a thoughtful pause.

"What is it about?"

"We understand," the agent said, "you were making some inquiries regarding Bruno Stettler of Hulot & Associates."

Another pause.

"How..."

"His business is under federal investigation," the agent continued. "We have his offices under surveillance. We record any visitors he has."

"I see," William said. "Yes, he is a person I knew in my youth in Germany. I'm on vacation in Orlando and when I saw that article in a newspaper about his company, thought I would look him up and talk about old times. Unfortunately, I never got to see him."

"We would still like to meet you to ask you a few questions."

"I'm a retired jeweler. As I said, I haven't seen him for years. I'm not sure I would be of any help."

"It is our job," the agent said slowly, "to follow up all leads. We'll meet you at your hotel tomorrow around 10:00 a.m."

William half hesitated. "But... I've got plans."

"It won't take long. Thank you for your cooperation, Mr. Wingort." He hung up.

William was thoughtful for a moment. *Pavlenko is under federal investigation.* Could this be his chance to expose the monster and see justice done?

Two men in conservative business suits were waiting in the lobby as Wingort walked out of the breakfast buffet the following morning.

"Mr. Wingort?" one of the men said. He extended his hand. "We spoke yesterday. "Clyde Taylor, special agent. This is my partner, Juan Martinez."

William looked at them. "May I see some identification?"

"Sure." The plainclothes agents showed him their badges.

"Please follow us," one of the agents called Taylor said. "We've got a car waiting to take you to our office downtown."

"How long will this take?" William asked. "I've got a tour at 1:00 p.m."

"Not long," said the other agent. "It's pretty routine. We'll drive you back in time for your tour."

The two men led William to a charcoal-black Chevrolet Impala with tinted windows parked across the street. Agent Martinez slid in behind the wheel, and Taylor moved into the passenger seat. Wingort sat in the back.

William felt in his pocket. "Sorry," he said, "but I forgot my cell phone and heart medication in my room. Could you wait a minute while I get them?"

"Sorry," Martinez said. "We're on a tight schedule. I'll have you back in no time."

William shrugged. *Strange. What could be so urgent that they could not wait five minutes?*

"Okay," he said. "If you say so."

They had been driving south for over an hour. Overhead the white clouds piled on top of the other in the Florida sky. A few cars flashed by. Slowing gradually in the deceleration lane, agent Martinez exited the highway and drove the car down a secondary narrow road toward a pine-forested area.

Willliam looked over at him, frowning. "Where are you taking me?"

Martinez moved his head. "We told you. To our office downtown." None of them said a word. William leaned back in his seat. He didn't mind the silence. It gave him time to figure out what was going on. Figure out who these two guys were. What they were up to. What they wanted with kidnapping him. Only God knows where they were driving him. He looked across at Taylor. A funny little smile was playing on his lips. Liars, William thought. They are big fat liars. When the two men came to the lobby of the hotel and showed him their badges, something seemed off about them.

William couldn't put his finger on it. He didn't know what to make of it. Something was not right.

Their faces were blank, expressed no emotion. Nothing. And it was the way they had acted; they had been pretty insistent on having a meeting with William in the hotel lobby and later on, when agent Taylor wanted him to stay seated in the car and told him they could not wait for him to get his pills he left in his room, that had switched on a lightbulb inside his head. It was conspicuous to say the least. William was beginning to have his suspicion that they could be fake cops.

There was one possibility William could come up with; obviously, these guys were hired. Obviously, they were hired by Stettler and behind all of this was Stettler's motive to stop any information from getting out. Given the facts that Stettler knew about William knowing about his past, it was a high possibility.

The two agents didn't seem to notice William's scowling mistrust.

Inside the car, William sat there listening to the two men talking about going on vacation and some other small talk as though everything was a pretty routine thing. A day-to-day occurrence. But it wasn't for William. Not a day-to-day occurrence. And not after driving around aimlessly for an hour. "It won't take long," Taylor told him. "We'll have you back in no time." Back in no time? It won't take long? Who was he kidding? Taylor had been driving over an hour by now and after looking at his watch he noticed that he was too late for his tour now. A qualm of apprehension rose in his stomach and the suspicions started to flirt around in the back of his mind, telling him; *They are playing you, Dumbkopf.* And a little later, w*ho knows what things these two rogue agents are plotting against me? I don't trust them with a penny.*

Weighing his options William kept an eye out for a passing cop car, hoping to draw attention. But agent Martinez was driving through a sparsely populated, desolate looking country with some clumps of grass and some young cypress trees along the road and not a living soul in sight. Not a cat, not a dog, no nothing.

A couple of miles farther on, Martinez turned his head and said to William with a note of reassurance in his voice, "We are almost there."

William looked up and ahead he saw a few couple of sprawled houses interspersed with some stands of young trees.

He wondered. *That's where their downtown office is? Where is the downtown area? All I can see is scattered small houses and some stands of trees. This doesn't look like a downtown area to me.* He felt a strange uncomfortable feeling rise up in him again.

Five minutes later, Martinez turned the car into a small side road and braked to a stop in front of a two-story gray-painted wooden farmhouse with green shutters. He switched off the engine. Taylor and Martinez got out of the car. Martinez opened the rear door on William's side. He took a pistol, a Beretta 92, out of his pocket and said harshly, "Out of the car, Wingort."

Slowly, William got out of the car. About 12 yards away from him stood an elderly man in his middle seventies, tall and silvery haired, next to the wooden farmhouse.

William turned his head. He found himself looking into the icy-blue eyes of Bruno Stettler and felt a chill. He had walked into Stettler's trap. *They outfoxed everybody. They have set me up. And there's no way out now.*

Glancing around, William figured out his chances of escape. Near him, agent Martinez kept the pistol steady on him and Taylor, smiling a sardonic smile, also kept an eye out. And Bruno Stettler stood there in front of him, his eyes boring into Willam's intently.

"I wouldn't," Stettler said softly, menacingly, "try it if I were you." Instinctively, William looked away a moment, avoiding to look this man in his face. But then swung his eyes back on him and found himself staring at the most brutal and coldest set of eyes, chin and lips that he had ever seen on a man's face; the true picture of a ruthless driven former Nazi. Knowing what Stettler knows, William was certain that his life was in danger. Stettler was not going to let him live and let him ruin his life. Never. Not in a million years.

William watched apprehensively as Stettler walked over to a green-painted side door leading into the hallway of the two-story wooden farmhouse. He opened the door. The group stepped into the house.

3

Seated in his Manhattan apartment, Matt Wingort, a lean, strong-featured man in his early thirties, well above medium height with a square jaw and intelligent gray eyes, was trying to work on his investigative piece on corruption in bitcoin business for *Vanity Fair*. But he kept thinking about his dad and his ten-day trip to Orlando.

It had taken him months to convince his father to take a vacation. After his mother died, his father closed up his business and retired. Once a boisterous, outgoing man much beloved by friends and colleagues, he became withdrawn. His father seemed to have retreated in an emotional bunker. He lost touch with his friends. He rarely went out. Matt was the only person he would see. Resolving not to push any further, Matt hoped as time passed that his father would gradually open up to him. He hoped the trip would help him relax and get back to his old life.

Matt's father never shared his emotions or talked about his past. All he knew was that he immigrated to America after WWII, started a jewelry business, met his mother, and made his life in here. When Matt asked him about the war or his family, the answer was always, "It's in the past. Better you shouldn't know, son."

Matt had spoken to his father when he arrived in Orlando and got some photos of his excursions, but that was it. He guessed he was having a great time, too busy to call. Then three days before his father was scheduled to return home, Matt's phone vibrated with a text message: *Tried to call you but couldn't get through. Got some unfinished business to attend to. May stay a few more days. Will call back later.*

Matt shook his head, frowning. *Unfinished business? What could he mean? He's been retired for years.*

Two days went by and not a word. He kept calling but got his father's voicemail each time. Something was not right. He could feel it.

Matt checked his watch: 7:00 p.m. His father would certainly be back in his room. Matt called the number of the hotel where his father was staying. On the fourth ring, a male voice answered the phone. "Thank you for calling the Courtyard at Marriott Orlando. How may I help you?"

"I'd like to speak to William Wingort, please."

The clerk patched Matt through to the room. The phone rang ten times. No answer.

Matt hung up and called again.

This time a female voice answered the phone. "Courtyard Marriot in Orlando, good evening."

"Could I speak to William Wingort, please?"

The hotel room phone rang ten times. No answer again.

Matt put the phone down. *What's going on here? Something definitely doesn't add up.* He called the hotel again and asked for the manager.

"Dean Crawford, manager. How may I assist you?"

"My name is Matt Wingort. I'm concerned about my father, William Wingort. He is a guest. He is not answering his phone. He is elderly and has a health condition. Could you send someone to check on him in his room?"

"Maybe he's just out, sir. It is not that late."

"It is too late for him to be out. Please."

"Of course, sir. What is your number?"

After half an hour, Matt's phone rang. "Mr. Wingort? Dean Crawford of the Marriot. We had housekeeping check on him. He didn't answer. When she opened the door, he was not in his room. All his belongings were thrown around the room."

Matt sat in stunned silence. "Could you check when was the last time he accessed his room?"

"I'm sorry. We don't keep track of our guests in that way."

"I understand. Could you leave an urgent message for him to call me?"

"Of course. Don't worry," Crawford said, "I'm sure he's fine."

"Thank you," Matt said and hung up.

Dad was fastidious to a fault. He'd never leave his room like that. Where could he be? He bit his lower lip. *Why won't he return my calls?*

After a thoughtful moment, he booked a flight to Orlando and a room at the Courtyard Marriott. Then he texted his father's cellphone: *Arriving in Orlando tomorrow afternoon. Meet me at the hotel. Love, Matt.*

The Orlando-bound Boeing 747 was about half full. Uncomfortably settled in his seat with a glass of orange juice in his hand, Matt tried to relax but was too keyed up over his father to open his laptop and work on the draft of an article. It wasn't like his father to be out of touch with him for so long. He just hoped it wasn't his health and that he was lying in a hospital somewhere. He'd find out more when he got there.

Matt Wingort had been born and raised in New York City. He went to Manhattan high school where he worked on the student high school's newspaper. He discovered that he much enjoyed the work. At 23 he graduated from Berkeley College with a B.A. in journalism. Soon after, he became a reporter for the local newspaper *The Today's Gazette*. His next move was to apply to the *Messenger's Tribune* where a year later, he joined the staff as a reporter. Two years after that, he began freelancing for the paper.

His father was a jeweler, his mother helped her husband in the business while raising the boy. After school, Matt frequently visited his father's business in midtown Manhattan, watching him and his mother at work. The family lived in a five-bedroom apartment on the Upper West Side. They enjoyed a comfortable lifestyle.

His father was a caring father who saw to it that the family took their vacations together and traveled together. Matt loved New York. He enjoyed the constant hustle and bustle of the city and made friends easily. He hung out with them at a popular Club on Broadway which featured weekly performances by big-name musicians.

On the weekends at college, Matt would go rowing or canoeing on the river with friends. Or attend favorite baseball games at the Yankee or Shea stadium. There were the movie theaters, dance halls, and jazz clubs. And there was the midtown theater district and restaurants.

During the cool summer evenings, the youngster would sit with grown-ups around the wide wooden outdoor tables in the backyard of the tall brick buildings and would listen to them talk about the "Holocaust." About another world, a world where unholy, frightening things were happening. The men were seated at the table in shirt sleeves, would take sips from their cold beer bottles, lean back in the chair, and talk about Nazi Germany. About The National Socialist German Workers Party that dominated much of Europe till the end of World War II. The youngster would sit there wide-eyed and listen intently to the men talk about their families. About uncles and aunts and sisters and brothers that had been taken from their homes in broad daylight and were sent to extermination camps where the Nazis slaughtered them. Like animals. Because they were Jews.

"And the world," they would exclaim heatedly, "stood aside and didn't give a damn." *Slaughtering innocent people?* the youth wondered disbelievingly. *Like animals? Thinking about it, good Lord, can you believe that?*

Matt was 19 years old when he dated Sandy Rubin. He had met her at a New York charity ball. She was one year younger than Matt.

Sandy was a tall, slender woman with high cheekbones and shoulder-length curly blond hair. She was the daughter of Jewish parents that fled Nazi Germany for fear of persecution. Sandy attended Columbia University and wanted to be a lawyer. They had gone steady for almost two years and had talked about marriage. Then her family moved from New York to Seattle and Matt lost touch with her.

One day, they went to watch a movie together. Sometime after their cup of coffee at a midtown coffee shop across the street from the theater, seated at a corner booth, Sandy started talking about her parents' life in the Old World, explaining why her parents moved to the United States.

She looked at Matt across the table. "Did you ever hear the term *Kristallnacht*?"

Matt's eyebrows drew together in a frown. "Kristallnacht?"

"Yes."

He shook his head. "Tell me about it."

Sandy looked down at her drink, turned her cup on the table, wondering where to begin. Looking up she said, "Back in November 1938, the Nazis in Germany unleashed a vicious pogrom against the German Jewish population. The event was called *Kristallnacht* because of the shattered glass that littered across the German streets." She took a small sip from her cup then set the cup back down and paused a moment.

"Go on," Matt urged her.

"Well," she said, turning her cup some more, trying to find the right words, "after Hitler's power grab the growing antisemitism in Nazi Germany reached a racial dimension the country never experienced before. There were large-scale antisemitic acts of violence; Jews were brutally beaten; riots raged for many days; Nazi stormtroopers rampaged throughout the country destroying everything Jewish in their path." She gave an involuntary shudder and her mouth quivered a moment. "Jews were snatched off the streets," she said in a trembling voice, "in broad daylight and transported to the concentration camps. When it was over, countless homes, synagogues and businesses were looted and burned down. Apparently, a Jewish-Polish teenager assassinated a German Diplomat at the German embassy in Paris. That was a welcome excuse for the Nazis to launch their violent pogrom. Mom told me that it was a sign of bad things to come."

She paused. "It was a wake-up call for my parents," she said, looking at him steadily across the table. "Yes," she said, taking a deep breath and sighing it out, "they were lucky, very lucky. They obtained an immigrant visa to the US and escaped by the skin of their teeth."

Sitting in silence, absorbing her words, it was at that moment that Matt made up his mind to be an investigative journalist.

When the plane landed at the Orlando International airport, Matt collected his bag from the carousel. He walked over to the Hertz car rental counter and arranged for a car. He studied the roadmap and drove straight to the hotel. It wasn't difficult to find. Matt pulled into the parking lot, entered the long lobby, and checked in.

The clerk handed Matt the register card. "Would you fill this out, please?"

Matt signed his name and gave her his credit card. She put it through the processing machine and handed him a plastic key card. "Your room is 315. I'll have someone take your bag to your room, sir."

"No need," Matt told her. "Thank you. My father is staying here at the hotel. Can you call his room and find out if he's here, please?"

"Certainly." She looked up. "The name, please?"

"William Wingort."

"William Wingort?" She glanced at the computer screen and paused.

"Is there a problem?"

"Please wait a sec, sir." She reached for the desk phone, spoke a few words into it, then turned back to Matt. "Mr. Crawford, our manager would like to have a word with you, sir." She gestured for Matt to follow her. "This way, please."

What's going on here? He followed the young clerk along the deep, dark blue-carpeted hallway to the manager's office. He was beginning to have a hollow feeling in the pit of his stomach.

As he entered the spacious office, Dean Crawford, a tanned, round-faced, polite-mannered man in his fifties rose to greet him. He smiled. "We spoke a few days ago concerning your father."

"Yes," said Matt. "I remember. Is everything..."

"Please, have a seat, Mr. Wingort."

Crawford paused a moment and looked at Matt across the desk. "It's not unusual for guests to use our hotel as a home base while they visit the various attractions our city has to offer. However, it is highly unusual for them to stay past their reservations without informing us. Have you been in touch with your father recently? His reservation is three days overdue."

"No," Matt said, "that's why I'm concerned and flew down to see him."

"Yes," said Crawford, "quite understandable. As you can imagine, we would like to know the disposition of his stay with us."

Matt swallowed. "I understand. Can I see my father's room?"

"Of course." The hotelier pressed some keys on the computer. "It's room 102. I'll have housekeeping let you in."

Matt nodded. "Thank you. Since he hasn't been around, I'll pack Father's things and move them into my room. Please, feel free to close out the charges on his credit card."

Matt turned away toward the door.

"Yes," Crawford said. "Thank you."

Matt stopped and turned. "And could you tell me, when was the last time anyone here saw my father?"

"I'm afraid not," the hotelier said. "This is a busy place. And our staff can't keep tabs on all our guests. I hope everything is all right, Mr. Wingort."

"Me too," Matt said, and headed for the door.

His father's room was on the first floor. The housekeeper unlocked the door and they stepped inside. The room had large windows, three armchairs, a night table, and a king-size bed. His suitcase sat on the luggage stand. It was empty. Matt glanced around and frowned. Dresser drawers and closet door were open. His father's pants, shirts, underwear lay scattered on the floor. Matt picked up his father's navy-blue shirt and stared at it. He remembered the shirt. His dad wore it on the day of his departure to Florida.

He checked the bathroom. Toilet articles and medications were arranged on the shelf next to the sink. He noticed a glass of water on the night table with a half-smoked cigarette in it. *Strange.* His father didn't smoke. A growing sense of alarm washed over him. *Someone had been here, looking for something. But what? And where was his father?*

Matt packed up his father's things and brought them to his room on the third floor. He emptied his father's suitcase on the bed and laid everything out on the bed. There were his clothes, his father's leather-bound agenda book, some souvenirs from Disneyworld, his phone charger, his phone, and a weekly pill organizer filled with different pills.

Matt felt a cold hollowness growing inside of him. *He would never have gone anywhere without his phone or the medication.*

He sat down in a chair and tried to turn on his father's phone. It was dead. That explained why he never returned his calls. He plugged it and waited for it to charge while he examined his father's daybook.

Mostly, it held dates of the various events he planned. Of course, there was a record of what he spent. Matt smiled. He was always meticulous about money. Then Matt scanned the last page. He had written: *Bruno Stettler, Hulot & Associates,* with an address in Orlando. It didn't seem like a vacation tour.

A photo fell out of the daybook. It was of an older, distinguished man and a tall attractive younger woman. It looked like it was taken outside in front of the hotel. *Who were these people?*

His father had been missing 72 hours, well beyond the legal limit to file a missing person's report. He needed to go to the local police.

4

Matt drove up to the front of the old, gray-and-brown-walled brick building on South Hughey Avenue of the Orlando Police Station. He parked and went inside.

A uniformed officer sitting behind the desk glanced up. "Can I help you, sir?" he asked.

"I'd like to report a missing person," Matt said to him.

"Your name?"

"Matt Wingort."

"Name of the missing person?"

"William Wingort, my father."

The desk officer wrote it down. "How long has he been missing?"

"Three days."

The man nodded and scanned a sheet. "Detective Debra Garfield is the person you need to talk to," he said and picked up the phone. He spoke into it for a few moments then turned to Matt. "First floor, third door on the right."

Matt walked down a long hallway until he reached the third door. It was ajar. Matt stepped inside.

The room was filled with male police detectives. Detective Garfield was the only woman. In her early thirties, slim and attractive, her auburn hair pulled back in a ponytail, she was seated at an old wooden desk talking into the phone, the receiver wedged between shoulder and ear while she took notes. She gave him a nod, indicated a chair, and continued speaking into the phone.

After a minute or two, she hung up. "Detective Debra Garfield. How can I help you?"

"I came here," Matt said, "to report my father, William Wingort, as a missing person."

The detective nodded. She pulled out a form. "Your name, address and phone number?"

He gave her the information.

"How long has he been missing?"

"Three days," said Matt.

She was silent for a moment. "And what makes you think he's missing?"

"He left on a ten-day vacation from New York. We spoke every day until three days ago. Then, suddenly he stopped calling or answering any voicemails or texts for the last three days."

"Maybe he's just having fun," she said, trying to be optimistic. "He's on vacation after all."

"My father is not the partying kind," Matt said. "That's why I flew down here to check up on him. I went to his hotel and inquired. The hotel manager said he never checked out of his room, well past his reservation date."

Debra Garfield listened intently and started taking notes. "Do you have a current photo of your father?"

Matt nodded and removed from his wallet two pictures of his father and handed them to her.

Debra studied the photographs of a tall man in his early seventies, white-haired and angular-faced with slightly prominent cheekbones and a gray mustache. She stared at the photos, looked up and asked, "You mind if we make copies of the photos?"

"Please do."

"Is he married?" she asked after a moment.

"Widowed."

"Retired?"

"Yes."

Debra looked at him thoughtfully. "Is he in a relationship?"

"No."

"Does he have any medical problems?"

"He suffered a heart attack and needs to take several medications regularly."

"Does your father have a drinking problem?"

"No."

"Does he gamble?"

Matt shook his head.

"When did you last hear from him?"

"By text, last Thursday morning... April 22. He said he needed to extend his trip a few days to take care of some business."

"I thought you said he was retired."

"That's just it," Matt said. "He doesn't know anyone in Orlando. It's his first visit."

"I see," Debra said. "Did he seem depressed?"

"No more than usual. He hasn't been himself since my mom passed."

"Maybe," she went on, "you can remember something else? Maybe something out of the ordinary your father said?"

Matt frowned. "Like what?"

She made a gesture. "Anything unusual that might give us a lead?" Debra paused and folded her arms over her chest and waited.

Matt spread his hands, palms up. "I keep thinking about it but no, nothing comes to mind." There was a thoughtful pause. "Actually," he said, "he looked forward to the trip."

Detective Garfield sat tapping her index finger against her lips. "Do you know anyone he might have contacted down here on his trip?"

Matt thought for a moment. "Not specifically."

She looked at him. "What does that mean?"

"I found an agenda book with a note about someone named Bruno Stettler at Hulot & Associates."

She watched as Matt pulled the calfskin agenda out of his

inside jacket pocket and passed it across to her. She flipped through pages. "He seemed to have a pretty routine vacation trip. Disney, SeaWorld, etc. Hulot & Associates is a big investment firm here not associated with vacation activities. Maybe he had business there."

"Unlikely," Matt told her. "I control my father's assets. No, he has no account with that firm. As I said, he's been retired for years."

"We'll check them out anyway." She paused a beat. "I'd like to keep the book also for further review if that is all right."

"Could you make copies? I'd like to keep it."

"Sure. Wait right here." She left the room and returned a few minutes later and handed him the book and photos.

"We'll do whatever we can to find your father. We'll start by checking local hospitals and see what we can find out. Let's hope he is all right."

"Yes," said Matt tightly. "I hope so too."

She handed him her card. "Call me if you think of anything. Otherwise, I'll be in touch."

"Thanks. I appreciate it."

5

One week passed. After a quick run, Matt took a shower, changed into a pair of faded jeans, a blue polo shirt, and black loafers then made his way downstairs to the restaurant for breakfast. There were a few guests, mostly business people who read newspapers or conversed with other guests at the table.

Matt had just started reading the *Orlando Sentinel* and took a bite of his toast when his cell phone buzzed. He sat down the cup of coffee and pulled out his mobile.

"Mr. Wingort? This is police headquarters, Detective Garfield's office."

Matt's heart skipped a beat.

"Detective Garfield would appreciate it if you would come down to the station later today at 2:00 p.m. to meet with her."

"Is there any news about my father?"

"You'll have to discuss it with Detective Garfield." She hung up.

When Matt walked into the station, he said to the desk clerk, "My name is Matt Wingort. I have an appointment to see Detective Garfield."

"Wingort," the officer said, looking at a paper on his desk. "Yes. Detective Garfield is waiting for you in her office. "First floor, third door."

Matt nodded. "I know the way."

When he walked in, Debra rose to greet him. "Thank you for coming. Please sit." Debra hesitated. "I am afraid I have bad news."

Matt swallowed.

"A boat tour found a body fitting your father's description. In a swampy area a few miles outside the city."

Sitting in a state of semi-shock, he looked at her in disbelief. "Are you sure? Was it my father?"

"It is highly likely."

"That makes no sense," Matt blurted out. "What the heck was he doing in a swamp area? All alone?"

"Sometimes older people wander out, get lost, have problems. We see it all the time down here."

"Were there any signs of a struggle?" Matt asked. "Robbery?"

"Not according to the preliminary report," Debra said. "It appears that the cause of death was sudden heart failure."

It took Matt a moment to digest what he was hearing. Father did have a heart condition, but it was under control so long as he took his medicine. Then he remembered. *His medications were in his room.*

Matt glanced over at her. "Where is he now?"

Debra looked at him blankly. "At the county morgue," she said. "You'll need to confirm his identity as he had no identification on him." She gave him the address.

Heading south to the morgue at the Regional Medical Center hospital, Matt kept asking himself: What possibly could have happened? Why would he leave without his medications? His cell phone was dead. He wasn't one for nature. He'd never go to a swamp just to walk around, especially on his own. His room was trashed. He had no wallet. His hotel key was missing. Maybe someone robbed him and left him for dead, then went back to the hotel, looking for more money.

At the Orlando Regional Medical Center hospital Matt walked with a uniformed cop and a medical examiner into a long, cold, white-walled room. Off to one side, beneath fluorescent lights was a wall of stainless-steel draws.

The medical examiner, a big, lanky man with a small mustache and raspy voice checked his list, pulled open one of the draws and waited. Matt moved towards the draws, stopped and stared.

The man was a total stranger.

The doctor turned to him. "Can you identify this man?"

Matt stood there, his mind in momentary turmoil. "He's not my father," he said slowly. "I have never seen this man before."

"You have never seen this man before?" The doctor looked at him.

Matt shook his head. "I have no idea who this man is."

The doctor shrugged. "Okay," he said. "Sorry to have bothered you."

Leaving the hospital, Matt's mind was on overdrive. The more he thought about it, the more he was convinced his father had been kidnapped and could still be alive.

Matt headed for police headquarters to Detective Garfield's office.

Detective Garfield met him in the lobby. "Mr. Wingort, is everything okay?"

Matt shook his head. "No," he said tartly. "Everything is not okay. The body in the hospital was not my father. I think my father has been kidnapped, and robbed."

The detective frowned at him. "Mr. Wingort, that is a serious accusation."

"Well, when I got here, the hotel manager let me into his room. I found it trashed. All his personal possessions were thrown around as if someone was in there looking for something. His medications were in the bathroom. His cell phone was dead. He never went out without his medications or cell phone." He paused. "He may still be alive."

"Yes." Debra thought for a moment. "Why didn't you tell me this at first?"

"It was before that body was found. I guess I was hoping he'd be found alive. I didn't know what to think. Now, it seems obvious."

"It does sound suspicious. Our office handles kidnapping cases like this." Her tone was firm. "Come up to my office and make an official statement."

After making the statement, Detective Garfield said, "Now that it is a criminal investigation, I'll try to get things straightened out ASAP."

"Thank you," he said. "I'm flying tomorrow to New York." He was silent for a moment. Matt decided to make a stop at his father's apartment in New York. There was just an outside chance that he might find any piece of information that might be helpful.

"Oh?" she said slowly. "You are?"

"Yes. I want to go to my father's place. I want to check it out. Maybe I'll find a lead which may help to discover what happened to him."

"That's a good idea."

"Yeah, you have my cell," he told her. "Please keep me informed."

"Of course." She handed him her card. "Call me if you think of anything else."

"Will do." Matt paused. "By the way, did you ever follow up on Stettler and his company?"

"Yes, they have no record of your father's visiting their offices or trying to contact Mr. Stettler."

6

Back in New York, Matt took a cab to his father's apartment. He entered the large living room, stood in the still and peaceful silence and looked around at the precious things his father so much cherished. There were souvenirs from the foreign places he had visited with his mother; the antique-style cuckoo clock on the wall from Frankfurt, Germany, that struck the hours with a cheerful cuckoo call. A photograph of his parents and him at his college graduation stood on an end table. He stood there lost in thoughts. *Who on earth would kidnap his father like that? Who? Why?*

He wandered into his father's small study. Photos of him from high school and at holiday dinners covered the wall. On his desk was the laptop he'd bought his father a few years ago so he could stay in touch with his friends by email. Sticking out of one of the USB ports was a thumb drive. *Odd*, Matt thought. *Maybe he had copied something onto it and forgot to take it out.*

He knew that like a lot of guys his age, he was a bit clueless about technology. He took the thumb drive and put it in his pocket. *Maybe there's the piece of information on the flash drive I want. I'll check it out when I get home.* A few minutes later, he walked out of the room.

Back at his place, he answered a few emails, got a beer. Tried to work on his article, but couldn't concentrate. *What*, he thought for the umpteenth time, *could have happened? And who did this you? Dad will be all right,* he thought. *He'll be fine. But where is he?* Matt was resolved to find out. He took out the thumb drive. "Let's see what you copied, Dad," he murmured out loud, then plugged it in and opened the file. The first words he saw were: *This story is dedicated to my son, Matt. Now he will understand.*

A lump came into his throat as he read this, and he began to scroll down and read.

PART II
REMEMBRANCES

7

My name is William Wingort. I was born in Frankfurt in Germany. My father, Victor Wingort, a broad-shouldered man of medium height, had strong features and a quiet, friendly manner. He had grown up in Frankfurt and was a jewelry wholesaler. My mother, Rachel Wingort was a slender and dark-haired woman. She was thoughtful and serious-minded with sensitive features. She had been born in a small town in Galicia, in Poland. She was a housewife. Her family moved to Frankfurt for her father to find work as an artisan. She met my father at the Jewish congregation their families attended and fell in love. After they married, she gave birth to three sons, Eli, Josef and me. We were happy and lived a good life. Until Adolf Hitler came to power in Germany. Then things began to change. Anti-Jewish slogans appeared on the walls. Hateful antisemitic propaganda littered the streets. The SS started their chilling torchlight parades through the dark German streets. I heard my parents whisper about the new laws that took away our rights as citizens because we were Jewish. My father was afraid for our safety and moved our family to Amsterdam, where small numbers of Jewish refugees fleeing the Nazi regime in Germany were able to settle in safety. We lived in a modest apartment in the district Zuid, the middle-class southern section of Amsterdam. My father found work through his jewelry contacts. Life in the new country was not easy. There was widespread unemployment, and acclimation was tough, learning a new language, finding a new place to live, finding the right schools, adjusting to a new culture. However, we felt lucky to have gotten out of Germany, as the stories we heard from our friends and neighbors were horrible, especially the destruction of Jewish shops and synagogues through Germany known as *Kristallnacht*.

The day I had the awakening to how much danger we could have been in if we had not left Germany was when I walked into the living room and found my parents and brothers crouching before the radio listening tensely to Hitler's hysterical rapid-fire shrieking. This man, who was an Austrian, represented, my parents told me, the personification of evil. Only then did it dawn on me what this person was capable of doing. It was actually the first time that I heard the bone-chilling words of Hitler planning to annihilate the Jewish people in Europe. Just listening to this hateful diatribe, listening to him shouting in German, made chills run through me.

The dark clouds of war loomed over us and in less than a year, the Nazis invaded Poland, and declared war. I remember my mother crying as many people in her family still lived there. We thought we would be protected in the Netherlands, but as the Nazis stormed through Europe, we worried he would target the peaceful country also. Jews from all over the city began to line up at foreign consulates for visas, and immigration papers. My father stood on long lines at the US consulate in Amsterdam, hoping to get visas for the family to travel to America. The Great Depression had left countless millions unemployed in the US and the visa people at the American consulate told everyone that the annual immigration quota for the United States had been filled. Jews (with minor exceptions) faced great difficulties getting into the United States – or anywhere else.

As the American journalist Dorothy Thompson wrote in *Refugees: Anarchy or Organization?* in 1938: "It's a fantastic commentary on the inhumanity of our times that for thousands and thousands of people a piece of paper with a stamp on it is the difference between life and death."

But before it had all started, life in the city of canals and tulips was pleasant. We made plenty of friends and there were other days in the Netherlands, nicer and more memorable days, such as going with Dad to his tiny midtown office and to the public library that was beside his office to get a book by Robert Louis Stevenson. *Treasure Island* was quite popular and similar to the books Mom bought me to read during the long wintry Friday evenings.

I remember a fine spring day – I must have been nine years old – when I was walking home with my father from his office. We passed the fish market on the Koningsplein, where people stood or sat at wooden tables eating raw herring dipped in onions. My father had stopped walking and said to me, "Wait here a moment, I want to buy some herring for Mom."

While I waited, I was mesmerized watching a group of men and women eating the herring. Holding the fish, called *maatjesharing*, by its tail, they would throw their heads back and slide the fish into their mouths. I could see their Adam's apples bob up and down as they swallowed the herring, and I thought to myself, *Oh, my God, ugh*. I hated the smell of this raw fish, but herring was (and still is) hugely popular in the Netherlands.

In the spring of 1940, my family and friends took a weekend vacation to the pleasant town of Hilversum. We stayed at a Swiss chalet-style building, and after dinner one evening, we all took a walk. The lights in the cafés and restaurants had come on, and walking past the crowded tables, we could hear that all the talk was of war. Was a war with Nazi Germany imminent? By now the Germans had occupied Czechoslovakia and invaded Poland, Denmark, and Norway. The latest news was that Great Britain and France had declared war on Germany. Why would Germany spare the Netherlands? The Dutch military had recently mobilized, and people were clutching at straws.

There was a humming sound that hung like a cloud as a group of customers discussed the situation across the tables. Would the Germans go ahead and attack the Netherlands? Yes, that was the question, and if they did, would the Netherlands be able to ward off the attack? The Dutch Water Defense Lines – a system of dikes that could be flooded in a controlled manner – were considered to be the bulwark to ward off attacks from German forces.

"No, no," one of the guests sitting at the tables exclaimed, "the Germans won't attack. Of course not. They won't dare." He folded the newspaper he had been reading and slipped it into his pocket. "It would be a foolish thing to do," he went on heatedly. "The Dutch military will open up the floodgates, inundate the low-lying areas, and cut the Germans off from the rest of the country." He gave an emphatic nod. "This," he said, "will deter any attack. And don't forget, we have the Maginot Line fortifications built by France. No, they won't dare. Besides," he pointed out, "Germany will not violate Dutch neutrality."

Even though I was just a child (I was eight at the time), I had studied enough history to know that this sounded like the story of the young boy who stuck his finger in the hole in the dike to forestall a flood.

Another customer seated nearby was raising his voice. "Rubbish," he shot back at them. "I'm telling you, there will be a war. The Germans could easily outflank and attack us." He glanced around the tables. "So we had better be prepared."

The following day, as we checked out of the hotel to take the train back home to Amsterdam, we heard over the radio that the Dutch forces had been put on alert.

In the predawn hours of Friday, May 10, the first German forces crossed the Dutch border at Limburg and invaded the Netherlands via land and via air without a formal declaration of war. I was awakened in the early morning darkness by the shrill noise of an air raid. I heard the throbbing, humming sound of low-flying airplanes coming closer. Then there were the distant detonations as the first bombs fell. We heard first the piercing whistle and then the thundering blasts of the bombs, followed by roaring echoes that made the windows rattle. I lay in bed, thinking back to the people at the restaurant. As the sound of explosions got nearer, I closed my eyes and covered my ears, pulled my knees to my chest, and thought, *stop it, stop it, please,* and lay there praying we would survive the attack. God, I was scared to death. Across the room from me, my brothers were sitting up in bed, groaning, "It is the Germans, it is the Germans!" And then: *Crack boom.* Then again: *Crack boom.*

My parents tried to calm us. It took a while until the sirens and mortar shells and echoing anti-aircraft guns had subsided.

We hurried into the living room in our pajamas and sat transfixed before the radio. "In the early hours of May 10, Germany attacked the Netherlands, Belgium, and Luxembourg. Dutch troops are blowing up bridges to slow down the German advance..."

The Netherlands was at war.

That same day, the government proclaimed a state of emergency.

In the days that followed, the country seemed to hold its breath. We stayed at home, mostly in front of the radio, listening to the nonstop reports that were coming in from all fronts. There was heavy fighting up north in Groningen. And in the south, there were reports of German planes dropping parachutists near Rotterdam.

In Amsterdam, the streets were nearly deserted. Now and then a truck filled with uniformed soldiers roared by, and little groups of people stood on the street corners huddling together. It seemed people gathered together more for comfort than for news.

During those days, Dad would be sitting in his chair in a corner by the window, playing with a fountain pen. Mother, a cup of coffee in hand, would sit down beside us in front of the radio. Nothing happened over the next few days, but I was constantly on edge, wondering when the next bombing would occur.

The schools remained closed, and we neighbor kids found ourselves looking for grenade fragments of the artillery rounds that lay scattered across the streets. We would collect them and then trade the pieces among ourselves just as we had traded soccer cards.

On the third day of the war, the fighting took a turn for the worse; the front lines had collapsed, and the Dutch forces had started a full retreat. We heard Dutch radio announcers saying, "The German planes have dropped tons of bombs on the center of Rotterdam. Nazi paratroopers have landed near military fields of The Hague, the capital city. Dutch troops are withdrawing from the east front..." And the broadcasting of bad news went on and on.

The town of IJmuiden had come up in the newscasts since the war had started. IJmuiden is a port city in the Dutch province of North Holland.

As events unfolded, Jews as well as non-Jews were trying to flee by boat to England. Rumors were spreading that the Dutch government was providing ships for the transport of Jews to England. Our parents decided to travel to the port city to get across to England.

The following morning, while packing our bags, we heard on the radio that German Panzer divisions were advancing in the direction of Rotterdam, and Dutch forces were suffering big losses.

We hired a cab and set out for IJmuiden. Tens of thousands of people had packed up their belongings and left the cities – especially Jews who had fled Germany earlier – all resolved to get out of the country and seek asylum in Great Britain.

The distance between Amsterdam and IJmuiden was usually a 30-minute drive, but with German surveillance planes swooping out of the sky and the massive flow of terrified civilians often coming to a snarling halt, it took us more than an hour.

Finally, we arrived at the harbor, where the quays were overcrowded with people trying to escape the Nazi onslaught.

Upon our arrival at the port, we tried to locate a ship to get us across and saw in front of us the ship SS *Bodegraven*, depart right before our eyes, leaving us behind ashore. This ship, a passenger freighter, was the last boat that left the Netherlands for Great

Britain. Watching the boat sailing out of the harbor was like saying goodbye to a loved one you knew you would never see again.

I remember people standing near me, exclaiming a kind of a "Oh, no!" wail of despair. Dad and Mom's faces showed nothing. They just stood there staring silently after the departing ship.

We had been so near and had missed the boat by seconds.

All around us, there was chaos. In the distance, explosions from mortars could be heard, and children were crying. We heard the anguished wails of mothers unable to soothe their terrified kids. Planes attacked a group of cyclists. As we looked up, we saw German Heinkel and Stukas fighters passing overhead in the deep blue sky.

Following a nerve-racking *boom*, we saw in the distance plumes of gray smoke shooting into the sky.

The constant rumbling of distant mortar and the rattling of gunfire scared the daylights out of me. All we wanted now was to get out of this mess as fast as possible.

When there was a lull in the gunfire, we started to look for a spot to sit and rest. We settled ourselves on a patch of field beneath a stand of trees and ate egg sandwiches and drank tea from the thermos bottle we had taken along for the ride.

Holland's brief military resistance was over, and the future didn't look particularly bright. From refugees who had tried to get across, we learned that Dutch outposts were now firmly in German hands.

A young uniformed Dutch soldier sitting with his back against a trunk near us, his helmet lying near his feet and his rifle leaning against the tree, was talking to us – or perhaps just to himself. He took swallows from a water bottle attached to his shoulder strap and kept repeating over and over in a monotone voice, "Yes, it's over. We have lost. Those damn Germans. We surrendered. It's over." He kept saying it again and again in a weary, apathetic, resigned voice: "It's over, all over."

So that was it, I realized with dread. Life as we knew it was over.

Night had now fallen. Our trip to IJmuiden had been in vain. We found a cab again and returned to Amsterdam. The landscape framed by the black sky was bleak. We passed destroyed buildings still aflame and saw many bridges blown up. Vehicles lay abandoned on the road. I felt it all in the pit of my stomach. Holland had lost, and Germany – the Nazi Germany we had fled – had won.

For a while, we were driving in silence along a road winding back and forth with trees on each side. Through the open window floated the stench of burning buildings.

"Good God," our driver muttered to the windshield. "Good God, look at that, look at what these Germans did to us." His disturbance was met with silence. The members of my family were each brooding.

During the next two or three days, Mom sank into a morose melancholy. Father prepared the meals and we sat around the radio listening to the grim news. The country surrendered to Nazi Germany the next morning on May 15, and two weeks later, it was placed under the *Reichskommissariat*, a Nazi Civilian Government.

These were dark days. The blackout papers had disappeared from the windows, for there would be no more bombs. We had given up the fight.

Now, German soldiers in field-gray uniforms, rifles slung over their backs, could be seen patrolling the streets everywhere.

There had been food rationing already before the war. Now that the Nazis had occupied the country, the rationing got worse. Everyone received coupons from the distribution office (which was controlled by the Nazis) for bread, meat, sugar, shoes, and clothing. We scraped by like the rest of the people we knew. Generally, the majority of the Dutch population kept their heads down, particularly the Jews, just trying to survive.

Until the beginning of 1941, the German authorities had lulled us Jews into a sense of false security, didn't make themselves noticeable, were friendly and polite and sometimes would even be helpful, carrying heavy bundles to buildings for the elderly.

Then came the sudden change.

In the second half of 1941, the Nazi occupation government in Holland established a Jewish council called *De Joodse Raad*. Its purpose was to mediate the Nazi government's orders with the Jewish community. Before the change, there was very little to negotiate. Basically, life just went on. The country was placed under the German civilian government headquartered in The Hague, and German military forces were stationed at bases in different localities.

But then in the summer of that year the Nazis started to target the Jews. The rules got more stringent for the Jews; every month, a tsunami of new regulations and measures was announced.

The Nazis mandated the registration of all Jews living in Holland. The first anti-Jewish laws and measures were issued; Jews were no longer allowed to take advantage of air-raid protection shelters. Jewish newspapers were closed down. A few months later, all civil servants had to sign a declaration of Aryan origin and all Jewish civil servants were dismissed. Every Jew that lived in Holland had to register himself or herself, including "half Jews" with one Jewish grandparent. (This data would help the Nazis later on to round up Jews and send them to Nazi extermination camps). Their passports were stamped with a large red *J*. Assets of all Jewish businesses were registered. Bank accounts owned by Jews were blocked. Jewish Dutch citizens were allowed only 250 guilders ($455) a month for private use.

In May 1942, like a thunderclap out of the blue, the most humiliating order was issued (or we thought at the time it was the most humiliating; we would learn much about humiliation as time went on); each Dutch Jewish resident from age six and up was required to wear the yellow Star of David on their outer clothing. That decree was passed to us, as all the rules were, by the *Joodse Raad* (Jewish Council). It was followed by notification that we were no longer invited to attend entertainment events or soccer championship games. This was a bucket of cold water. The new decree seemed to proclaim: *Jews! Go away! All of you. You are not wanted here!* It was like a punch in the gut. *You are different from us.*

You are an outsider. You don't belong here. You are not one of us. Go! Go away!

Dear Lord. It was a pretty awful sight, watching Mother sitting there at home in her armchair nervously sewing the yellow star on our clothes. Each Dutch Jewish resident from age six and up was required to wear the star given to us by the Jewish Council on our outer clothing. At home, we kept silent, we didn't talk much, but Mom's face spoke volumes. The emotions inside her must have been whirling. I did not yet know the meaning of the word *anxiety*, but it was spelled out on her face.

Father, too, hardly spoke a word. Haggard-faced, he went about his business. My two brothers continued going to the HBS (higher civic school), and I walked each day to elementary school.

The first time I laid eyes on that yellow star was unsettling. The sight of the yellow star with the black letters *JOOD* in the center of it was disturbing; I felt like now I was a hunted animal, a target. I was fair game, a very uncomfortable feeling.

In hindsight, I realize I did not know what conversation went on behind my back; were they talking about me at home? Did their parents object to them playing with me? Subconsciously, an uneasy feeling had started hanging around me. The Nazis had prevailed with their star because I did feel like I was somebody different.

Deep down I felt violated, molested. It was a sense of indignation and humiliation. I felt as if I had been stripped naked in the street in full view of the world. When I first put on my coat with the disgusting star on it, automatically my eyes lowered from shame and embarrassment. I wanted to walk down the street, curious to know how people would react. The Dutch people – my neighbors whom I saw every day – would they see me the way I was seeing myself?

The truth was, they hardly looked up, didn't seem to care (which was a relief), and when I caught someone casting a quick, guarded glance at me and then looking away, that was okay. Over time I learned to put up with it, live with it. The star became part of my life, like eating and sleeping.

The first day back at school wearing the yellow star taught

me much about my people. As I entered the classroom, a group of girls and boys were laughing and talking together. Suddenly the room fell silent. One of my friends was glancing up, nudged his friend who sat beside him, and both stared as though hypnotized by the yellow star. Then quickly, almost guiltily, they looked away. Soon angry murmurs of protests could be heard: If the Nazis were so unfeeling and inhuman, they would pay a price.

I was astonished hearing them talk this way about the Germans and how the NSB, the Dutch Nazis, behaved toward the Jews. I was awash in total gratitude. Perhaps the Nazis' attempt at humiliating the Jews would not work. But I was shy by nature, and the whole class was looking at me. The entire scene was all about me. I did not want to blow it out of proportion. So I just sat down, nodded, smiled, and kept silent.

When class was over and the bell rang, I was the first one to walk out the door.

In the corridor, my soccer team buddy Gerrit Peters stopped me. "Our game," he said to me in a casual tone, "tomorrow six o'clock." He looked at me. "All right?"

"Sure." I nodded. Then mumbled happily, "All right."

Gerrit smiled broadly and slapped me on the shoulder. "See you later."

Filled with a feeling close to love, I watched him turn and walk away.

I continued playing with my non-Jewish friends like before. It made me feel confident. They never acknowledged the star.

One month later, new orders were issued. A curfew for Jews was imposed: between the hours of 8:00 p.m. and 6:00 a.m. we were to remain at home. The new state of the country was frightening. Our family and friends were scared to death. People started to disappear. My family was very lucky. In 1942 with the help of a friend, my father had acquired Paraguayan passports provided through the Paraguay Embassy in Switzerland. He had heard that anyone who held a passport from any Latin American country was assured protection from deportation to the Nazi extermination camps and would be exchanged by the Nazis for Germans held in captivity.

Nightly raids were common and we lived in constant fear. More and more Jewish men were sent to labor camps in the Netherlands, creating the initial impression that they wouldn't be sent to any feared concentration camps, because they had already been put to work in the Netherlands.

In July 1942, the Nazis began transporting the first Jews to Westerbork, a transit camp in the northeast of the Netherlands. At the same time, the occupation officials announced that Dutch Jews failing to comply with orders to report to German labor camps would be dealt with by the Gestapo. As the transports began to roll, the Dutch police actively collaborated and assisted the German authorities in rounding up Jews on the streets and in their homes.

One morning, a Jewish neighbor family was taken in. I had witnessed the raid, as Dutch policemen arrived in a police truck and took them away. A couple of days later, standing by the rear window, looking out at the other side of the corner building, I saw a young man in shirt sleeves and black trousers descending a rope hand over hand, then lowering himself onto the missing neighbors' balcony. He broke a window and climbed into the vacant apartment. Soon he reappeared with dinnerware in his hands and put it into a large woven basket attached to another rope, which was then hauled up by his family members to their fifth-floor apartment. They were Dutch fascists. In this way, they had robbed the apartment of many valuables.

We figured we'd better keep a low profile, so we decided not to call the police.

And the transports kept rolling.

In those dark times, the official radio programming in the Netherlands was under German control, glorifying the offensive warfare of Nazi Germany's early military successes.

As columns of Nazi soldiers marched along the streets, my parents sat listening to the latest war bulletins from the clandestine BBC radio, careful not to get caught by the Gestapo. People who got caught listening were immediately shipped off to labor camps.

We felt desperate. Jews were no longer safe in the Netherlands and had to get out. But there was no way to escape.

My parents considered their options. I heard them discuss in low voices the possibility of fleeing Nazi-occupied Holland.

One idea was that Dad would try to cross the border into Switzerland (with a smuggler who'd been recommended), and send us a coded message to follow him once he'd made it safely. But Mom fiercely objected to the plan, pointing out that the "recommended" smuggler might leave us stranded at the border, or worse, hand us over to the Gestapo after he collected his money.

"What then?" Mom's voice rose at the very thought of what might happen to us. "No, no," she told Dad firmly. She was dead set against the plan. It was too risky, too dangerous. Maybe my parents figured, possessing the Paraguayan passports would save them from deportation.

However, their hopes were quickly crushed when, in July 1942, rumors started buzzing around town that the Gestapo had obtained direct orders from the Reich Security Main Office in Berlin to round up all Latin American passport holders and deport them to the camps in the east.

These documents that were supposed to be a key to freedom, to help protect the holder from getting rounded up, became the opposite.

On that September morning, there was a feeling of tension in the air as two men arrived at our doorstep on bicycles. They had been sent to the southern section of Amsterdam carrying the list of "exchange Jews" – people who could be used to negotiate for German prisoners of war. They came on a Wednesday morning, at 9:00 a.m. as we were about to go into hiding. Dad was not with us; he was outside the city to complete the escape. He had spoken to a colleague who was willing to help get us to a safe house in Apeldoorn in Gelderland, 87 kilometers northeast of Amsterdam.

The middle-aged woman had arrived a few minutes earlier to take us to the hiding place.

We had always dreaded the knocks on the door. When they came, they were loud, followed by an authoritative voice that called out in Dutch, "*Politie, open de deur!*" [This is the police. Open up!].

Mother, turning pale, exchanged a quick glance with us and opened the door. Two tough-looking Dutch Nazi policemen in plain clothes pushed their way inside. They looked around the room and one of them took a list from his pocket. Standing close to him, I could see all of our names written on the piece of paper: Father's, Mother's, my two brothers', and mine.

The officer looked up and nodded toward the woman standing a few paces away. "Who's that?" he growled.

"The cleaning lady," Mom replied casually.

"The cleaning lady?"

The policeman studied her for a moment, glanced at the list, and then shrugged. Before he could say anything else, the woman slipped out the door.

Then he read off our names. "Where is Victor, your husband?" he snarled at my mother.

Mom looked down at the ground and kept quiet.

The second policeman turned to her and snapped, "You heard him. Where is your husband?"

"He's visiting some relatives," Mom said, after a hesitant pause.

"Where?"

Mom hesitated.

"Amstelveen," my brother Eli said.

The second policeman motioned with his head to his friend and he searched our three-room apartment then came back, growling grimly, "*Verdomme* [damn], he is not here." To my mother he added, "You have 30 minutes to pack your things."

They ordered us to pack our belongings and come with them to an assembling point, a Neo-Renaissance municipal theater building named *Hollandsche Schouwburg*, located in the center of Amsterdam. Ironically, it was often used to celebrate Jewish holidays and festivities.

"Take only what you can carry. One suitcase, one handbag, and one rucksack. *Now!*

Mom nodded and furtively wiped her eyes with the palms of her hands. She started bustling about, packing our things while the Dutch officers stood looking on with expressionless eyes. We boys helped as best we could.

We didn't know if we should pack for summer and winter or how long we would be gone. We helped Mother, putting stacks of clothing in the suitcases.

One of the men was guarding the front door and the other wandered into the kitchen, whistling a Dutch song. He stepped up to a cupboard, pulled open the top drawer and glanced inside. He found half a dozen eggs stored in a carton. He gave his companion a conspiratorial wink and reached for the raw eggs, tipped his head back, and cracked them open one by one directly into his mouth. He wiped his mouth on his sleeve. I watched him in horrified fascination as bile rose in my throat.

When we had finished and were about to leave the apartment, the officer who had been cracking open the eggs coldly stared at Mother, held out his hand, and harshly demanded the keys.

She meekly handed them over. In all likelihood, once we were shipped off to the camps, the *Reichskommissariat* [civilian occupation regime] would give the two men official permission to rob our apartment of all its valuables.

"Now, move!"

The two Dutch policemen hurried us out the door into the street. As we waited for a streetcar, our friends and neighbors knew what was going to happen to us. They turned their faces away, too afraid to acknowledge us as if we were strangers.

The moment we boarded that streetcar, I felt like I was caught in a nightmare. My family had been deprived of our home and our belongings and our freedom and now, we were officially declared prisoners and would be deported to God only knew what horrible place. None of the passengers seated next to us in the streetcar would nod and reach out or say a friendly, encouraging word. Not one of them.

The majority of the Dutch population had stayed passive and remained silent in the early years of the occupation. Any form of resistance to the Nazi occupation took time to evolve. But it must be said that there was a growing number of good Dutch people who risked their lives saving Jews by hiding them in their homes during the war. More aggravating was the way the institutions responded. The police and civil service willingly cooperated with the Nazi agenda. *Nederlandse Spoorwegen*, the Dutch railway company, would eventually be forced to pay compensation to those who were deported to concentration camps on the trains it organized, at a profit.

The roundups and deportation were usually executed in a dispassionate and methodical manner. The two Dutch policemen who arrested us were passionless, hard-hearted beings, showing no compassion.

When we got to the Hollandsche Schouwburg, a squat angular three-story stone building with a dark gray facade located in the center of Amsterdam, we were hustled inside and stood in line with other people wearing yellow stars. When it was our turn, the police handed the Nazi soldier at the desk the list of our names. He confirmed it with my mother, then stamped it.

"No husband."

She shook her head. He made a note on the list and stamped it as confirmed.

"Move along!" he shouted. "Next!"

We were kept there in a large auditorium for an entire week, with little to no food.

The grueling wait of seven days and nights in that overcrowded, devastatingly depressing theater felt like an eternity. It seemed to go on and on. I kept wondering what had happened to Father. Where was he? Was he safe? Mom wasn't a big help either. I couldn't know how frightened she was, since she tried to hold herself together for our sake and didn't say anything. She simply sat there, downcast and hollow-eyed, with a dispirited expression on her haggard face.

My brothers and I spent most of the time wandering the

length and width of that high-ceilinged, large theater auditorium, or sitting and sleeping in the brick-red plush theater seats. During the day, Dutch nurses who worked for the Jewish Council passed out meager meals and drinks. We had to share the toilets and long queues formed in front of the washrooms. Kids ran up and down the aisles. Mothers tried to calm their crying babies. From where I sat, glancing around, I saw no one I could talk to, no boys I knew, just more and more families sitting there, waiting.

A growing number of people poured in. The smell of hot coffee, sweat, and traces of perfume lingered for all the days we were in the auditorium. The air was thick with a sharp, almost tangy odor of not knowing what lay in store for us.

Every now and then, an elderly person would faint and would be rushed on a gurney down the hallway to a makeshift hospital ward on the ground floor.

Late in the evenings (and sometimes at night), uniformed Nazi officers would strut about on stage and bellow crude German insults at us. I couldn't understand them, but their screaming would send cold shivers through me, and I would clap my hands over my ears to block those coarse profanities.

One of the ways these monsters delighted in entertaining themselves was ordering women on stage and forcing them to sing a song while standing on one leg.

One evening, one of the SS glanced about and picked a young, blonde woman who was seated nearby, and gestured for her to come on stage.

Beneath the stage lights, I could see the terror in the woman's eyes as she stood there on the podium and began to sing a Dutch folk song: "*Daar bij die molen, die mooie molen* [Oh, there at the mill, that beautiful mill...]."

Standing there, trying hard to keep her balance, her shaking voice faltered. One of the Nazi louts standing near gave her a brutal shove from behind which sent her flying across the stage floor.

Fellow guards who stood nearby broke out into ribald laughter. The young woman laid there for a moment, shocked, gasping for breath, then scrambled to her feet, ran back to her seat, and, burying her face in her hands, burst into tears.

By this time, the theater had become a crowded mass of people, all wearing the yellow star on their clothing.

After seven days of this torture, the SS had enough people rounded up. They ordered us over the loudspeaker to grab our possessions, head for the exit, and get ready for departure. Now what seemed like hundreds of people, old and young, parents carrying babies in their arms or holding hands with their little scared kids, started shuffling toward the arched exits, thankful to escape the oppressively stifling room.

It was a clear, chilly September day. Many people had gathered across the street to watch us climb into local buses while Nazi officers and Dutch fascists armed with automatic weapons impatiently ordered us to move along.

"*Verder gaan, mensen! Verder gaan!* [Keep going, people! Move along! Move along!]" they called out with impassive faces. "Clear the way! Clear the way!"

"Where are you taking us?" I heard one man ask.

"Shut up and move!" a Nazi said stonily, pushing the man into the bus.

"Mom," I asked, "where are we going? How will Dad find us?"

She didn't answer. I saw the tears welling up in her eyes.

Minutes later, we got off the bus at the large Central station and were herded into ordinary passenger cars.

Not knowing what awaited us out there filled us with fear.

My mother had barely spoken a word during the ride across the Dutch countryside. She just sat there motionless, staring emptily out the window at the changing Dutch landscape sliding past us: brown-stone windmills at the edge of stream beds; large patches of birch forests; little green meadows with cattle grazing in the trees and brightly colored flower fields alternating with ditches crisscrossing flat farmlands. We did not ordinarily drive out of the city, and the countryside might have been beautiful scenery for me. But my father's absence – and what it was doing to Mom – took away all my spirit.

We rode all through the night, sleeping on seats, with nothing to eat. The black-uniformed *Marechaussee* – the Dutch Military Police – were guarding the train. We were grateful they were Dutch and not Germans. Unlike the Dutch police, the Military Police were neutral, and we considered them as being on our side.

That morning, our train pulled into the small railway platform of the transit camp Westerbork, in the northern part of Holland. The black uniformed *Marechaussee*, were outside to meet the train. They loaded us into wagons and trucks to make the 15-kilometer trip to the camp.

WESTERBORK

Camp Westerbork was surrounded by forest grounds and looked deceptively bucolic. The green and brown colors of the trees hid the camp's guard towers and layers of barbed wire. Later I would learn that we were situated in the middle of the eastern province Drenthe, about 80 miles (130 kilometers) north of Amsterdam.

After we entered the camp, men and women were separated and lived in different quarters, but were allowed to mingle freely during the day. Children under 12 were placed in the women's barracks. My brothers, who were older, were placed in the men's barracks.

Besides being imprisoned and robbed of our human rights, it needs to be said that life in Westerbork was tolerable up to a certain point and was not like what you would call an extermination camp. We got enough food and were treated fairly.

We seldom saw the dreaded SS with the grisly skull-and-crossbones insignias. The compound itself was run by members of a Jewish council which was made up of Jewish elders deported there, the majority of whom were German Jews who had been in the camp from the very beginning. The camp was guarded by the *Marechaussee*.

There was a pharmacy, a hospital with doctors, a dental clinic, a hairdresser, and the police (not very popular) with "OD" badges (standing for *Ordnungsdienst*, order maintenance) pinned to their left breast pockets. My brothers and I enjoyed sport-filled days with soccer games. There was also some entertainment every Tuesday night including cabaret and theater performances with German and Dutch Jewish inmates who were top performers with professional theater experience before their deportation. Every Monday night, there was a *Bunte Abend*, an "enjoyable evening" to distract the inmates from the dreadful transports of Tuesday morning. Later we would learn that all of these events and services were staged to maintain a sense of calm among the Jewish prisoners, give them a false sense of normalcy and hope of survival.

But fear was never far away, a threatening shadow following every move. We worried about the days that laid ahead of us.

Around mid-July 1943, our family was part of a group of 600 prisoners who were transferred by train to Camp Amersfoort, in central Holland to make room for an influx of new arrivals in Westerbork.

To get to the camp we had to walk from the railway station through Amersfoort, a quiet, peaceful town surrounded by a thick oak and birch forest. We passed gardens and white farmhouses with low roofs and open fields where kids were playing soccer in the sun. But once outside the town, the dark nature of the place became clear. It started as a transit camp from 1942 to 1943 for prisoners destined for the Buchenwald extermination camp, but had since become more of a forced labor camp. We lived there for 30 days in makeshift brick and stone barracks and slept in narrow iron frame beds arranged in double tiers, and passed our days doing a variety of jobs like camp maintenance. Time went by, and we tried not to think what other horrors lay ahead.

After the short stay in Camp Amersfoort, we were shipped back to Westerbork in early August.

Uppermost in people's minds was the war, how long it would last. In the meantime, the mantra in the camp was "Hang in there" and "Don't let your heads hang down."

That was the beginning.

But soon things began to change: The deportation of inmates from Westerbork to the concentration camps in Germany and Poland began to roll...

With growing fear, we watched as the passenger cars arriving at the camp were replaced by freight cars, and uniformed SS men disembarked.

I still remember when the first long windowless freight train with the metal train sign "WESTERBORK-AUSCHWITZ – AUSCHWITZ-WESTERBORK" pulled in. The cars were emptied out by a cleaning crew of inmates, going from car to car, cleaning the buckets used for toilets and picking up garbage and litter from the floor.

The cleaning crew in Westerbork discovered concealed messages scribbled on little scraps of paper hidden in the cracks across floors and wood benches of train cars. These notes described the hideous conditions of camps at Auschwitz and Sobibor. We listened in horror as the messages were read to us: the starvation, the beatings, the gas chambers that exterminated thousands of prisoners and the ovens that burned their bodies.

Apparently, these notes were put there by the cleaning work unit of prisoners at Auschwitz who cleaned the train cars that would return to Westerbork. As this information was shared throughout the camp, our fear increased, and we wondered who would be next.

And today, many years later, as I sit here writing these words, it seems surreal to me that despite all this, despite the fact that the Dutch Jews in Westerbork knew what was happening once they were put on the deportation list, knew that they were going to be shipped off to extermination camps, they didn't resist or try to escape, but embraced denial instead, and tried to ignore the unbelievable monstrosities happening around them.

But what else could they possibly have done? Rebel? Fight the armed SS guards? Attempt to escape? Many of us tried. But those willing to fight were too few, and anyone who tried, was cold-bloodedly shot by the SS. On the spot. We had witnessed this, the ruthless killing and lack of humanity in these creatures sent to make sure we stayed where we were told and followed every order. Bit by bit, the Nazis groomed us into accepting one wretched change in our lives after the other, each one a step lower down the abyss, until we willingly walked onto the train knowing where we were headed. We had nowhere else to go. We were powerless.

Until we stepped onto that train, ignoring reality was our only option.

I can see now that the Auschwitz inmates leaving warning notes for the next group of passengers that were going to be in the same situation were both courageous and desperate. They were trying to save whoever came after.

On days before the train came to deliver people, and sometimes on other random summer nights, the prisoners played the accordion. The evening air was mild and the notes rose high above the heads of dancing couples as they moved around to the beat of the Dutch folk songs. Despite being prisoners, for a few minutes, they were unconcerned about their future. These were touching moments.

I remember as clearly as if it were yesterday how we youngsters would nimbly climb up the wooden support beams underneath the slanting roof of the barracks and watch the performances from up high, as though we had orchestra seats with the best view. In hindsight, I wonder how people who knew what lay in store for them could still laugh or dance to cheerful music. *How – how was it possible?*

Maybe they did not believe that people could do such horrible things to each other. Maybe they thought it was all a lie, that the Nazis would put us in labor camps, "resettle" (the Nazis' term) and relocate us to the east. Heck, they might even have believed that the war would be over soon and everything would be just fine.

Yes, maybe, maybe not.

But every Tuesday, the brutal reality would set in when deportation started.

TUESDAYS

From July 1942 until September 1944, transports left Westerbork for Auschwitz at about 11 in the morning on Tuesdays. That is when the greatly feared transport list made its appearance, and everyone fervently hoped not to be on it.

Every Tuesday around 3:00 a.m., a member of the Jewish police force (OD) came into the sleeping women's and men's barracks. The lights would turn on, and everyone would anxiously awake. The OD officer would glance around, climb onto a chair, and begin to read the names of prisoners that had been selected for deportation to one of the death camps.

The Jewish police were forced to make these lists, but we never learned how they made their choices. I remember sitting there and listening to the names, my heart pounding in my throat, thinking, *will we be next in line?*

We watched helplessly as our fellow inmates' names got called out.

The call-up usually lasted 30 minutes. Then the lights dimmed and the police left. Those called up would hug their friends and relatives in between sobbing.

We, the lucky ones holding South American papers, were being exempt from deportation for the time being.

As they came to know what awaited them, anyone without these papers who had the means would have done anything to get off the dreaded lists. Some would bribe Jewish police, offering their wedding rings, expensive jewelry, their bracelets, watches, and gemstones. Sometimes, young girls would go so far as to offer their bodies if it would grant them exemption.

Some were fortunate enough to find a doctor who would get them on the sick list and into the hospital ward, which meant they would be barred from getting on a transport. Others tried and succeeded in joining the OD and so could delay the transport to the east for another couple of weeks. But in the end, almost every Jew would be shipped off to the extermination camps located in Poland, to Auschwitz or to Sobibor. Or to Bergen-Belsen in East Germany.

During deportation day, there was a curfew until the prisoners were on board. People stayed inside the barracks and watched through the windows.

We could see the long line of rusty brown cattle cars parked on the empty railroad, waiting for the hapless prisoners to come struggling up the narrow platform with their paltry belongings: a rolled-up blanket, a suitcase, or a bread bag dangling down their backs.

The policemen walked alongside them, calling out: "*Doorlopen!* Move along! Move along! Keep it moving people! Keep it moving!"

Invalids were wheeled or carried on stretchers by the OD officer to the waiting cattle cars.

Prior to departure, several SS officers gathered on the platform to check the lists and make sure that everyone was on the train. They stood on the platform, stone-faced as families pushed their way into the crowded cattle cars, trying desperately to stick together. Once everyone was accounted for, the Nazis slammed the doors of each car shut and locked them.

Then the train driver climbed up into the locomotive and blew the whistle. The train started to move, and SS men, rifles slung over their backs, swung up onto the single Nazi guard carriage while the commandant, SS Obersturmführer Gemmeker, stayed the platform in his brown leather overcoat and riding breeches next to his little dog, and watched stolidly as the train pulled out, heading eastward toward the death camps.

After the trains began moving, everybody started coming out of the barracks. I recall seeing prisoners standing outside on the platform, watching the train cars go by. Their arms were outstretched in desperation as they waved goodbye to relatives and friends despite the fact that they could not see them.

I remember one young, good-looking woman. Her husband was about to board the train to Auschwitz alone. They stood two feet away. He had put his arm around her as she began to cry. As he stood there comforting her, she kept shaking her head from side to side. He told her that everything would be fine. They would see each other again soon, and maybe in a camp similar to Westerbork. Everybody tried to make the best of a hopeless situation. After the curfew, I saw her standing alone on the platform sobbing hysterically, tears streaming down her face after the train had left the station. That was the last I saw of them.

As I write this, I find myself wondering what those Nazi officers were thinking as they watched hundreds of people head to their deaths. Did they even care? What about their own families, their wives and children back home? Did they tell them what they did? How could they live with themselves?

After the war, when confronted with the monstrosities of their actions, former Nazis would shrug their shoulders and insist without remorse that they didn't know what was happening. Of course they knew, but what could they have done? Refuse following orders and face court martial or execution for treason? In many ways, they were just as imprisoned as we were.

After months of enduring this existence, our prayers were answered. We were thankfully reunited with Father at Westerbork. He found us in one of the long wooden barracks. We ran to him and we all hugged tightly.

"What happened to you?" my mother asked.

"I was at my friend's house, trying to arrange our escape. It came to nothing," he began. "I went back to our house, and used my key to get inside. Everything was taken by the Nazi bandits."

My mother stared at him disbelieving. "You went back to our apartment?" Her brow furrowed. "What about the neighbors? Weren't you afraid they would report you? Didn't they see you?"

"I had to take the chance," he told her. "I thought I'd find you there. I stayed hidden; I had no place to go. I avoided everyone and only went out at night."

"The police might have come back."

"Yes, but they didn't. I know one of the police officers at the Hoofdbureau. He said he would warn me if any cop went to the apartment." He paused a moment. "When I learned that you were deported to Westerbork, I didn't know what to do. I got word to my friend in the country, who was kind enough to send some food packages to you. Did you get them?"

"Yes," my mother answered.

"How did you get caught?" I asked.

"When I shopped for the parcels, I didn't dare wear the yellow star. In short, my friend at the *Hoofdbureau* [Head office] lied. A week ago, the police surrounded our street and started pounding on doors. I was walking to the house. As soon as I saw them, I tried to run, but they caught me. They arrested me for not wearing the star and put me on the train to Westerbork. You know," he said, showing us the white *S* on his jacket sleeve, "as a *Sträfling*. Upon arrival I was put in the Penal Block. Once they checked my Paraguayan papers, they let me out and put me in the barracks. They released me earlier today. I've been looking for you for days."

My mother broke into a broad smile. I had seen her smile for the first time in many months. We all hugged Dad tightly. We were all happy to have him back.

BERGEN-BELSEN

January 11, 1944. We were next in line now. The Nazis assembled us at daybreak to announce the next group to be sent to the death camps. We listened as the OD officer called out our names for transport. Mother began to cry and Father tried to comfort her. My brothers and I were silent, paralyzed with fear.

Unlike others on the list, we were deported to Bergen-Belsen instead of Auschwitz because of our Paraguayan passports. We started off at Westerbork as a group of over 1,000 people, boarded a regular passenger train – generally, third class passenger cars were used for prisoners holding Latin American documents from Westerbork to Belsen – and traveled through a seemingly unending long night through the German countryside.

We stopped once at the dark deserted railroad station in Bremen. When we arrived, there wasn't a soul in sight, we only saw a couple of steel-helmeted SS soldiers, rifles slung on their backs, pacing the echoing empty platform back and forth, back and forth.

A German voice over a loudspeaker was booming out across the empty platforms: "*Das Betreten des Bahnhof-Areas ist verboten.*" [Entry to the railway station is forbidden to the public].

Looking out the window at the bleak, empty station in front of us, the passengers in our compartment figured that the reason must have been because of us passing through.

Near dawn the train stopped at a narrow loading platform in the middle of nowhere surrounded by a sea of deserted gray wintry farmland. We were cold and hungry and frightened. We were ordered to disembark from the train in the freezing early morning.

Dozens of machine gun-toting Waffen SS soldiers some with growling German shepherds straining on their leashes packed us into a waiting fleet of military trucks. After driving 20 minutes through the snow-covered Lüneburger heath, we reached the desolate Bergen-Belsen camp.

The caravan of trucks stopped.

The SS shouted at us to get out of the trucks. "Get off the trucks! *Runter! Vorwärts! Alles raus!* [Out! Everything out!] *In Reihen von fünf aufstellen.* [Line up in five! Line up in five!] *Los! Los!*" We lined up as the vicious dogs snarled and barked just a few feet away. It was frightening. Male and female prisoners were separated. My brothers and I stood there, looking for my father who was luckily in line behind us.

"*Vorwärts! Schnell!*" one officer hollered as they marched us through the high front gate like sheep to the slaughterhouse.

My first impression of the camp was chilling. I felt my chest tighten.

Menacing-looking wooden lookout towers behind barb wire fencing sat at intervals of about 30 meters and were manned by SS soldiers with machine guns who watched the camp through high-powered binoculars. As we stared at the chilling sight spread out before us, it seemed as if the gloating devil herself was sneeringly welcoming us inside.

The entire camp was encircled by a 13-foot-barbed wire topped razor sharp concertina wire. Later we would learn that the fence was electrified. Long rows of low wooden barracks filled most of the grounds. We took all this in as we debarked from the trucks under a hail of this abusive SS yelling and dog barking,

We waited for maybe 30 minutes with the hundreds of other men in front of the murky barracks. Broken in groups of a hundred, we were herded into each barrack. The low, unheated buildings had small windows on both sides and wide enough for three long rows of three tiered wooden bunks down the sides. The block elders – Jews who had been selected by the SS to be in charge of the barracks – handed us a small ration of bread with a scoop of soft white cheese on top but nothing to drink. They informed my father and me, we were assigned Barracks 98, and ordered us to go there. My brothers were sent to Barracks 105, a few buildings down. We hugged my brothers and went off, eating as we walked.

The filthy barracks was 50 meters long with hardwood floors. There was only one medium-sized toilet stall in each barracks and attached were cast iron wash basins. There were a few beat up tables with wooden benches surrounded by dozens of rows three-tiered bunk beds. Dad got the bottom and I got the middle of one bunk toward the back. Outside, about 90 meters (100 yards) from the first barrack, stood a large door-less wooden shack, the camp's outdoor latrine.

A man named Joseph "Joop" Weiss, the deputy Senior Jewish Prisoner, told us how the camp worked; every morning, all prisoners, male and female assigned to the work details had to wake up at 5:30 – make their bunks then attend a "head count" at the *Appellplatz*, a large open area located in the center of the camp compound across from the entrance gate where they would be counted off by the SS before going to the workhouses. Workhouses were co-ed. The rest of the prisoners had to assemble at 7:00 am. After roll call, the children returned to the barracks with adults not assigned to work details.

"There are three meals a day delivered to your barracks," Mr. Weiss told us. "Coffee, and two slices of bread early in the mornings; soup or vegetable stew around noon; and at night, a piece of bread with a bit of cheese, jam or margarine. Working prisoners eat at the workhouses."

As I stood there listening to him, my heart sank, and I shuddered at the thought of what lay ahead of us. Two, three slices of bread a day? How long, I thought, would we have to stay in this miserable, godforsaken hellhole?

"Any food parcels sent through the Red Cross are supposed to be distributed to the addressees," Mr. Weiss informed us. "But," he added laconically, "the Nazis take them."

"You are allowed to keep your luggage and clothes. Everybody here continues to wear the clothes they arrived in. This section of the camp is called *Sternlager* [Star camp]. You must wear the yellow star at all times."

"Men and women work together. After the workday, men and women are permitted to meet." He paused a moment. "Follow the rules and there won't be any trouble."

And that was it. No questions.

My parents and my two brothers worked in the workhouse *Schuhkommando* [the shoe work group], located a short ride out outside in the camp. It was 11 hours of dirty, tedious work, salvaging usable leather from old shoes or sorting buttons to be used on German uniforms. After work we usually met at mother's barracks after dinner and before curfew.

When Dad returned to his barracks late in the evening, he was so tired he could barely eat. When we joined Mom, she sat there silent and looking disconsolate and haggard with dark circles under her sunken eyes, staring dully down at her hands.

To this day, these memories have me asking, "What did we do to deserve all that happened? We were just people, leading our lives as best we could. I keep wondering about the evil in the world, why people are so bestial to each other and why they keep fighting and destroying each other? Human beings are capable of such great and wonderful things such as beautiful art and culture, great advances in medicine and science, building magnificent cities, love and friendship, yet they are the most destructive force on the face of the earth.

Why is that? Good question. And the further question then arises; will humans ever change? *Can* they ever change?

Two months had gone by.

Over the next two months, winter had set in. The weather in north Germany is cold, real cold, *frigid*, teeth-chattering cold. It chilled us to the bone.

The temperature in the winter often hovers below zero, but once the temperature turns milder and snow is falling in silent flakes, it plunges the sloping barracks roofs and heavy forest and watch towers into a white, peaceful silence.

Obligatory roll calls usually would go on for hours, until the count turned out the right way. Often standing in snow, we endured abusive and degrading expletives. Many were so weak they fell to the ground.

My parents were already gone when we heard the SS yell, "*Appell! Appell!* [Roll call! Roll call!]"

One of the SS officers standing near the entrance of the barracks would join in, blowing the whistle, yelling: "*Raus! alle Leute raus!* [Everyone out!] Get it moving!"

The roll calls seemed to go on for hours, until the count turned out the right way. All kids below the age of 15 and the elderly, male and female, hastily lined up outside in the camp square while a group of SS officers huddling in the snow-covered quad conferred in low voices and then started counting, striding briskly up and down the line of inmates, who stood shaking in ranks of fives.

One of the SS officers, a stocky, thick-chested colonel with thick eyeglasses, holding a metal clipboard in his gloved hand started counting the prisoners methodically, pointing with his second finger. He was followed by two groveling staff sergeants, mumbling, "*Hundertzehn*, 110... 120... 130... 140..." Then suddenly the group of three men stopped, turned around, and moved toward the group of SS men who stood huddled together in their fur-collared winter coats in the middle of the quad.

As all the prisoners stood in the frigid air, the colonel deliberated with the group of SS men, first glancing at his clipboard and then glancing up at his fellow officers. The officer shook his head uncomprehendingly. Then he turned and walked back toward the inmates and started the roll call again. This this time he was followed by three uniformed subordinates who joined him in the counting.

The colonel bundled in his warm coat, his thick eyeglasses often fogging up, counted us slowly and methodically, one by one, while we stood there at attention. We weren't allowed to move or to speak even one word out of the side of our mouths. And the snow kept coming from the overcast sky – thick, soft flakes wrapping everything up in a furry-wool stillness as the inmates stood there in silence, shivering in their thin overcoats and inadequate shoes.

If someone dared to stamp his feet or flap their arms to ward off the cold, all hell broke loose. The four SS apes started hollering at us, accusing us of being slipshod, not showing up on time for roll call and not properly standing in a row of five, or whatever their excuse was for why the counting as so often had turned out incorrect. This disruption would cause the colonel to lose count. Instead of starting the count again, they decided to take a break. Good Lord! A break! Often, so often, the SS had counted too many or too few prisoners and now would have to start all over again till they got the numbers right. They would go into a huddle and start talking in hushed voices, their breath rising in clouds of steam in the center of the quad and then went into their barracks nearby presumably to warm up. In the meantime, we had to stand there with chattering teeth in our worn-out clothes without food and drink (or whatever substances they eventually gave us that stood in for food and drink) and wait till the SS would get back. It was torture. Many got sick from the exposure...

Dusk was falling when the wrought-iron camp gate opened. The different outside labor details returned from work, and we still stood there shivering in the numbing cold. Now the work details were marched through and were forced to join us and stand ramrod-straight in the middle of the quad to be counted again, to make sure no one had escaped. It took hours until the lucky moment would arrive when the SS finally got their numbers right.

"*Wegtreten! Abtreten! Dismissed!*" Finally the sound of the harsh voices of the SS would sweep across the freezing roll call quad, reverberating like a bugler's notes through the air. *W-e-g-t-r-e-t-e-n!* [Dismissed! Dismissed!]

Almost frozen stiff, we returned to our barracks, nursing our numb feet and hands, and sat on the edge of our beds or at the long wood table trying to warm ourselves with a tin cup of hot "coffee" and a slice of bread and a teaspoon of jam.

Each day, I remember seeing a young Lithuanian SS guard, not much older than my brothers stand guard by the gate, watching attentively as the inmates returned forming up for roll call. I shall never forget him. He stood there wide-legged, hands locked behind his back in his steel-gray SS uniform wearing the gray field cap with the Nazi emblem for the SS Death Head Unit, a human skull and cross bones.

He stood there silently, his stone -cold blue eyes paying close attention to the inmate count, waiting for someone to step out of line so he could punish them with a fierce beating. He had an ugly scar which ran from his left eye down to his chin. His gravelly voice caused a cold shudder to run up your spine. I can hear him to this day, barking orders or degrading us with contemptuous, vicious comments. His hateful behavior made him infamous among the inmates.

His name was Lukas Pavlenko.

Today, as time goes by, I can clearly recall how an evolution, a barely perceptible development in the prisoners' attitude had taken place. It was the realization that once you stepped inside the camp (read: death camp), it was the same as a death sentence, and you'd better accept the cold reality that one day you would end up dead here. It was a truly unsettling reality to live with.

Admittedly though, tiny glimmers of hope would shimmer

through the haze of suffering that if you were lucky, then one day you might come out the other side sane and alive. But the preponderance of prisoners lived with the grim reality that they were condemned to die here. The change in their attitude typically manifested itself in a gradual apathy, a posture of indifference to what was going on around them. The policy was to do whatever the SS orders you to do; stand at attention for hours on end at roll call and keep your mouth shut; go to work and obediently do what the Nazis command you to do; and say to them, "*Jawohl, Herr Obersturmführer*," and say it over and over, and as time passes, listen to your masters' commands like an automaton.

Actually, we began to change after months of living in the camp. Our attitudes slowly went from abject fear to a kind of numb acceptance, even apathy about our plight. We lost hope. Our status as exchange Jews grew more distant as time wore one. We learned to live like slaves and do whatever the SS ordered us to do, no matter how inane or difficult. Obey, or suffer the consequences.

And pretty soon, you may very well think and act like a robot (or slave) and accept your fate, though maybe deep down you still harbor hopes that miracles will happen and one day you will survive this god-awful hellhole. But you *obey*, and that's the main thing; you *obey* or else – "We have the means to *make* you obey, prisoner, *understand?*" – you keep nodding your head silently and sullenly, and you say, "*Jawohl, Herr Unterscharführer*," or "*Bitte schön, Herr Obersturmführer*," and you bow your head obsequiously and you say, "*Danke schön, Herr Standartenführer. Danke schön.* Please, thank you, sir, thank you, sir. It was like a broken record, always with the repeating refrain of German subservience.

As the warm weather approached, the face of the camp changed.

The SS had been rarely visible. Here and there they could be seen walking singly or in pairs or riding on motorcycles with sidecars on the camp's main road. Many of the SS troops assigned some of the routine guard duties to a group of black-bereted prisoners called Kapos. We recognized them from their white arm bands with bold black lettering KAPO and black berets. These overseers, generally a bunch of former Polish convicts and all sorts of vicious criminals were selected by the SS to keep the prisoners in line by whatever means necessary. They treated us with verbal abuse and cold disdain and we hated them almost as much as the Nazis.

As dawn broke, these *Kapos* would barge in yelling, "Get up. Get up. *Los, los.* Wake up. Fast, *schnell!*" and the prisoners would get up, get hastily dressed, gulp down the cup of "coffee," swallow the piece of bread, and then would be marched off to several places, always accompanied by two or three *Kapos* or armed SS guards. Then by sundown, looking tired, humiliated, beat, miserable, and irritated, they would be back inside the camp. By then the gates of the camp would get locked by the SS from the outside.

This was the way prisoners spent their days. Most inmates kept to themselves. That was true of my two brothers – they'd get up in the morning, would get marched off, and many hours later got back from their work shifts. Actually, we didn't see much of each other.

I hardly can remember the time we spent together outside of seeing each other when sitting and eating on the bunk beds or at the table next to other cheerless inmates who hardly would talk except of their tedious, endless hours' work. And then the next morning like a broken record, the new day started again; getting up, gulping the "coffee," swallowing the slice of bread, and then already being aware of what was lying ahead, they would go apathetically off to work – and well, that was it.

The one thing that we were grateful for was that our family was together in one place, unlike so many others who had been broken up and sent to different camps.

Looking back on it now, our lives in the camp, following orders blindly, was somewhat analogous to the fate of a soldier on the frontline of battle. He couldn't escape his fate and had to accept it, even if it could mean his death. Setting his jaw firm and gritting his teeth, he just had to continue to endure, and keep on fighting, and not giving into his fear. That was the same way many of us lived by in the camp, doggedly and obstinately following orders and surviving day to day. But while the solider could protect himself to some extent, we had no such luxury. The shadow of the camp's cremation plant loomed over us, spewing its ugly black smoke, poisoning our hope for a future. When would we be next? This week... maybe next week... maybe a month...

I recall how I often stood there and wondered, *how much longer, how many days?*

What will the future bring? But the thought of death never entered my mind. What I wanted was to get out of this filthy hole and be where there was food, enough glorious food. But there was a darker side of this the horrific life of servitude.

Our fellow prisoners started to become mean and selfish, willing to turn on their fellows Jews to get a crumb of better treatment. There were fights over little details like a blanket or a scrap of food or a cup of water. Trust and goodwill began to erode.

There's one occurrence that's indelibly etched on my memory.

One morning – it must have been around late July – a transport of a few hundred French people arrived from the Drancy transit camp, outside Paris. They were mostly young men and women. One of them, a tall, dark-haired, slim Frenchman, about 19 years old, who had been assigned to our barracks was sitting across from me at the empty table. He contentedly ate his bread ration, *the entire portion* he received upon arrival (the slice of bread with a scoop of white cheese on top) in several huge bites as if he were sitting back home at the kitchen table having a quiet breakfast snack. We other prisoners sat there staring at him with wide eyes. Apparently, the man had no idea what lay ahead of him.

A few months later, we were sitting one evening at the same table in the barracks spooning our watery cabbage soup when Leo, a hollow-cheeked Dutchman in his fifties, looked around at the bunks just across from the table, then suddenly got up and dashed as fast as his painfully thin legs could carry him to the Frenchman's bunk where he'd left a slice of bread on the pillow.

"Hey you!" yelled Michel the Frenchman. "Come back here! Come back! That's my bread!"

Leo stopped dead in his tracks, turned and began to curse.

We sat there and watched in stunned disbelief as that bony, skeletal Dutchman stood there momentarily hesitating, mulling over his options. He could give it back and shut up, or he could try to talk the Frenchman into letting him have a piece, which was improbable.

Seeing no other way, the Dutchman suddenly broke a large piece off the bread, quickly stuffed it into his mouth, hastily chewed, then broke off another piece, a larger one, and jubilantly wolfed it down. Now, the Frenchman jumped to his feet and together with another inmate tackled him (though it must be said, a little puff from someone's lips and the Dutchman would have drifted away in the air like a feather) and punched him in the jaw. Leo fell to the floor, gasping for air, then shrieking and kicking away at the two of them, trying to hold on to his beloved little piece of bread. The Frenchman's comrade wrenched it away from him and handed it over to Michel, who, cursing viciously, started kicking the Dutch guy in the head. Leo lay there writhing and moaning and crying in a weepy voice, "D-don't hurt me, please."

They finally let him up and the Frenchman yelled, "Filthy thief!"

Most of us just sat there looking on in sullen silence. No one interfered. We had seen it too many times before. Hunger and desperation drove people to act like animals. And in the end, despite this desperate, teeth-grinding resolve to survive, many faced the inexorable cruel death from the conditions of the camp.

We youngsters – aged between 12 and 14 – stayed back in the barracks. I had made three friends and we spent a lot of time together. One was blond Kees Graaf, the other was Henk de Vries, and then there was small, curly-haired 13-year-old Uriel de Jong, who hailed from Rotterdam. We talked hopefully about the days when we would be free again, and thought nostalgically of the freedom we'd once known.

Since we were too young for work details we would sit in chairs in the sun in front of the barracks and would fantasize about delicious mouthwatering hamburger sandwiches dripping with grease or delicious sunny-side up eggs and juicy steaks with fluffy mashed potatoes served up on silver trays, and we would say to each other, "Hey, take your pick," and one of us, usually Henk, would smack his lips with a long slurping sound, miming that he was munching on something succulent... As I sat there listening to their reminiscing, I suddenly found myself thinking if only I had wings and could fly, I would soar like an eagle so high, soar through the deep blue sky, away from this godforsaken place. If I could just glide like a stately ship to the free world and *be free* like a bird, oh, how wonderful that would be. But then my thoughts would switch back to where we were now, and I asked myself *what will the next couple of months bring*, and then the thought of freedom quickly disappeared, faded away.

And then again, as lots of rumors swirled around the camp about an Allied landing, and we were thinking maybe in a few weeks, maybe in a month, maybe even sooner – perhaps as early as next week – yes, who knew?

One morning, after our roll call, I heard the piercing sound of an air raid siren. The German soldiers in the camp were running about. I frowned. Something big must be going on.

Then a distant humming filled the air. It grew louder as the minutes passed, moving closer and closer, and then boom! A deafening roar passed over the camp that made the ground under me shudder as though an earthquake was about to split the earth apart.

Seconds later came the second thundering sound of an aircraft flying over. I glanced up and saw two planes circling overhead. They swooped out of the deep blue sky with an ear-splitting roar and then the rattling of machine guns began. Then another flame-spitting plane roared past. *Woosh!* And *boom*. The plane was twinkling in the sunlight. Frightened, I ran behind the outdoor latrine for cover as the bullets rained down on the camp.

Filled with a sudden euphoria, I thought, *the camp is under attack! Maybe the rumors have been true after all. Maybe the Allies have come to free us.*

One hundred meters from me a small group of youngsters had appeared outside the barrack. They were shielding their eyes with their hands from the sun, staring excitedly into the sky. Then scattered like pins in a bowling alley when another fighter plane leapt over the forest tree tops, firing at full blast at the lookout towers, blowing it up into a huge fireball.

As I watched a line of bullets furiously stitched across the asphalt kicking up small stones and dirt and deathly afraid of being killed, I hit the ground and lay there frozen in fear. The low-flying planes continued to strafe the camp. Then, as quickly as they appeared, the planes were gone and an eerie silence had settled over the camp.

I got up and looked around. The camp was in chaos. On the asphalt road beyond the barbed wire fence command vehicles pulled up and SS men leapt down out cursing and hollering at the prisoners to get the hell back into the barracks. I ran back to the barracks to find my friends.

Luckily, none of us was hurt. We talked excitedly about the attack. *Could the rumors be true? Were the Allies winning the war against the Nazis? Could our freedom be close at hand?*

We saw a column of black smoke rising slowly into the sky behind the pine forest and later learned that the planes had bombed and destroyed an ammunition depot and a fire range. There was much discussion of the prisoners' disappointment that the planes hadn't bothered to bomb the SS barracks. Why had they spared the Nazi barracks? I heard one man say he felt like a bride waiting with excitement at her wedding ceremony only to have her groom not show.

A few weeks later, during September 1944, we learned about the Allied landing in Normandy on the west coast of France, and rumors were buzzing that the Allies had already invaded the first villages in southern France and now pushed deeper and deeper into the country. When we went to bed at night, we could hear the humming, droning sound of Allied fighter planes flying overhead above the clouds on their way to Germany to drop tons of bombs on the German cities. Picturing it – actually *seeing* in my mind the pilots opening the bay doors of the planes, releasing their loads of bombs upon the hated German towns – filled me with immense satisfaction. One glimmer of hope kept blinking at us like a flickering neon tube: *Could the rumors be true? Were the Allies winning the war against the Nazis? Could our freedom be close at hand?*

And that kept us going and breathing and hoping.

A LIGHT IN THE DARKNESS

Summer and autumn had passed, and we faced another cold winter in Bergen-Belsen.

On Tuesday evening December 27, my father told me in a low voice that tomorrow on my 13th birthday, I would have my bar mitzvah. I remembered my brothers' bar mitzvah ceremonies and the time they spent studying for the Torah reading.

"But Dad, in this place? What if the Nazis find out?" I knew that any demonstration of our Jewish faith was strictly forbidden.

"Don't worry. I asked our men friends to form a minyan in barracks tonight when the monsters are not awake to say a brief blessing. It will be safe."

Father had set aside his daily bread ration and had asked some acquaintances to come to our barracks for a minyan and a brief celebration of my bar mitzvah.

I was excited to become a man in in our religion and around midnight,

ten men quietly gathered in silence between the three-tiered bunk beds as I softly recited the blessing my father had taught me earlier, which men recite when called to the Torah.

"*Barchu es Hashem hamevorach.*"

And the men responded, "*Baruch Hashem hamevorach l'olam va'ed.*"

I continued, "*Baruch Attah Hashem Elokeinu Melech ha'olam asher bachar banu mi'kol ha'amim v'nasan lanu es Toraso. Baruch Attah Hashem, nosein haTorah.*"

Then my father said the special blessing of *baruch shepetarani* said by the father of a boy who has reached the age of bar mitzvah. There was a hearty mazel tov. Father proudly slapped me on my shoulder and then he gave everyone a piece of the ration he had saved up for a bar mitzvah "meal." Afterwards, everybody returned to their bunks and went back to sleep.

It had been a pretty tense moment doing this ritual, hidden between the silent rows of three-tiered bunk beds, making sure that no one would see us. All religious practice was forbidden by the Nazis and harshly punished. I don't know if they had any religion other than that of conquering and killing.

That day when my parents came back from work, a great surprise awaited me. Gray-haired Joop Weiss, the head of the barracks, presented me with a big smile on his face my bar mitzvah present: *a delicious fresh loaf of bread!*

Staring at it, my eyes nearly popped out of my head and my mouth started watering just thinking of eating a crusty piece of that bread. I'm not kidding, holding the loaf in my hand, I felt like the owner of a 24-karat gold bar. This present was irreplaceable. I would not have traded it for anything in the world. For nothing. Period.

Anyone who hasn't been in captivity in a Nazi camp suffering from this awful gnawing hunger can't imagine what it was like to receive such a present. A whole loaf of bread! Can you believe it? *A loaf of fresh bread!* Oh, boy. I did not spend time wondering how Mr. Weiss had managed to obtain it, though as I write this, I try to unravel whom he would have had to bribe – and with what – to find me this priceless gift.

I thanked Mr. Weiss profusely, then unable to wait any longer, I tore off a piece and stuffed it my mouth. Everyone laughed at my eagerness.

Smiling gently, Mom extended her hand for the bread. "Will, don't eat it all at once. We need to save it as the food rations are getting smaller each day."

I wanted to keep the bread for myself, and was about to say,

"Hey, that's my present," but wisely kept my mouth shut and handed it to my mother

and watched with a sinking heart as mother, biting her lower lip in concentration, started arranging for little portions, making notch marks with the knife along the top edge of the loaf of bread. She hid it under her bunk.

Later in the day, when we were all together, we shared the momentous news with my brothers. They all were so happy for me. We shared this bright moment in the darkness along with my bar mitzvah bread.

ANOTHER ACT OF CRUELTY

It was about one week later on a particularly cold January morning. Dad had left for the work detail and I joined my friends sitting on a bench near the door of the barracks. They were unusually quiet.

"What's wrong?" I asked them.

Kees stared at me. "It's about your mother."

I felt my stomach plummet. "What about her?"

"I saw that pig Pavlenko dragging her in front of the commander. From what I could hear, she missed the work detail."

"When?"

"A few hours ago. Remember that guy from barracks 16? When he missed the work detail, they made him stand all night long at the electrified barbed wire fence. They'll probably do the same thing to your mother tonight."

"What?" I was shocked, didn't know what to say. Standing in front of the gate in the icy wind all night till daybreak while SS guards were patrolling in front of you, was a nightmare. I knew that quite a few prisoners had been punished this way. When they became weak or began to shake or almost fainted and dropped to the ground, the SS guard kicked their faces and clubbed them, forcing them to stand up. Sometimes, it pushed them over the edge and they flung themselves on the fence and got electrocuted. In fact, I had watched one morning as prisoners pulled the corpse of an inmate who got electrocuted across the stony square toward the crematoria. I could not bear to think about Mom being–"

"Where is she now?"

Kees shrugged. "Probably back in the barracks."

I panicked. "I've got to see her."

"Don't. The Kapos might report you."

"Bastards," I spit. "I don't care."

That afternoon, I went to see mother at her barrack. She stood there in the corner of the room as Mr. Weiss was speaking to her. I moved toward them.

"They want you to feel intimidated," he told her. "Don't be scared. There's no reason to be afraid of anything. You'll be fine. Take these," he said, handing her a pile of old German newspapers.

I stared at the papers. I vaguely recall reading the headlines. *Immer mehr Bomben* [More and more bombs], *Deutschland im Kriegszustand* [Germany in state of war], *Der Landsturm* [The reserve forces]...

"Put on several layers of clothing," Joop Weiss advised her, "and put the newspapers between your clothes and wrap your entire body and feet in them to keep warm."

She thanked him.

"Stay strong for your children," he said and turned and went across the long room and out the door.

"Mom," I said softly as I walked out of the shadows.

"William!" She turned to me. "What are you doing here?"

"I heard about the punishment because of Pavlenko. I wanted to see you before."

She hugged me. "Don't worry," she said. "I'll be all right."

I nodded. "Mom, I..."

I sat down and we talked for a few minutes. I looked across at her and saw the tension in her face. Dad and my brothers had also come to see her. She told me again that everything would be fine.

Before I left, she looked me in the eye and said calmly, "Don't worry, Will. I'll be all right." She gave me a thin smile. "It's only one night."

Filled with dread, I turned away.

At dusk, when Dad got back, I told him that I went to see Mom.

"That was brave but foolish," he said. "You could have been punished as well."

"I was careful," I said to him. "Mr. Weiss gave her newspapers to stuff under her clothes to keep her warm. She said she'd be okay."

Dad cursed. "That bastard Pavlenko. I wish I could–" He stopped, knowing it was futile to even think about fighting back.

About an hour later, we watched from the front door of the barracks as Pavlenko dragged Mom out to the fence. It was bitter cold. I could see her standing there when the searchlights shone on her position. Pavlenko and another Nazi stood guard. My heart broke for her, but there was nothing we could do.

"Don't worry," Dad said, patting me on the back. "Your mother is strong. She will be all right." He nodded. "God will protect her."

I hoped he was right. We watched as that miserable monster and another soldier screamed at Mom, hitting her with their rifle butts. She stumbled, but they forced her to stand still. The bitter wind howled.

We tried to stay awake as long as possible, but it was too painful to watch. Exhausted, we went back to our bunks. I had a hard time sleeping.

Next morning, I got up with Dad and watched as he assembled for the worker roll call. I looked for my mother, but she wasn't there. I was worried. Was she okay? After our roll call, I went over to her barracks.

One older woman told me she was in her bunk.

My mother was lying under the blanket on her bunk, shivering.

I touched her shoulder. "Mom?"

She turned to look at me. She could barely speak. Her teeth were chattering from the cold. "Wil...il...iam..."

I looked at her and asked how she felt.

She just stared back at me, unable to speak. I reached for her ice-cold hand. She was too sick and weak for work. I took a deep breath and tried to calm myself down. These Nazis, I thought, these vicious beasts. They abused prisoners as if they were nothing more than discarded trash. At least, I told myself, they let her rest.

I looked at the empty bunk above her, pulled down a blanket folded there and covered my mother with it. I took a seat across from her, and she explained what happened. Among the SS who had been on duty during the night was Pavlenko, who had kept watching her like a hawk, taunting her and prodding her with the tip of his rifle, while making sneering comments. While fighting sleep all night, she would take deep breaths and try to control her emotions and as she stood shivering in the icy cold, and she would think about us having a wonderful new life in peace, owning our own little home and never returning to Germany. In her mind, she could see the Swiss Alps in summer which she often had visited as a child. She immersed herself in seeing the peaceful scenery of lakes, forests and mountains and imagining hearing the soothing sound of the distant cow bells...

The last one or two hours she had been shivering uncontrollably and was almost too weak to move or stand. All she needed, she said, was a little crumb of bread or something to drink. When the first light of dawn light had appeared, a prisoner-foreman had escorted her back to the barracks, where, physically and emotionally exhausted, she had fallen into bed and instantly gone to sleep.

When prisoners standing at the fence for about eight hours straight as a punishment became weak or began to shake or almost fainted and dropped to the ground, nothing delighted the SS men and *Kapos* more than to kick their faces and club them senseless with a baton or with the butts of their carbines. It was a game they enjoyed.

Now Mother lay there silent, her eyes closed.

I heard a Kapo yelling at another inmate for something.

"Bye, Mom. I'll be back," I said and then left.

We sent to see my mother that night after Dad got back. Tears were in his eyes as he saw her weak and still shivering. He fed her some cabbage soup and we all tried to keep her spirits up.

Despite her weakness, the Nazis forced her to go to work the next morning. I got up with dad at dawn and stood there in the freshness of the early morning air as he assembled for the worker call. I looked for mother and watched as she stood next to a group of other women in line. She looked exhausted and could barely stand up during the roll call. A young woman who stood beside her carefully held her up.

"Let her go!" Pavlenko yelled at her.

I watched as the young woman pleaded.

Pavlenko came over and hit her. She backed off and fell to the ground. As I watched, my heart caught in my throat.

"Get up," Pavlenko roared, "get up, you Jewish whore, or…" He pulled his pistol from his holster and pointed it at her. Aiming the gun, I could see murder in his face.

My mother slowly got to her feet.

"Move! Move!" he yelled to the group and I saw them march away. My fists clenched hard. I felt plenty of anger and hate towards Pavlenko.

I thought, only God knows what that SS bandit Pavlenko would have done if my mother had disobeyed his orders. The flat, murderous look that passed across his face stayed in the forefront of my mind. It stuck there like a postage stamp on an envelope ready for delivery. It took me a while to get used to visualize Pavlenko's mental image. I tried hard to get rid of it, but it kept following me. No, it pursued me like a shadow and stuck with me and I couldn't get rid of it. It was mental torture.

DESPERATION AND DEATH

The conditions in the camp had deteriorated; the number of prisoners greatly increased, and our camp was expanded to accommodate people who had been evacuated from the camps in the east, mainly from Auschwitz. Barracks that usually would house about 120 prisoners were now filled to overflowing, with prisoners lying on the floor and tents set up outside. The Nazi guards could hardly keep order with so many more inmates. It was total chaos. The camp oven was working overtime; dead bodies were piled on top of each other. Everything that happened seemed haphazard – whether you lived or died, were lucky or unlucky, it looked like a throw of the dice.

Water and food supplies continued to shrink. The head of the barracks, it turned out, had been informed by the SS that truckloads of food moving across the autobahn had been the target of air strikes. (Later we would learn that this was a false report.)

The mood and behavior of the people grew uglier while tension and fear were high. People had become cold, inconsiderate, and quarrelsome. More quarrels over small details sprung up almost hourly. Even the Kapos couldn't keep up. Everyone looked out for his own interests. Everybody. It was a zero-sum game – it's either me or else. It's you who stands or falls. Like two boxers fighting in the ring for the championship. Usually, the stronger one wins and the weaker one loses. But it's *you* who *wants* to win, it's you who keeps throwing hard punches, keeps jabbing and feinting and weaving and throwing a hook or a crossing right, hoping to get the title. You want to *survive*, that's what counts, *survive at all costs*.

When it came to food distribution, tempers exploded. Frequently there were quarrels between the secular and observant Jews, who weren't particularly fond of each other.

I recall that one day at dinner time in the evening, a large metal container filled with kohlrabi soup arrived in our barracks from the camp kitchen, and prisoners rushed at it like a throng of shoppers at Macy's Black Friday sale.

Some of the observant prisoners would wait out the rush and stood at the end of the line. Generally, the guy who would ladle the soup into our bowls wouldn't stir enough and naturally, the soup would get thicker toward the bottom of the container and prisoners standing at the end of the line would get more vegetables than those who were standing up front who would get miffed about it and shout out loud: "Hey, you, holy ones! Waiting for some thicker soup, eh? Don't stand there and wait, get in line like everyone else, *vrome rotkoppen* [pious knuckleheads]!"

It's impossible to describe people who were subjected to starvation and had been degraded to the humiliating life in the camp would stoop that low. Sadly, even in these horrific living conditions, people would stick to biased opinions. Non-believers would keep mocking: "Where is your God now?" while observant people replied: "Only God will keep us alive now."

After an ugly, unruly fight between the two groups, I had walked out of the barracks one early evening and heard the sound of metal against metal. I was watching as a youngster – maybe 16 years old – was bending over a large food container which was left outside the barracks waiting to be picked up. He was scraping and scraping and scraping with a metal spoon, hoping to find some leftovers at the bottom of the pot. But as usual, it had been in vain; the container was totally empty. And now he moved to other containers standing outside the barracks waiting to be brought back to the kitchen across the road, desperately scraping their bottoms, hoping to find some leftovers. But there was nothing left, so he moved to other containers standing outside the barracks. He scraped like a madman and finally, with a hopeless gesture, threw away the spoon, slid down the wall of the barracks, and sat on the ground with his arms wrapped around his knees, just staring into space.

Everyone was so starved, we kept hunting for food, *any kind* of food, even potato peels, and any leftovers that in another life we would carelessly have discarded – absolutely anything edible. We daydreamed about food. Eventually, we had hallucinations of food, such as succulent steaks dancing before our feverish eyes. And we kept hoping...

SICKNESS AND LOSS

Dysentery began to ravage the camp. Many people died.

I remember feeling pretty sick. The food – if you can call this murky brown liquid and the few slices of stale bread food – must have caused it. Whatever I ate, which had been dismally little (unfortunately, the bar mitzvah bread was long gone), poured out of me like water, and I headed for the outdoor latrine almost 24/7. I recall staring down at my body in horror, seeing the ribs and chest bones protruding through an almost yellowish transparent skin. Fortunately, after a little while it passed. My family got sick also, and like me were able to survive.

But some, such as my buddy Kees Graaf, were not so fortunate. He was thin as a rail and his face had turned almost gray. I never forget what happened to him. The image that stays imprinted on my mind was that cold frosty morning as he was sitting in a chair in the barracks, his eyes closed as thought he had fallen asleep. We had been talking about Dutch soccer games and what we were going to do once we got back home after the war.

I leaned forward. "Hey, Kees!"

Silence.

I looked across at him. "You okay, Kees?"

He did not respond.

I shook him by the shoulder. "Hey, Kees. Wake up!"

I stared at him. His head slipped sideways and didn't move. His mouth was slightly open. I then realized that he was dead. I ran to get help and shortly afterwards, two men of the special unit that handled dead prisoners arrived, lifted him onto a gurney, and carried him away. I never had a chance to say goodbye. He had died sitting in his chair across from me talking about Dutch soccer players and the Dutch Champions League.

A few hours later, I was outside and stood watching an open trailer loaded with piles of corpses passing by. The truck was on its way to the crematorium. As it passed, I spotted Kees on top, his bony arm dangling. I stood staring after the truck and watched until it was out of sight up the road. Kees, my buddy who not so long ago, had daydreams of food, imagined eating strawberries with whipped cream and delicious pastrami sandwiches, smacking his lips with relish, had ceased to exist. Fourteen years old. And now he was gone. Like dust in the wind. I wanted to cry, but couldn't. At that point, I had gotten so used to death, grief and loss that I was numb.

As the dysentery ran its course, a brutal reign of terror took its place. Swinging their hardwood truncheons with sadistic pleasure, the Nazis beat up prisoners at random. It was as if they wanted more of us to die to relief the crowding; they would order us to stand as straight as a pole during the roll calls, and at daybreak they'd wake us by rattling their truncheons against the metal bedposts, their voices snarling: "Off your beds, you lazy swine! No Sabbath today. Hurry up! Hurry up!" And the rattling sound of their wooden clubs along the bedposts seemed to go on incessantly.

Seated in my apartment today, I am still flooded by memories of the camp; we were deathly afraid of the *Kapos* and the vicious SS. Just observing their demeanor toward us was enough to strike terror into brave hearts. We feared that at any given moment, one of them would calmly remove a gun from his holster, take aim at one of us, squeeze the trigger and shoot us in the head in cold blood. This would not be in the least surprising.

Anyone who has been incarcerated in a death camp under some other ruthless dictatorship knows. He knows of the evil slumbering in human beings. Hand a whip to this or that person and tell him he is in command of another person and see, just watch how this man will change in a short period of time. He will turn into a cruel, vicious brute; he will feel superior and will wield his power ruthlessly. No, surely not everybody will act this way, but this definitely was the case with these Nazi officers, who had joined the ranks voluntarily. An SS officer would commit the most barbaric crimes and then go back home to his family and behave like an ordinary human being. Like a father or husband, he loved his devoted wife and at night tucked his little children into bed and sing sentimental lullabies to them.

The camp became even more of a horrific nightmare. Mortally sick prisoners, eyes sunk deep in their heads, their bones sticking out like flagpoles from their bodies, wandered the grounds in a dazed state unable to work. They were living skeletons, looking inhuman with smudged faces, eyes gazing and mouths hanging open. Yet, the Nazis beat them, accursing them of being lazy or not followed orders. I hadn't been seen my friend Uriel de Jong for a few days and it didn't take us long to find out why. As Henk and I entered his barracks, we noticed two men from the death detail at his bunk.

"What happened?" I asked.

A man shrugged.

We watched as they took Uriel by wrists and ankles and lifted his body off the bunk bed onto a makeshift stretcher. He was curled up and they were unable to straighten him. Then they carried him off to a truck waiting outside.

Watching people that you knew die had become a daily habit. You just got used to it. Like tying your shoelaces or wearing your everyday shirt. It became part of life in the camp.

I often found myself listening to prisoners sitting on the edge of their bunk beds debating the unpredictable whims of fate, discussing why Ruben so-and-so and not Simon so-and-so died. There was no reason in the end. In retrospect, it seems to me that in a war, when bullets and shells are flying about, and your friend Chuck or Billy or Gary standing near you cries out, "I got hit!" and suddenly crumples like a floppy rag doll to the ground dead, and you keep going, hoping to survive this hell and stay safe, if you had a moment to think, you might be filled with wonder at the baffling unpredictability of death. Why does one person live through this hell and others don't? Quirk of fate? Maybe you were the lucky one and drew the winning ticket, but others didn't get that far. You tell me.

The prisoners kept debating and hoping... There were people who were observant and held onto their Jewish faith, convinced that God would look after them, and would keep them safe. Others would shrug it off unimpressed and say, how can you still harbor any belief in God after all this anguish and death and horror? Everyone held onto to whatever they could whether it was religion or bitter self-reliance, trying to persevere and survive.

HOPE CRUSHED

We'd been at the camp for two years at this point. Our only hope was that as "exchange Jews" we'd be taken in by the Allies so that

German Nazis would be released. It was the only thing that kept us going in the face of all the sickness, cruelty and death. All we could do was wait.

Then one day, the word circulated around the camp that an exchange with German prisoners of war was imminent. The commandant's office informed us that inmates recorded as having South or Central American passports should pack their bags and get ready to report to the gate at ten o'clock the following morning to be sent to Switzerland.

Filled with excitement, my parents, my brothers and I hugged one another and we sat up a long time talking excitedly what we were going to do, where we would go. We went back to our barracks and packed.

Not many of us slept that night. Our minds were racing. Had the horror and dread of the past years finally come to an end? Was this really the end of our misery? We found it hard to believe. But it was the truth. It was not like when you wake up from a bad dream and you think, *thank goodness it was just a dream*. No, this was real. This was liberation. This was freedom. What words. *Freedom. Liberty*. Very soon, we would stop seeing the hated SS guards and the *Kapos* and the camp gates. We would be different people.

The inmates who didn't have "exchange" status looked at us with barely concealed envy and hatred. They didn't even wish us well. I understood their feelings. I'd probably feel the same way. I felt truly sorry for them and understood their disappointment that they were left behind.

But not everyone was so bitter. Our friends came over, shook hands with us, smiled, and wished us all the best with a wistful expression on their faces. We thanked them, patted their backs and told them to keep their chins up. The war couldn't last forever. They'd be free again soon. It was a moment of mixed emotions as we stood there, shook hands and said goodbye.

That Sunday morning at ten, we stood with packed bags and huddled together in the chilly air. Helga Krumm, one of the few *Aufseherinnen* or female SS Waffen overseers, dressed in a dark green jacket, green skirt, green SS cap and black boots, emerged from a black Volkswagen in front of the gate and entered the camp. We didn't see her often, but knew she could be as brutal as any of the male officers. She was followed by Pavlenko. A cadre of empty military transport trucks idled at the gate. Armed SS guards disembarked from the trucks and waited, smoking a cigarette. Pavlenko, stony-faced, his arms folded across his broad chest, stood there in a wide-legged position watching everything attentively. He saw to it that everything would go like clockwork, without a hitch.

Krumm stood in front of us, holding a list of names in her hand. She addressed us in German. "Answer when your name is called. Anyone who does not answer will not be going. Any sick prisoner will not be permitted to leave." This was significant; since the mass influx of deported Jews from the east, many prisoners had fallen ill with pneumonia, tuberculosis, and uncontrollable diarrhea.

Krumm paused a moment then raised the clipboard and began to call the first names. "Isi Cohen…"

A hand went up. "Here."

Helga Krumm nodded at Pavlenko who motioned him to the first truck of the convoy.

"Reuven de Vries…"

Another hand went up.

"Samuel Horwitz and Sarah Horwitz."

Two hands went up. Sarah Horowitz turned to Pavlenko who pointed with his forefinger to the waiting truck.

Krumm studied the clipboard a moment. "Philip Wagenaar…"

"Yes."

A beat of silence.

Krumm took out a pen and wrote something down.

"Benjamin Klaassen and Leah Klaassen."

"Yes."

The first truck began to fill up.

This went on for ten minutes. We waited impatiently for our names to be called. Friends who stood beside us were called up. They raised their hands, smiled at us, and happily boarded the truck. We looked after them, shivering in the cold, and wondered how long we would have to wait for our names to be called.

I watched a flock of white birds circling overhead. They were flapping their wings, wheeling and swooping, then soared in the air and flew away into freedom... Longingly, I stared after them. The minutes crawled on. We stood waiting in the shivery weather wondering how much longer.

Then SS Aufseherin Krumm's voice barked: "Wingort, Victor." And then: "Rachel, Joseph, and William."

All of us immediately raised our hands and shouted, "Here."

And then she called out, "Eli."

My oldest brother who was 17 years old then, put his hand up and said, "Here."

Suddenly, a large woman pushed through the crowd dragging a little girl behind her and started screaming. "My daughter was left off the list. It was a mistake. Wagenaar."

Before we were able to proceed, we had to wait for an affirmative nod from SS Aufseherin Krumm, so we waited.

What we were able to make out from their rapidly spoken German was that Aufseherin Krumm had omitted reading the child's name off the list, even after the mother had pointed a finger at the scared little thing who was now standing beside her with lowered eyes.

"Get back in line!" Krumm shouted at her.

Pavlenko stepped up and raised his baton. "You heard the order. Step back, scum!"

The woman stepped back.

After that, Krumm paused a moment, then went back to her clipboard. "Wagenaar, Lea," she said.

My father stepped up. "Our names were called and we answered: Wingort."

Krumm looked at her list. "I called Eli and no one answered."

"*Nein*, no, no, no," mother exclaimed, pointing a finger frantically. "*Das ist falsch!* That's wrong! That woman got in the way after you called us."

The SS woman's narrow eyes stared stonily down at her. "What? You dare to question my authority?" Her coarse face set coldly.

"Yes," one man said. "They are right. You called them and they answered before the woman…"

Pavlenko stepped forward and pushed the man. "Shut up you," he growled. "You are off the list like the rest of these lying vermin."

Helga Krumm studied the clipboard again, glanced up at the group, and said, curtly, "Elias Holles didn't answer my call." She shrugged, "*Na schön*, too bad, apparently the young man is sick." And with a crisp flick of her wrist, she drew a line through his name. Then glancing up again, said unemotionally, "The family is crossed off the list."

What?! We looked at each other, dazed, not yet fully comprehending what was happening.

"Go back to your barracks!" Krumm shouted. "All of you. Right now. Move it! *Vorwärts!*[Forward!]"

Wringing her hands, mother kept imploring the Nazi warden. "We are here and answered. Please…"

The whole group turned toward us.

We looked at each other, dazed, not yet fully comprehending what was happening. Wringing her hands, my mother kept imploring the Nazi warden. "We are here and answered. Please…"

Krumm looked over at the SS guard and gave him a slight nod of the head. He confronted my mother. "Troublemaker," he snapped. "Move it!"

My mother went down on her knees. "*Bitte, bitte…* [Please, please.]"

Pavlenko stepped forward, stared at mother, then quietly removing a hardwood truncheon from his belt, and as a sort of a warm-up switching the club from his left hand to his right, callously began to hit Mom in the head and shoulders. My mother holding up her hands protectively, sank down onto the cold ground.

My father rushed at that Nazi guard to stop his insane beatings.

Pavlenko, looking startled, turned toward my father, dropped his club, then pulled his pistol from his black holster flap and jammed it into my father's face. Dad froze and put his hands in the air.

"Back off, Jew swine!" Pavlenko bellowed. "Get back to the barracks. *Sofort!* [Immediately!]"

My father slowly lifted Mom to her feet. Her head was bleeding. He put her arm over his shoulder and walked back toward us. My brother helped him. An SS soldier marched back us all to the barracks along with the unfortunate man and the screaming woman and her daughter.

Pavlenko stood there imperially, arms crossed over his chest, a cold sneer on his face and nodded to Krumm, who continued to call names.

From that wretched day on we had given up hope we'd ever make it out of that camp alive. The other inmates were angry, but were as helpless as we were. They tried to be supportive, telling us we'd get another chance when the next exchange came up. It was a false hope and we all knew it.

In hindsight, I can say with 100-percent certainty that this episode changed our lives forever. It was as if the jury had cleared the defendant, but the judge sent him back to prison.

How on earth were we going to face the daily gloomy routine, the freezing roll calls, the filth and dirt, the lice crawling in the seams of clothing, and starvation? How were we to keep going?

By some bad stroke of luck, this Nazi overseer with outstretched arm, pointing a finger at us, ordering us to remain, to shut up and stay put, had changed everything. Everything. Call it fate or tough luck, call it Divine Providence. You may call it anything you want. It didn't matter anymore.

And from this moment on, things started to go downhill.

My father became withdrawn. Mom slowly recovered from the brutal beating, but had severe headaches. When coming back from work detail, Dad lay down on his bunk, crossed his arms behind his head and brooded. We tried to get him to talk, but he mumbled a word here and there, and barely ate.

The Dutchman who had spoken up for my family and was taken off the list began behaving strangely irrational. Once a tall, handsome young man, with unruly sandy hair and a good-natured, friendly smile had become deeply depressed. He kept muttering to himself, "I can't take this anymore. I can't. It can't go on like this." Shaking his head despondently, he kept repeating it to himself over and over. "Something's got to give... something's got to give."

He began to refuse to attend roll call. Then he started to talk back the guards, refusing to follow orders. Grateful that he has stuck up for us, my brothers tried to reason with him.

"You'll get yourself killed," Eli said.

He laughed derisively. "Well, I'm already dead."

Joseph said, "Be careful. The SS might punish the entire barracks and withdraw our pitiful bread rations in retaliation."

But De Wit refused to listen.

One day, seated at the long wood table in the barracks, drinking the dirty brownish water, he was coughing from time to time. Then all of a sudden, his eyes glittering madly, he lifted up his cup and poured the hot coffee with a contemptuous I-don't-give-a-hoot sneer onto the table. Then jumped up from his chair, pranced around, cursed and yelled, climbed onto the low table and started dancing, laughing maniacally, talking gibberish.

We sat watching him and at first thought it funny, but soon, it wasn't funny anymore.

Another time, having saved his quarter loaf of bread, De Wit started scattering around crumbs like confetti and watched with roaring laughter as the men dived for the crumbs and then again started frolicking on the table. A group of prisoners managed to calm him down and put him to bed. He fell asleep peacefully on his bunk. When he awoke the next morning, De Wit was his mild self again and acted normally.

This odd ritual or quirk of De Wit's happened every few days.

Joop Weiss had reported him sick to the SS staff, and for a couple of days De Wit didn't attend roll call.

Then things took a turn for the worse. One morning, the SS started the count and found one prisoner missing. When they consulted with the head of the barracks, Joop Weiss, and found out prisoner De Wit hadn't shown up for the morning roll call, they hit the roof.

"What?!" SS Unterscharführer Hugo Walters, a narrow-hipped

man with a long neck and broad shoulders, roared at Joop Weiss furiously. The officer's thick eyeglasses were soaking wet from the morning sleet. "He's *refusing* to fall in for roll call?" He took a deep breath, adjusted his glasses with thumb and forefinger, then half bent over at the waist, his nose almost touching the barracks leader's startled face, repeated, unbelieving, "*Was? Er weigert sich auf dem Appellplatz anzutreten?* [What? He refuses to fall in for roll call?]" He stared across at Joop Weiss from under his thick brows as though Weiss had gone mad.

Weiss, smart enough, said nothing.

"And," the SS officer said in a sardonic tone, "may I ask why he refuses to report for roll call?"

Weiss kept quiet.

"*Antworten Sie!* [Answer me!]," Walters barked, his breath clouding the freezing air.

"The prisoner," Joop Weiss replied hesitantly, "has reported sick. He's unable to stand on his feet for a long time."

"Oh, I see," the SS officer countered sarcastically, knuckles on his hips, not yet sure how to react. "That's just great. He's not able to stand on his feet for a long time. Well, well." Thick glasses stared in utter disbelief at the prisoners lined up in front of him. Then turning back to Weiss, the SS man fumed, "And now he thinks he can–" He paused a moment, groping for the proper word, "do what he wants? And he thinks that that is all right with us, huh?" Enraged, both arms crossed over his chest, the officer placed his feet apart and glared at Weiss in utter fury and cold contempt.

No one moved. Not an eye wavered. Everyone remained silent.

"*Nein, Herr Unterscharführer,*" Joop Weiss ventured diffidently.

My mind drifts back to the camp when I think of those words, "*Herr Obersturmführer*" or "*Herr Unterscharführer.*" It makes me think of the Nazis' rigid obedience and the vile obsequiousness of Nazi soldiers standing at ramrod attention, obediently clicking their heels and raising their hands in holy salute. It would have been laughable, had they not been capable of such devastating destruction.

"Very well," Walters said crisply. "I think that is what he thinks. We'll see."

The SS officer turned to his subordinates standing submissively like squatting birds in the rain and spoke to them briefly then turning back, he gave us a five-minute angry speech about how he was going to make an example of malingering prisoners.

Actually, that night just like the previous nights, the prisoners had seriously advised De Wit not to anger the SS any longer and told him he'd better report to roll call. They'd argued that beyond punishing De Wit himself, the SS in their fury would punish the entire barracks and would withdraw their pitiful bread rations in retaliation for De Wit's maddening stubbornness. But in vain.

De Wit remained adamant and decided not to attend roll call. Stubborn like a mule, he refused to listen. He had lain on his bunk, arms behind his head, eyes glaring madly at us. "Get out," he had growled, "and leave me alone!" There was no way to make the man listen to reason.

The next day, the SS found him comfortably lying on his bunk in the barracks, stubbornly refusing to attend roll call. This time the SS meant business. They were not going to monkey around. They definitely were going to make an example out of this man and show us what happened to someone who didn't comply with SS orders.

We were ordered to line up in ranks of five in the numbing cold in the roll call square.

And we waited. Nobody moved. Nobody said anything.

I watched bull-necked and wide-shouldered Hauptsturmführer Josef Kramer accompanied by Lukas Pavlenko plus two husky SS Scharführers, armed with wooden clubs and side arms, march into our barracks.

The tough-looking SS-*Totenkopfverbände* [Death's Head Units] armed with Mauser rifles and pistols stood spaced along the barbed-wire fence near the gate.

One of the *Häftlinge* [prisoners] standing in the row behind me whispered, "What do they think they're doing? Do they believe we skeletons are going to attack them so they can kill all of us?"

The SS stood there across from us with flat, no-nonsense looks on their stolid faces, hands resting on the guns in their holsters, and they waited. And we waited.

Several minutes went by. Then we could hear a hoarse howl coming through the open door of De Wit's barracks. And then a scream.

These Nazi guys were not kidding.

The beatings and the snarling voices we heard went on for a couple of minutes.

When the door opened, the Dutchman was dragged out by the two grim-faced SS Scharführers, followed by stolid-looking commander Kramer, and contentedly smiling Pavlenko. The Dutchman's face had been beaten so badly that it was barely recognizable. He was bleeding profusely. Then they threw him on the dirt in front of us.

"Defiance is useless," bellowed Kramer. "This will teach all of you to obey orders." He looked from one to the other. "Taking the side of the enemy will be punished accordingly."

The Dutchman, lying there in the dirt, began giggling idiotically.

Pavlenko went over to him and kicked him in the gut.

De Wit grunted and was silent.

Small wonder they hadn't dragged him into the open square and shot him in front of us as a deterrent to other recalcitrant. Obviously, the SS were satisfied showing us how they were going to deal with any insubordinate behavior in the camp.

Later, we were told that Pavlenko had hit him in the head with the wooden club over and over as his cohorts stood there watching him hum a Lithuanian tune while he was inflicting this savage beating.

A couple of minutes later, as we stood lined up in columns of fives, De Wit, barely able to stand up straight, was being held by his arms by two fellow prisoners.

The SS officers, looking very pleased with themselves, started the recount. They worked their way slowly and methodically through the line of prisoners, counting each one slowly and meticulously until they came to De Wit. They stood back to admire their handiwork.

"*Na schön.* [Very well]," said SS commandant Kramer amiably, turning away from De Wit, looking steely-eyed at the inmates standing near him. "I hope this will teach you prisoners to obey orders."

De Wit, supported by the two prisoners, stood there in silence, slightly rocking back and forth on his heels, staring dreamily into space as though listening to the sound of some beautiful distant music. Then suddenly, he threw his head back and let out a roar of uncontrolled, maniacal laughter.

Caught up short, the officers gazed at him dumbfounded.

De Wit stopped his hysterical laughter. He simply stood there grinning at them.

The SS officer shook his head pityingly, perhaps concluding the guy was a complete lunatic. Then he walked down the line of prisoners, the other SS apes following him obediently.

When the call *Wegtreten* [Dismissed] was sounded, and both fellow prisoners let go of De Wit's arms, he collapsed as though he'd been kicked in the back of his knees.

Two inmates rushed to help the Dutchman, but Pavlenko stood in their way, gun drawn. "Let him lie there in the dirt." He made a slight motion with his head. "Now get the hell going!"

That night, I woke up to a brief series of machine-gun bursts. German voices were calling out a warning. I looked out the door, but it was pitch black and could see anything. We couldn't make out what it was all about, but we knew for sure something bad had happened.

When stillness fell, a few prisoners went looking outside in the black night. They came back without having seen anything abnormal.

The next morning at daybreak, we learned that De Wit had been shot dead.

When the labor detachments got lined up in the gray dawn light, they saw the Dutchman's bullet-ridden corpse hanging in a grotesque lifeless position, entangled in the barbed-wire fence for all the camp to see. He looked like he'd been crucified. Nobody knew for sure what happened. Rumor had it that in the dead of the night, De Wit in his deteriorating condition was seen talking to an SS guard outside the hospital barracks.

When he was about to make a dash across the deserted grounds toward the barbed-wire fence, guards in the watch tower who swept their blinding searchlights across the square caught him seconds away from leaping at the electrified barbed wire, barked commands – which fell on deaf ears – and opened up, riddling him with bullets. The SS staff had left his body hanging in the double wire fence as a warning to all prisoners.

We speculated that he had tried to escape, or what seemed more logical, had gone off the deep end and committed suicide.

It was later that we found out that De Wit had been suffering from severe tuberculosis. It didn't matter really. In the end, the man had found his peace.

DAD

It was March 1945. We heard rumors that the Allied forces in Western Europe were making rapid progress. We could hear combat aircraft flying overhead above the clouds and the distant rattling machine-gun fire growing nearer. Perhaps the war would be over soon and we'd be set free.

Other rumors said the Nazis were ready to create diplomatic channels to open negotiations for a separate peace with the western Allies and all the prisoners in the camp would be exchanged for German prisoners of war and hard cash. *Hard cash? All right*. Another path to freedom, or so we hoped.

Then the darkest rumors began to circulate that Berlin had sent direct orders to the SS Hauptsamt, that all inmates in the camps were to be eliminated rather than have them fall in the hands of the enemy. Hearing this shocking news struck cold blade of terror into us.

"Any truth to these reports?" we asked Mr. Weiss, running into him outside of the barracks.

He shook his head. "Nonsense. How do you suppose they can do this? Forty thousand prisoners and tens of thousands more pouring in from the east every day? Be sensible. Besides, the Germans know that the war is lost." Pausing at the barracks entrance, he assured us: "If this were true, I would know about it."

And we kept trudging along like stubborn men and women wearily slogging through heavy rains, mud and storms, day in and day out, hoping to survive, knowing the storm eventually would pass over and lose steam. But after each day's storm passed, a new black ominous one loomed up ahead. We clenched our teeth and kept plodding on, not giving up, hoping that this one would be the last, the final one. And in that spirit, we lived.

Then one morning, the roll calls ground to a complete halt.

As the enormous flood of prisoners arriving daily in open-topped freight cars from Auschwitz and other camps further east kept pouring in unabated, too many people were dying. Who was going to count the corpses lying sprawled on the barracks floors?

The Nazis couldn't keep up and the lists became useless. Anyone able to work was just pulled out of the barracks and herded into groups. There was no system. It seems like pure chaos reigned…

My daily morning routine during those weeks in March consisted of getting up together with the grownups before they went off to work and heading to the freezing sanitary facility to wash beneath the open taps of the steel sinks. After that, and after drinking the brown liquid called coffee and wolfing down the slice of bread (we still obtained our food rations at the time), I made my bed in proper military style (*You'd better pay attention, boy, and make sure that the corners of the blanket are tucked in as tightly as they can be underneath the straw mattress*).

This was followed by the sickening task (which often made me want to throw up) of checking the seams of my shirt, my undershirt, and my pajamas for any wingless lice that might be crawling around there. The kids in the camp who weren't sick would start sweeping the floors with frayed straw brooms.

There was great relief when we first heard the rumor that the

Allied forces were fighting their way into the heartland of Germany. But my father's mood was not heightened by the news. During this period, I watched him slowly change from a relatively healthy person to a gravely ill man.

Ever since the incident with Krumm and the exchange list, I watched as my father got worse. We had been so close to freedom, and then *bam*, like a bolt out of the blue, everything had changed. With the casual wave of a Nazi's hand. And now Dad was lying here, emotionally shattered, demolished like a smashed house after an air strike, without hope, without any resolve, and because the strength of will he had possessed before had left him now, his condition was deteriorating rapidly. He'd lost so much weight from not eating, he looked like many of the other skeletal prisoners in the camp. He had developed a limp from who knows what altercation or run-in with the wrong guard which made it difficult for him to work and subjected him to beatings. The worst part was the change in his face. Once lively and expressive, it now bore a blank, almost detached expression, which I was not able to read. At night, he would return exhausted and went straight to his bunk. He didn't speak to anyone, even my mother. We were all worried. I talked to Mom about it. With her eyes fixed on mine, she confirmed my anxiety and said, "Yes, Will, I don't like it at all the way he looks and acts."

The gravity of father's condition became evident the day he stayed in the barracks and didn't go to work. The next day, his face was flushed with fever, his skin was blotchy, and he had a racking cough.

It was unbearable to think that the British forces (according to Joop Weiss) were battling the Germans practically on the doorstep of the camp now, and we soon would be free, but father was falling victim, as many others had, to a frighteningly debilitating disease known as hunger edema.

I felt my heart sink within me. I was terribly afraid we would miss out again like on that terrible morning when Krumm with an indifferent shrug had refused to let us board the trucks to freedom.

Not again experiencing this bitter irony, this injustice, this pointlessness. Please, no. I refused to think about it.

This time, I told myself, Dad will be okay. He will be lucky. He will be all right. Of course, he will. We need to get out of here.

The next morning, his condition hadn't changed.

I sat down at his bedside and asked, "Dad, how are you feeling?" (I still can see the scene in my head, almost can hear the dialogue).

He shot me a weak smile. "I'm good, son. I'm doing fine. I'll be all right. I just need a little rest and–" His body shook from a severe coughing fit.

I sat and waited until it was over.

Then he told me, "Your two brothers. They came to see me yesterday evening after they got back from work."

I nodded. I didn't see them in the morning. They had left early for work and lived in another barracks. In general, as strange as it sounds, my brothers and I didn't see much of each other. They went to work, were gone all day, had their circle of friends, and the only time we saw each other was at "supper" at the beat-up wooden table in the barracks. When we talked, our conversations were limited because they were exhausted. That's the way the days went by in the camp – just enduring.

I had often heard people say that willpower can work wonders, and I was struck by an idea: maybe there was a way to lift my father's spirits.

I turned to him. "Dad, we learned from Joop Weiss that the Allied forces are winning. They are battling the Nazis and are practically on the doorstep of the camp. Everybody expects the war soon to be over."

"Really?" he said, his eyes lighting up like two candles in a dark cathedral. "Well, good." He smiled weakly. "That's very good."

He didn't believe me. It was plainly written, like a billboard, across his face.

My father was lying here, emotionally shattered, demolished like a smashed house after an air strike, without hope, without any resolve, and because the strength of will he had possessed before had left him now, his condition was deteriorating rapidly.

I thought for a moment. *What else would encourage him to hang in there?*

"We all will be free soon, Dad," I said lamely. "Very soon."

"Yes," he said, "that's good, very good."

"Aren't you glad, Dad?" I asked, watching him curiously.

"Yes, I am." He nodded.

"We all will be free soon, Dad. Just get better."

He didn't answer. Soon afterwards another cough shook his body. When he stopped coughing, he looked up slowly and asked, "Could... you bring me a cup of coffee, please?"

A cup of coffee? What cup of coffee?

"Of course, Dad," I said, though as I got up, I was thinking, *where in this hellhole do I get a cup of coffee?* "I'll be right back."

I went to look for Mr. Weiss and found him in one of the barracks talking to a prisoner. I approached him, excused myself for interrupting, and told him about my father.

Joop Weiss turned to me, nodded his gray head gravely and looked me in the eye. "Your father needs to be in the infirmary," he said. "He can't lie there like this. He needs to be under a doctor's supervision."

I stared at him blankly. *What good would that do? Everyone who went there just died.*

"Will they do anything?"

He shrugged. "I hope so. I let them know." Then he added: "I noted his condition making my sick report. You know, the roll calls."

"There haven't been any roll calls lately," I told him.

"Nevertheless," he said, "I need to make my reports. They're still checking the work details."

Of course. "He asked for coffee," I said. "Is there any?"

Mr. Weiss looked off for a moment. "I'll get him something. Wait here."

Five minutes later, he came back, holding the cup of water in his hand.

I looked at him.

"It doesn't matter. He won't know the difference," Joop Weiss told me and handed the cup to me. "I'm really sorry about your father."

I nodded and went back to his bunk. Mom came by and sat there talking to him, giving him a pep talk. But he lay there motionless, eyes closed. She tried to make him drink.

He opened his eyes for a moment, drank a few swallows from the cup, then started coughing, spraying the water all over. We sat for a little while longer as he lay there listlessly with his eyes closed. Every now and then he would nod his head, but otherwise he kept silent and soon he fell asleep.

The symptoms of hunger edema were all too familiar to me, and my heart felt heavy.

We watched as the men from the infirmary entered and carried him away. We followed but were not allowed in. My father was admitted to the pitifully overcrowded camp infirmary. The filthy wards (divided in two by sex) offered little to no medical treatment. There was squalor and disease, shortage of bedpans and blankets. No medicine. No doctors. Prisoners died of hunger, edema and typhus and had little hope of survival. Two harried female prisoners who had trained as nurses walked around in a daze, not knowing what to do next for all the sick patients.

To distract my mind, I went outside to take a breath of fresh air.

It was windy and cold, and the ground was covered with two inches of snow. Huddling deep in my thin winter overcoat, I took deep breaths and looked around me. Everything looked white, and the snowflakes kept falling silently on my hair and face, whirling around me in gusts of wind.

I spotted the stiff body of a dead prisoner lying half hidden beneath the blanket of snow. His hand was thrust out as though he had been begging for mercy. For a long moment I could not take my eyes off the body. Then I turned and spotted more twisted bodies, lying there like thrown-away junk. I was surrounded by death.

These prisoners most likely went out of the barracks to get a breath of fresh air just as I had. They must have dropped from sheer starvation, their malnourished bodies unable to hold them up. The snow and the silence enhanced the gruesomeness of that creepy sight.

I was about to go back to the barracks when I heard the muffled sound of a motor. I turned. An open truck of the crematoria detail was pulling up, and three gravediggers, still looking to be in relatively good shape (due to their extra food ration), climbed down and started to collect the dead on makeshift stretchers.

I remember standing there for a long minute watching with almost rapt fascination as they loaded the dead like a heap of garbage upon the roofless lorry. Once their job was done, they swung up and drove off through the thickening curtain of falling snowflakes.

I looked after them for a long moment. Then I turned and headed back toward my barracks. I wondered what the next few days would bring.

Thanks to Joop Weiss, I was allowed to visit my father the next day. He was lying in a dirty bed, pushed up against a wall. I had to walk around several other patients in beds or lying on the floor.

I stood there staring at him. The big, muscular boisterous man I knew as my father lay there, listless, eyes closed, emaciated. His face had gotten swollen, his belly was bloated, but his limbs looked like poles. I knew he was dying. He looked like so many other prisoners in the camp that hadn't made it.

"Dad…"

He turned his head slightly, opened his eyes but was unable to speak.

"You've got to hold on."

He sighed, then closed his eyes again.

"Can I get you anything?"

"Water," he whispered. His voice sounded hoarse.

Dehydration was another symptom of the disease.

"Yes, of course," I said, and rose to get him some water. I stood there, hoping to find someone to help.

A young female inmate hurried by carrying some dirty bandages.

"Excuse me," I asked her. "Where could I get some water for my father?"

The woman paused a moment. She looked at me, threw a quick a glance at my father, and nodded. A couple of minutes later, the woman returned and handed me a cup of water. She waited and looked on for a moment as I put the cup to father's lips. He took a few slow swallows then he laid his head back down on the pillow.

"Thank you," I said to her, handing her back the cup.

I sat there silently at his bedside, and flashed back to the years before the camp. And before the war. In the spring and summer, Dad would take us hiking. In the winter, he would take us ice skating on the frozen canals in Amsterdam. Afterwards we would have hot chocolate and sitting around the table playing the cards. We laughed and munched on cookies. He always did things to make us happy. Blowing out a long wistful sigh, I thought, happy, happy, merry cheerful days. Where are they? Would we ever see happy days again?

I left him sleeping and went back outside to the freezing barrack.

Joop Weiss was standing at the entrance. "How is your father?"

"He's very sick," I told him. "And I'm worried he won't…"

"I'm sorry," he said. He shrugged his shoulders in a gesture of resignation. "All we can do now is hope and pray."

That was little consolation. Dad was dying and there was nothing anyone could do. "How do you mean?"

Joop Weiss confirmed that the trucks carrying medical supplies had been bombarded. "The plant that has been pumping out drinking water for the camp was bombarded." He sighed. "Everything seems on the verge of collapse." He added: "I am completely powerless. Hopefully the Allied troops will soon reach the camp."

It was a distressing situation, to say the least. My father was lying there helpless, and Mr. Weiss had apparently no medical supply at his disposal.

Everything had stopped like a stalled engine in the desert, and contagious diseases were spreading like wildfire. The SS and *Kapos* were nowhere to be seen. Like wounded animals, they had crawled away into hidden holes trying to save themselves from the expected Allied onslaught.

When I returned to the infirmary later that evening, I found Mom and my brothers there also. We all stood there silent, staring down at my father. He was too weak to know we were there, and was barely breathing.

May the Lord forgive me, but I didn't feel a thing. Nothing. Maybe the reason, I thought, was because of all the death and squalor around me and constantly seeing people die from disease, from random punishments, and from starvation, I had become hardened to the suffering of others – including my father and now I felt numb, resigned to the fact that he was near death.

Mother leaned slightly forward and called out softly, "Vic? Victor… can you hear me?"

He just lay there, unmoving, unresponsive. Maybe a couple of seconds went by. Mother looked across at us with such anguish in her eyes we had to look away. We stood there for a few more minutes, then left.

Two days later, after midnight I woke up to the glare of a flashlight shining in my eyes. I slowly sat up and saw the dark outline of a tall figure standing in front of my bunk. Looking closely, I could see it was Hugo Decker, Joop Weiss's assistant. I rubbed my eyes trying to figure out what was going on and drowsily asked, "What's up, Decker?"

He hesitated for a moment. Then he softly said, "*Je vader is overleden, jongen.* [Your father passed away, boy] One hour ago."

It took a moment to sink in.

His hand patted my arm. "I'm sorry."

Slowly I slid off the middle bunk to the floor.

The Dutchman lingered for a moment. "Are you okay?"

I looked up and nodded.

We had expected it to happen, but when the message hit me, it was like a vicious punch to the stomach.

"Have you told this to my mother, or brothers?"

He shook his head. "No one." He paused a moment. "I think you'd better get dressed. Someone else is going to come here. He'll take care of it." Again, he patted my arm and then turned and walked down the length of the room out the door and into the night.

While I dressed, I thought about what was going to happen next. Were the men with stretchers going to take Dad's body and just throw it on the pile then take him to the crematorium? It made me sick to think about it.

Now it was up to me to tell mother. I got dressed slowly, stretching out the task so I could delay the moment when I would have to say the words to her. I glanced at the watch my parents had given me on my birthday in better times. It was 2:25 on the luminous dial.

Around me was deep silence. People were asleep. No one, I guessed, had heard us talking. I was thinking about what was going on at the hospital ward right now. The scenes were acutely familiar to me; I had experienced them more than once while sitting at my father's bedside. First off, there would be the authoritarian voice of a nurse calling out that whoever had died should be quickly taken away, since they needed the space for new patients.

More unsettling thoughts passed through my head when a curly-headed young Dutchman appeared at my bunk-side and whispered, "Wingort?" He motioned for me to follow him. "Come along." He was, I guessed, one of the men who belonged to the burial detail.

I looked at him. "What about my two brothers?"

He frowned. "What about them?"

"I thought that they should also know."

He gave a shrug and said that Joop Weiss had told him to tell me.

"All right," I said to him, feeling something drop inside me. "I will go alone."

He glanced at his watch impatiently and then looked up. "Let's go."

I felt a chill, and my stomach clenched. I put on my thin overcoat, and we walked in the heavy silence through the sleeping barracks and stepped through the door out into the whistling wet night. I shivered. Sleet and freezing rain beat down upon us like fists as we made our way across the deserted assembly ground past the silent barracks toward the infirmary.

I bowed my head into the driving, biting wind, following the man mechanically. After a five-minute walk through the wet darkness across the muddy grounds, we arrived at the low-slung hospital barracks. Two dim lights shone in a small window of the building as the man opened the door and I followed him inside. My heart started bouncing around like a ping-pong ball. The man was sensitive enough not to talk. As we made our way in the semi-darkness, I almost tripped over the body of a sick prisoner lying on his back on a mattress on the floor. Moans of pain or rasping breaths were all I heard. A woman wearing a white jacket rushed like a ghost past us, looking harassed, talking over her shoulder. At the far end of the ward, a second, younger man with closely cropped blond hair stood waiting beside my father's bunk. A stretcher was positioned on the floor beside the iron bed beneath a dangling bare bulb.

My father lay there on the narrow bed his body half covered with a soiled, torn sheet. The man lying there seemed like a stranger, yet it *was* my father. I felt a hollow sickness lurching in my chest. Here was my father – I had been talking to him only recently, and now he was gone. I looked at him and felt a hollow sickness lurching in my chest. Now as I stood there, the tears wouldn't come. I remember the only feeling I had was a cold chill shooting up my spine.

"This is his son," the man said who brought me to the hospital ward.

The other man with a blond crew cut handed me the few humble things that once belonged to father: a threadbare brown winter jacket, a pair of dark framed eyeglasses, a Swiss watch that had stopped, and a faded old leather wallet that had nothing in it.

"Thank you."

One of the odd things about the Star Camp was that the SS had been generous with regard to personal effects. We were allowed to hold on to such things.

Now, without Dad, these things, seemed like dead objects to me, and didn't mean anything anymore.

"Let's get on with it," the blond man said.

Moments later, we started off.

Both lifted up my father's body and put him on the stretcher. They covered him with a filthy sheet. Then without saying a word, they raised the stretcher, headed for the front door and moved into the windy, cold night.

I followed them, silent.

We walked along the rows of dark silent barracks toward the deserted, assembly square through the freezing rain and sleet that kept pounding us, the two men carrying Dad on the gurney and I his meager belongings. This was how I escorted my father on his last journey.

A few minutes later, we arrived at a small lean-to shed with a sloping metal roof. The two men stopped, put down the rain-soaked stretcher with my father on it. They paused at the closed door.

I knew what was inside the shed. I had seen the naked corpses stacked up like cords of wood inside, waiting to be dumped into open ditches or hauled off to the oven.

One of the men turned to look at me. "You can go now," he said.

Apparently the two wanted to spare me watching the grisly sight of them rolling my father off the stretcher and then flinging his body like a piece of trash upon the heap. Believe me, as God is my witness, I had already seen more of these sights than I ever wanted to.

I stood there pausing for another moment, and without saying a word, I turned around and headed with my father's possessions for my mother's barracks. To this day, I have never understood why I, as a young boy, was called after Dad had succumbed to starvation and not my mother or my older brothers.

Plodding my way through the cold night, a fleeting thought

entered my mind. Who would be around to say Kaddish for my father? So many people died each day. It seems like an endless, almost hopeless ritual to keep up.

RELAYING THE BITTER NEWS

It wasn't difficult to find mother's barracks. I knew it by heart, number 252. Inside, it was dark and silent.

Slowly, I approached her bunk. She was asleep when I reached her bed. My heart was beating in my throat. How was I going to tell her about Dad? How? After a moment's hesitation I reached out and lightly touched her arm and stood waiting.

She woke up with a start, and looked around with confused eyes. Seeing me, she quickly sat up. Alarmed, she brushed a strand of hair out her face and our eyes locked. "What happened, Will?"

I could see fear in her eyes. I took a deep breath. "Mom, Dad's gone."

"No, no," she said. "No, no." She shook her head from side to side while tears filled her eyes. She grabbed on to my hand and began to sob.

I just stood there not knowing what to do.

"When?"

"About an hour ago. Mr. Decker told me. I went to the infirmary and got his things."

As mother sat there, wiping her eyes I placed Dad's few possessions on the bunk next to her. "These things were all he had."

She nodded, but didn't look at them. I sat down at the foot of bunk. I wanted to say some words of comfort, but nothing came out.

"Those filthy monsters did this to him," she spat bitterly and began to cry softly, her voice choking. "They killed him," she sobbed. "Your father was a good man. He didn't deserve this."

As I sat there looking at her, a sudden flash memory picture of Pavlenko brutally striking mother with his truncheon rose up. That mental image would haunt me for a long time. My mother had been through so much, and now this.

Around us people woke up and soon sorrowful sighs followed when they found what the weeping was about. They had lost loved ones in the camp as well.

As my mother sat there wiping her eyes with the back of her hands, I took off my wet coat and sat down on the edge of the bunk bed. I sat there silent for a long moment.

I marveled at my cold detachment. Was this how my friends felt while we joked about the foods we would eat? I wouldn't know. I never talked to them about it. The things we talked about was food and the things we wanted to do after the liberation. We felt sick and wanted to leave. Leave this killing place, and be with people who lived without fear. In a place where there was cheerful laughter, a warm home and safe haven. We just wanted to enjoy doing the things we used to do in our former free lives.

Clinging to these thoughts, I closed my eyes for a long moment and found myself back in the sunny Dutch seaside resort of Scheveningen, where we used to spend our summer vacation. I could suddenly see the bumper boats and the thrilling water slide, the whirring carousels and the festooned arcades and cafés where the crowd sat and chatted and drank at little tables that ran out to the edge of the sidewalks. I could see the dazzling whiteness of the sandy beach and remember its strong scent of salty sea air. Most of all, I was swept up by the feeling of being *free*. *Being free.* What would it be like to live without the dreadful, awful feeling of being in captivity? To hell with all this misery. To hell with being imprisoned in a Nazi concentration camp.

I opened my eyes and took a deep breath. We sat in silence for a few more minutes. I shivered. The cold of the icy wind outside had seeped into my bones, and I wrapped my jacket more tightly around me.

Mom wiped her eyes and looked at me. "You'd better get back to your barracks and get some sleep. And," she added, her voice crumbling, "go tell your brothers."

"Yes, Mom." I got up and looked at her. "Are you alright?"

She nodded.

We both knew that she was not alright.

After I said goodnight and slunk back outside into the freezing rain and sleet, I stood there for a long moment on the muddy ground listening to the steady droning sound of the Allied planes that were flying overhead high above the clouds. *How much longer?* I thought. *How much longer?*

At the roll square in front of the barracks, I was able to talk to my brothers, Eli and Joseph, for a few minutes.

"I am sorry," I told them. "I have bad news." I paused for a long moment. "Father is gone."

Eli's face turned white. "Oh, no!"

Josef said nothing. He just stood there with a dazed expression on his face.

After a brief silence, Eli said softly, "When did it happen?"

"Around midnight," I told them. "Weiss's assistant came to fetch me."

Josef turned to me. Trying to keep his voice level, he said reproachfully, "Why didn't you tell us? We would–"

"It was Decker," I interrupted him. "He wanted me to come with him to the hospital. I went with him to the shed. Then I told mother." I was shivering. It was so damn cold on the assembly square.

Eli looked at me. "He seemed all right yesterday when I saw him."

I nodded. "It was that edema," I told him. "It went quick."

Josef turned to me. "How's Mom?" he asked, his face blank with the expression of flat refusal, and disbelief.

"She was pretty shaken when I left her."

Eli put his arm around me. "Dad was a great man," he said.

"Those damn Nazis," Josef said through gritted teeth. "Where is he now?"

"The squad took him to the shed."

"We'll see Mom tonight," Josef said.

The SS yelled, "Line up in fives! Line up in fives!"

Ten minutes later, after the SS officers had counted the labor units, the gate opened and they left for work.

Matt stopped reading and turned off the computer. He took a deep breath and thought, *I need a break.* He would read the second part of the story of his father's experiences as a boy in the Nazi camps later on. Now, he took the disk drive from the computer and put it in his pocket. He sat back in the chair and put his feet up on his desk. He needed to let it all sink in and digest the unfathomable. Matt had learned and read about the atrocities that had been committed over there in the old world, in Germany. But what Dad wrote was a total shock, a bucket of cold water. It was simply overwhelming, by God.

Recalling how his father had always enjoyed a glass of cold beer when sitting in the living room in one of the deep chairs, watching a TV show, Matt got up, walked across to the kitchen and took a bottle of Bud Light from the ice box. He poured the beer into a glass. Then he sat back down in the chair with it and put his feet up again. Need to give it some more thought, he told himself. Need to get a grip, and try to understand the immensity of what had happened to father in Nazi Germany.

It was hard to understand the enormity of atrocities that took place; Hitler and his obeying underlings. How was it possible? How come that nobody, no country and no elected leader of the free world realized what was going on? Well, yeah, there was Prime Minister Winston Churchill. Sure. But nobody would listen to him. Remember that fellow Neville Chamberlain flaunting Hitler's slip of paper pledge "Peace for our time," telling the world that Hitler was committed to peace? The Führer would keep his promise, he proclaimed proudly. Okay. What about the Jewish people? Well, don't be a nuisance (they said), nothing bad will happen. Everything's going to be all right. All will be well. Not to worry. Yeah, right.

Sipping his drink, letting his mind run all over it again what his father had written, letting imaginative pictures like movie shots run through his mind, he sat there silent. Suddenly something touched his mind.

He got up and reached for the daybook that lay face down on the table. Matt picked it up and thumbed through it till he reached the last page. His eyes fastened on the words that were underlined three times. It read: *Bruno Stettler, owner of Hulot Company. 121 S Sheridan Avenue, Orlando.*

Matt set the book aside. A frown appeared on his brow. Why did his father write down this address? Why underline it three times? Matt took out the photo and held it to the light to get a closer look. The elderly, gray-haired man had a scar running from his left eye along his jaw down to his chin. *That scar seemed familiar.*

He turned the computer back on and began to search through his father's memoir. His father described the cruel Lithuanian SS officer Pavlenko as having such a scar. Matt shot another glance at the photograph. *Could that distinguished gentleman be Lukas Pavlenko?* What connection did this picture have with Bruno Stettler and the Hulot Company? Matt's frown deepened. *Were they the same man? Had his father found the monster he feared was still alive, a fugitive from the justice he deserved?*

Matt laid everything down on the table, and leaned back in the chair.

It might well be that his father had seen him at his hotel and had recognized him, even though Pavlenko would be an old man by now. That's why he took that photo. He must have found out he was known as Bruno Stettler. Maybe he had written down the address of his company, intending to confront him and expose him. Perhaps this was the "unfinished business" his father had referred to?

But the police had followed up to see if he had gone to the Hulot offices, and there was no record of his dad's ever being there. Maybe he never got there. The question remained why was his room a mess, and why did he leave his medications and cell phone in his room, go somewhere and then suddenly vanish?

Maybe a Google search will find the answer to the question.

He opened his laptop and googled Bruno Stettler and Hulot &

Associates. Bruno Stettler was the founder and owner of the multinational electronics company Hulot & Associates. Founded in 1972 by Stettler, it manufactured digital pressure, sensor products, satellite and amplified transducers. He had turned Hulot into a major player in the industry. It's headquartered in Orlando with offices in New York and Frankfurt, Germany. Nothing out of the ordinary as corporate history goes.

But strangely enough, there was almost no personal information about Stettler himself, except for a vague reference to his having lived in Europe. No educational background. No past corporate achievements. No family. No official corporate photo. Usually, these corporate moguls liked to promote themselves and their accomplishments. He dug a little more and found some articles and interviews in various financial publications, but never any photos of the man himself. Why was that? It made no sense. However, if Stettler were Pavlenko, he would want to hide his true identity as much as he could. But how could he have escaped Germany after the war?

Matt knew very little about the Nazis and the Holocaust except for what he had learned in a World History class. One quick Google revealed that there were thousands of books, articles, documentaries about the Holocaust. He didn't have time to research the details of his father's story or the whereabouts of one particular SS officer. He decided that he needed to speak to experts to help him. He knew one of the largest Holocaust museums in the world was the Museum for Jewish Heritage in Manhattan. Perhaps he could find out more about Pavlenko there. He telephoned and made an appointment with the information manager, Mr. Sam Kluger for the next day.

The museum was a six-sided building with a pyramid-shaped roof located in lower Manhattan. He walked into the lobby up to the reception desk. Matt said, "Wingort for Mr. Kluger."

The middle-aged receptionist checked her computer screen. "Mr. Kluger's office is the second floor. The elevator is to the left."

A middle-aged man with a pleasant face was waiting, and rose from the desk to greet Matt.

They shook hands. "Thank you for seeing me on such short notice."

"Not a problem," Kluger said. "Please sit down."

Matt took a chair across from him.

"What can I do for you?" Kluger asked.

"My father," Matt began, "survived the Holocaust. Prior to emigrating to the US his family lived in Germany and Holland. During the war his family was deported from Amsterdam to Westerbork and Bergen-Belsen. He was liberated there at the end of the war."

Kluger nodded sadly. "Yes," he said. "He was one of the lucky ones."

"He has been missing for the last few days and nobody knows what happened."

Kluger stared at him a moment. "What do you mean *he just disappeared?*"

"Exactly that."

"I am sorry to hear that. I hope he'll be all right.

"The police are in on this," Matt told him. "My father never told me anything about his past. I found his memoir among the items he left behind."

Kluger sighed. "Unfortunately, many survivors kept their painful experiences inside, not sharing them with anyone."

"In his memoir he mentions a particularly brutal Lithuanian SS Officer named Pavlenko at Bergen-Belsen. "He paused a moment. "After the liberation of the camp, my father followed the Nuremberg process, looking for this officer among the Nazis tried. He was not among them and my father suspects he escaped somehow and emigrated to America."

Kluger nodded. "Yes, hundreds of Nazis criminals managed to escape justice. Simon Wiesenthal and host of others began to search for these monsters in the 1950s. They've successfully exposed and had convicted dozens of Nazis who have assimilated in society and remained hidden."

Matt looked at him. "Is there any way of finding out if this Pavlenko is still alive?"

"Well," Kluger told him, "there are lists of those still at large. But I'm afraid that they are not always complete. There were hundreds of Nazis who ran the camps throughout Europe. Many were lower-level officers like Pavlenko."

"Do you have access to them here?"

Kluger shook his head. "No. While we have a lot information about the camps, and the atrocities that took place, along with some of the eyewitness accounts shared by survivors, we don't have those lists."

"I see," Matt said. "Where would I find them?"

"Why would you want to find out about Pavlenko? He's probably dead by now."

"My father may have believed that he saw him alive, living in Florida."

Kluger looked at him and said, "That is unusual."

"I know. He mentions him in detail throughout his memoir as having a distinctive facial scar. While he was on vacation in Orlando, he saw a man with the same scar in his hotel and took a photo of him. His name is Bruno Stettler. He is the CEO of an international manufacturing company Hulot & Associates. I think he tried to confront him at his offices, but he disappeared before he could make contact. I'd like to know if Pavlenko is still alive. In memory," he said, "of my father."

Kluger thought carefully for a moment before he spoke. "In that case I think your best bet is the International Center on Nazi Persecution or The Tracing Center, in Bad Arolsen, Germany. It has the Arolsen Archives, the largest database in the world concerning Nazi persecution, forced labor and the Holocaust in Nazi Germany and its occupied regions. If there's any information leading to his life after the war, they'd probably have it. You can find the link online. You may need to make an appointment with one of the information managers to help you search."

Matt wrote down the name and thanked Mr. Kluger for his time.

They stood and shook hands. "I hope your father will be found safe," Kluger said, "and you find what you need and put your father's memories at rest."

As Matt rode back to his apartment. His head was spinning. Germany? Really? It's a long way to chase down some guy whom my father might have recognized. Maybe, he speculated, I need to follow up on Stettler first.

He decided to fly back to Orlando to pick up the trail and get answers.

Early the next morning, Matt boarded a Delta flight to Orlando International Airport.

8

After arriving in Orlando, he rented a car and booked a room at the Marriott again.

"How long will you be staying with us, Mr. Wingort?" the desk clerk asked.

"I'm not quite sure. I'm on an extended business trip."

"Okay," the clerk said, handing him the key. "It's room 212."

Matt went to his room, showered, changed clothes, went down to the restaurant for lunch, and returned to his room.

His first stop for the day was Detective Garfield's office.

"Matt Wingort for Detective Garfield, please," he said to the officer at the front desk.

"Just a moment." The officer spoke into the telephone, then looked up at Matt. "Have a seat," he said. "She'll be here in a minute."

Detective Garfield came out a few minutes later, and smiled at him. "You're back."

"Yes. Just following up on my father's case."

"I've been meaning to call you," she said. "We have some new information." She made a gesture. "Let's go to my office."

They sat on opposite sides of her desk.

After a moment the detective said, "The hotel clerk

remembered seeing your father meeting with two men wearing dark suits in the lobby of the hotel. They exchanged hellos, sat talking for a little after which the three of them went to a car and drove off. But the clerk doesn't remember seeing him after that."

"Do you know who these men were?'

Garfield shook her head. "The clerk said they looked official."

Matt regarded her for a moment. "And that's it? What about the CCTV cameras?" Matt asked. "Did they get their photos or a license plate?"

"Sorry, the cameras are cleared every few days. No record."

Well, Matt thought, *that's not much help to me.* He glanced over at her. "What's your next step?"

"We wait for a new lead."

"I may have one," Matt said, and shared his father's story with the detective while showing her the photo his father had taken.

"That's quite a story," Garfield said admiringly.

Matt looked at her across the desk. "My father wanted justice for the man who tortured his family back in the camps. Stettler and that SS officer seem like the same person – and he knew it."

"But there's no link," Garfield said, "between him and your father's death. We don't even know whether he made contact with him."

"Stettler and his company were the last entries in his diary before his disappearance. I'm sure he went to see him."

"Well," Garfield said, "they have no record of it."

"They are lying," said Matt. "I know it."

"Mr. Wingort–"

"Matt," he interrupted her.

"Matt. No offense, but Stettler is a major business force in this city. I can't just go poking around and interview him about some old man from New York who suddenly has disappeared while on vacation, an old man he probably never met."

"My father was possibly kidnapped." Matt's voice was calm and confident.

"There's no evidence of that."

"Yes. But I *know* he's involved somehow," Matt persisted. "Why else would my father take a picture of him and write down his address."

Debra Garfield was thoughtful. "I don't know. Based on evidence, we don't have enough information to open a kidnapping investigation. I'm sorry."

Matt was frustrated. "Okay," he said resolutely, "then I guess I'll just have to pursue it on my own."

"He's a powerful man, Matt," she cautioned, "with lots of friends and resources. Be careful."

The Hulot corporate offices were located near the central business district of downtown Orlando. It was not far from the hotel. Matt resolved to pay Mr. Stettler a visit. He took his father's diary and the photo, then headed for his car. Matt parked in front of the mid-sized office building. To the side he noticed several spaces reserved for Hulot. One was marked: CEO Bruno Stettler. A new black Mercedes was parked there. *Good*, he thought. *He's in.* He walked into the lobby, checked the directory and took the elevator to floor three.

Nobody was at the reception desk. *Odd*, he thought. *It's the middle of the day.* He glanced around. He caught sight of a partly open office door to the right. A woman sat inside, talking on the phone. Matt approached the office and knocked on the door.

The woman looked up at him and put up a finger. She said a few more words then hung up.

"Excuse me," Matt said, opening the door a bit more and entering. He waited a moment.

"May I help you?" she asked.

"My name is Matt Wingort. I'd like to see Mr. Stettler."

"Do you have an appointment?"

"No."

She studied Matt a moment. "Could you tell me what it's concerning?"

Matt hesitated. "It's a personal matter."

"I see," she said. "I am sorry. But you need to make an appointment."

Matt nodded his head. "Okay." He paused. "When might he be available?"

The woman looked at her computer, then picked up the phone, spoke briefly into it, then replaced the receiver. "Sorry," she said, "but Mr. Stettler is out of town."

She's stonewalling me, Matt thought. *I saw his car in the lot.* "When will he be back?"

"I don't have that information."

Matt took out his business card. "Please have him call me. I'll be in town a few days. I'm staying at the Marriott."

She smiled at Matt. "I'll be sure he gets it."

Matt nodded. "Thanks. Have a good day." He turned and walked out the door.

The woman watched him leave, rose and then went down the long corridor over the thick carpet to Carol Best's office. She knocked.

"Come in."

She walked into the office. "Here's his card."

"Thank you, Marie."

The young woman turned and then left.

Carol Best picked up the phone. "We may have a problem."

The next day, a tall, long-jawed man strode toward a dark brown Chevrolet Silverado parked in an empty lot at the edge of a grassy lawn across from a five-star-high-rise luxury building.

He opened the car door and spoke to the two men who were seated inside. One was a stout, deadpanned man who wore black sunglasses, a blue baseball cap, a button-down shirt, and dark slacks. The man who was with him wore a polo shirt with khaki pants. The younger one sat behind the wheel. Black sunglasses sat in the back.

"You have your orders," the tall, long-jawed man told them.

"Yes," black sunglasses said. Then: "What do you want us to do?"

"Here's the name and the address," the tall man told them. "And here's what I want you to do." He handed black sunglasses a slip of paper. "Take a look at it," he said. "Find him." His mouth curled into a vicious smirk. "Find out who he is and what he knows." He moved his head at the slip of paper. "And tighten his surveillance and report in."

Black sunglasses nodded. "We'll see to it. And," he added, "don't worry. We're good at locating someone."

"Good. Keep the slip."

Sunglasses shrugged. "No need," he said dismissively. "It's already engraved in our minds."

9

A black Lincoln Town Car stretch limousine pulled up in front of the small, elegant home in a remote wooded area in South Florida.

Miguel Santiago, a big chested Mexican man, in his late fifties with a pencil thin moustache, cold gray eyes and thin lips that rarely broke into a smile entered the house.

Inside, Bruno Stettler, tall and white-haired, dressed in open neck blue shirt and gray flannel slacks, was waiting for him.

"Welcome," said Stettler to the Mexican man. He went over to the bar and took out a bottle of Scotch with two glasses. He carried them over to where Santiago sat. Stettler filled their glasses. They both drank without toasting, then sat on the deep sofa.

"We got a problem," Santiago began. "A big problem."

"What kind of problem?"

Santiago's 's eyebrows shot up his forehead. "Do you know a guy at the bank named Schmitz?"

Stettler took a drink. "He's a low-level clerk in the wire department. Why?"

"My contacts heard he's been nosing around, asking questions about our operation."

"Yes, I understand he approached the director about it."

Santiago raised his eyebrows in surprise. "You knew?'

"Of course."

"Then why didn't you do anything about it?"

Stettler raised his shoulders. "He's harmless," he said. "He knows nothing."

"You make millions on commission," Santiago scowled, "for washing our money through the bank. We don't need any problem. Deal with it. Or else…"

Stettler stared back at him coldly. "Or else what? I don't respond well to threats. It is a business situation that needs to be rectified. That's it. I'll take care of it."

"So do it," Santiago snarled. "And fast." He put his drink down, stood and walked out.

"Spic scum," Stettler muttered to himself finishing his drink, then took out his cell phone.

A coffee-brown Jaguar XJ with Florida plates was parked into a turn off near a three-story white stucco house set among clusters of royal palms and waited for the lights to go out in the house.

At 2 a.m., two men, faces covered, one wearing a baseball cap and black glasses, the other a polo shirt and khaki pants, climbed out of the car and walked to the house. One of them aimed a silenced pistol at the security camera and shot it out. The house was silent. No lights shone through the pale curtains of the front windows. They walked along the edge of the gravel driveway, up to the front door. They stood still, listening carefully.

One man nodded, the other rang the doorbell and waited.

No answer.

He rang again, longer this time.

Still no answer.

Then they looked up and saw a light on the second floor. "Get ready," the man said.

Inside the large master bedroom on the second floor, Walther Schmitz rose from the bed, reached for his silk bathrobe and put it on. He turned on the light, walked over to the window and looked outside at the dead night. No sound, only scattered flickering lights twinkling from a neighbor's villa in the black palm trees.

A dark brown Jaguar XJ sat in the dim-lit drive across from the entrance.

Schmitz's frown deepened. He took the curving staircase and crossed the marble hallway to the front door.

Outside the house, the two men heard movement and saw the light go on in the foyer.

"Who are you and what do you want," a man's voice said through the door a few minutes later.

"Open the door, Mr. Schmitz," one of the two men said. "We've got an urgent message for you."

"It's 2 a.m. I don't know you."

"It's about your job at the bank," the other said.

There was a pause, the lock clicked and the big door opened.

"What could be so–"

Schmitz heard a muffled thump, then collapsed onto the stone floor. The gunman knelt on one knee and pressed the man's throat. He nodded, stood up and took a photo of the dead man with his cell phone and texted it to the number they had been given. Moments later, they got into their car and disappeared into the predawn darkness.

Coming down for breakfast the next day, Matt picked up a copy of the Orlando Sentinel newspaper in the hotel lobby. Scanning through the pages a headline read: NO LEADS IN THE INVESTIGATION OF BANK CLERK'S MURDER.

Matt went on reading. Apparently, several days ago, the body of Transfer Clerk Walther Schmitz was found with a bullet wound in his chest in his home in Winterpark in what appeared to be a burglary gone wrong. Police had no clues as to the killer.

The article went on to describe his background and listed some of his high-profile clients. One name stood out for Matt: *Hulot & Associates.*

This guy, he thought, was killed a few days before Dad disappeared. Was it just coincidence? Or could this murder be connected to the disappearance somehow? Was that the "unfinished business" my dad had with Stettler? I have to do some digging to find out more. Peter Sherman, a journalist with the Orlando Sentinel newspaper, lives in the Thornton Park district in Orlando. Matt had met up for lunch with him a couple of times. He decided to contact him to find out more. He looked up his phone number, and called from his room at the Marriott.

Peter answered on the third ring.

"Peter, it's me. Matt Wingort."

There was a brief pause. "Hi! How's it going, Matt?"

"I'm in Orlando," Matt said. "I wondered if you could spare a few moments of your time, Peter. I'd like to talk to you."

"Sure, no problem. When would be convenient to you?"

"Any time."

"What about tomorrow afternoon at two?"

"That would be fine."

"Okay. Grab a cab and tell the driver to take you to the Lake Stone restaurant." He paused. "I'll see you tomorrow."

The yellow-painted timber-frame Lake Stone restaurant was located in the central district of Orlando. It sat under a cluster of chestnut trees. When Matt arrived, Peter Sherman was waiting for him. Peter was a neat slim man in his early forties with an angular face and broad smile. Born in Chicago, he worked at the Chicago Sun-Times before joining the Orlando Sentinel.

"Good to see you, Matt," Peter said. "What are you doing in Orlando?"

"Long story," said Matt.

They took a seat at a round wooden oak table between two windows. The tables were covered with blue-and-white checked tablecloth with ceramic lunch plates, water glasses and porcelain coffee cups on them. A scent of wood, fresh-baked cake and hot coffee floated through the room. Country music was playing softly over speakers.

A waitress came to their table. "What can I get you?"

Both ordered a cup of coffee.

Peter looked at Matt across the table. "Well," he said, "what brings you here?"

"I wanted to talk to you about Bruno Stettler the CEO of Hulot Associates."

Peter's expression changed. "What do you want to know about him?"

"It's about my father," he said. "He's reported missing. I came here to find him."

"Missing?" A puzzled frown crossed Peter's face.

Matt explained what had happened.

"What can you tell me about a bank clerk named Schmitz who got shot dead in his home who was connected with Hulot & Associates?"

"Schmitz?" Peter stopped a moment. "Hulot & Associates? Hulot & Associates was a client of the bank where Schmitz worked. Does that have anything to do with your father?"

Matt nodded. "Might very well be possible. I found Stettler's and Hulot's name written in dad's diary."

"Well," Peter said, after a short silence, "word is that Stettler made a fortune laundering money for other people through the bank. The story goes that Schmitz, a transfer clerk in the bank, started shooting his mouth off about these transactions. When Stettler learned what Schmitz was doing he had him killed. Apparently, he arranged for Schmitz's death to look like an accident. A burglary gone wrong."

Matt looked at him. "Who are these people?"

Peter shrugged. "I don't know the entire story. Stettler is in some kind of business with them. Looks like everything is interconnected: Schmitz, Stettler, and more people."

Leaning forward, Peter's eyes fixed on Matt's. "Listen. Let me give you a piece of advice, Matt. Stay the hell away from all that. Whoever they are, these are not people you want to get mixed up with. Let the police do the job. If illegal activities enter the picture, it is a different kettle of fish." He paused. "Be careful. It's dangerous."

"Thanks, Peter," Matt said shortly. "I appreciate your advice."

Heading back to the hotel, Matt walked out of the restaurant and started up the street. When he reached the corner and stepped off the curb, he had the uncomfortable feeling that he was being watched. He could feel it. Someone stood behind him and stared at him, but as he turned and scanned the streets everything seemed normal. There was the usual vehicular and pedestrian traffic. Nothing suspicious. As he stepped into a side street, he stopped dead. His heart skipped a beat. Two menacing-looking men were standing across the street, watched him closely. One wore a baseball cap and black sunglasses and the other was dressed in a polo shirt and khaki pants. Matt felt a flash of recognition. He recalled seeing the two men as he left the Marriott and made his way to the restaurant to meet Peter.

Later that afternoon, when he returned to the hotel, the man in polo shirt and khaki pants stood there and pretended to be staring into a shop window. When Matt got closer, he turned away and spoke into a cell phone. The other man with baseball cap and sunglasses stood on the opposite side of the street, waiting. They watched as Matt entered the hotel.

Inside the lobby, Matt turned around and saw them walk up to an idling SUV, get in and drive off. He knitted his eyebrows. *What's going on here? Have they been snooping around? Have they been checking up on me? Were these two men connected to Stettler? Has it got anything to do with father?* Watching the SUV with the two men pull away from the curb, Matt tried to shrug it off. Maybe it was all in his imagination and he was seeing things? No, he was not mistaken. These two men had been trailing him.

A sudden qualm of fear and apprehension rose in him. He decided to get back to his hotel room and check again his father's diary. Who knows he might find a clue about what was going on. Maybe he would discover *something* in his memoir, a link that would help solve the mystery. Feeling himself drawn back to the computer, like a bee to the honeycomb, Matt found himself eager to finish reading his dad's memoir. Making sure he was not being followed, Matt crossed the lobby, stepped into the elevator, pressed the button for his floor and minutes later, back in his room, took another drink of beer and setting the glass aside, sat down in the chair, turned on the computer and began to read the chapter where he had left off...

THE LOST TRAIN

Rumors started floating around the camp that again exchange prisoners were going to be evacuated. The first transport with "exchange" Jews, mostly Dutch, had left the camp on January 20 without us. We would never forget that date. But maybe now it really was our turn to leave.

The rumors raised the tension. Especially now, as we all sensed the war was drawing to a close. We waited impatiently to hear the good news.

And meanwhile, the camp continued to deteriorate. Everywhere as far as the eye could see, there was deterioration, deterioration, and more deterioration. No roll calls anymore, no *Arbeitskommandos* [work squads] except for the death squads. People continued to die by the dozens. As spring slowly approached, the smell of dead bodies filled the air in the camp. We lived like animals with little hope, foraging for what little food or water was available. There was an abject wretchedness: filth, sticky muck and diseases, hollow-cheeked, starved prisoners shuffling about like scarecrows, little smudge-faced children wailing from hunger, desperate mothers lifting their hands, rolling their eyes to the heavens praying for absolution.

As the Allies got nearer, we heard that the SS commander of Bergen-Belsen was ordered to transfer what was left of the Sternlager inmates. The Sternlager prisoners still had value in future deals the Nazis high command might make with the Allies.

Two trains had already left the camp. The first one, on April 6, and the second one, made up of largely Hungarian prisoners, on

April 7. The third train was scheduled to leave the camp with 2,500 prisoners on April 11. My family and I were scheduled to be on it. Rumors kept circulating about the end of the war. It would be the last transport leaving Bergen-Belsen.

On a bleak, rainy morning, a dense, low-flying fog was like gray smoke drifting over the camp. I stood outside with my mother and my brothers excitedly talking to one another, waiting near the barracks for the trucks to be taken to the train station.

"I wonder what it will be like in the new camp?" I asked.

"Anything's better than this place," Eli said, trying to sound optimistic.

When the first gray-painted trucks came roaring alongside us, sending up sprays of slush from the wet concrete onto us, we all fell silent.

It was notable that the SS officers and *Kapos*, who during the last six days had been practically invisible, now suddenly reappeared to oversee a well-ordered departure, but this time without hollering voices or rude expletives. Rather calmly, they directed us toward the spot where we were supposed to board the idling trucks.

Perhaps the reason for this was the close proximity of the now rapidly advancing Allies, which must have scared the heebie-jeebies out of them.

In any event, despite the promising signs of the war coming to a rapid end, there was no excitement. Most of us had become emotionally apathetic. Just like the guards, who followed orders, we followed instructions mechanically.

The previous day, we had caught sight of Josef Weiss standing outside the barracks nearest to the gate talking to a group of prisoners. My mother and I joined the group.

Mr. Weiss apparently was about to board one of the trucks with us. As always, he kept his friendly calm and answered all our questions precisely. It had been Mr. Weiss who had ordered us to gather our meager belongings and get ready to leave. He had informed us that about 2,500 prisoners would leave the camp.

"Where are they sending us?" my mother asked him.

"Czechoslovakia," Mr. Weiss said. "Theresienstadt."

The name sounded unfamiliar.

"Will they send us to another camp?" asked a prisoner.

"Well," Mr. Weiss replied, "I hope not."

"Maybe it's not true," piped up another prisoner in the group. "Maybe they'll send us to the gas ovens."

"That's baloney!" Mr. Weiss shot back. An apprehensive murmur rose like a cloud of disturbed insects from the undergrowth.

"We have to believe them," Mr. Weiss continued quietly. "They didn't need to tell us anything. They simply could have ordered us to board the train and we would be on our way." He shrugged. "It's as simple as that. So why not believe them?"

Nobody answered him. "I don't trust their words," said the prisoner who before had mentioned the gas ovens. "You can't trust these animals."

"Oh," snarled another man standing near him, "for God's sake, shut up."

"Yes," said another nervous voice. "Please, shut your mouth."

The memory of Westerbork and the scraps of paper that were found in returning trains ran through our minds.

One by one, the open trucks lined up in front of the barracks. One SS walked my family to the second truck in the convoy. We climbed aboard and sat down on the truck bed.

There isn't a word to describe our feelings that cold morning as the soon-to-be passengers started off and headed for the gate, passing the open trailers stacked with bodies. I am sure all of us sitting there in the truck breathed a deep sigh of relief. We were really leaving this squalor, this death-ridden place. As the gates swung open and we turned down the road, I took one last look at the receding camp with its desolate barracks and barbed-wire fence and mentally waved a heartfelt goodbye, and I thought of my father. We were leaving without him. It was his dream and now we would had to live it for him.

Sitting huddled in the open truck moving along the winding road, my mother sat there in silence and stared out at the foggy, wintry landscape that streaked past us. She seemed resigned to whatever our future held.

I turned to glance at the longleaf pines and the country filled with heather rolling by and could hear above the sound of the motor noise, the crackle of small arms fire and farther off the rumbling of aerial bombardments. For sure the Allied troops were rapidly drawing near. (We learned later that the Brits entered the camp four days after we left). *Maybe we should have waited for them to free us*, I thought. *No*, I added, *the risk was too great. Better to get out when we could.*

Soon the trucks began to pull into the station, a narrow loading platform where a train composed of two-thirds passenger cars and one-third freight cars was waiting. My throat tightened: *Lord only knows where that train was taking us.*

We pulled to a stop. The SS drivers jumped down from their cabs, dropped the tailgates and ordered us to dismount. One walked over. He dropped our truck's tailgate. "*Los! Los!*" he said crisply. "*Alle raus!* [Everybody out!]"

People began to climb down from the truck. Taking my hand, mother turned to me and my brothers. "Let's not lose each other," she urged. "Stay close."

I was feeling pretty shaky and weak as we clambered down from the truck. Crossing the stony platform, now alive with SS carrying side arms and keeping a watchful eye, I saw a group of men dressed in striped prisoner clothes dismounting from the cars of the waiting train. *Who were they?* They spoke German, so I presumed, they were either German deserters or criminals who now would be sent to the camp we had come from. (One section of Bergen-Belsen had held German deserters.)

As we watched the group disembark, the word spread that they were carriers of a disease and had infected the train.

Actually, on that platform it was the first time I heard the words *typhus* and *tuberculosis*, though these epidemics had already been rampant in the camp for weeks due to its poor sanitary conditions.

I followed mother across the platform, now packed with people carrying backpacks or dragging suitcases, to one of the empty third-class passenger carriages. I felt sweat dripping from my armpits down the sides of my ribs and experienced a stabbing headache and a dizzy spell that made me stop short in my tracks. Was I running a fever?

SS officers with pistols in black leather holsters on their hips, speaking German to each other, passed by.

People were frantically trying to find pieces of luggage. The SS were busy directing us to train cars. Before boarding, I noticed a group of SS officers standing in a semi-circle around the body of a man in prison garb lying on the bloody concrete floor in front of them. No one seemed to take notice of the group.

Curious, I stepped forward to get a closer look at the body that was lying there, and I could see through the men that the chest was moving, rose and fell, rose and fell, the body was drawing deep breaths, and as I stared at it, my mouth went dry and a chill shot down my spine. *What had these Nazi savages done to this man?*

As I was trying to digest what I was seeing, the SS was standing there casually talking among themselves. I recognized SS guard Pavlenko among them. He casually joked with the other officers over the dead man's body. Then looking around, making sure everybody was watching, he stepped forward and tentatively nudged the body with his booted foot several times. Then stepping back, threw his head back in uproarious laughter. The SS surrounding him cheerfully joined in with ribald wicked grins. Pavlenko must have said something funny. Yes, that SS officer Pavlenko was a funny fellow.

"Will?" My mother was calling me. I turned and saw her standing nervously in the train doorway. "Hurry up," she said. She had put the luggage away and looked across at me. People were pushing past me. When I reached the train, I glanced up at her.

"Where are your brothers?" she asked me.

I shrugged. "They probably got on another car."

"All right," Mom said. "We'll find them later." Her eyes searched my face. "Are you okay?"

I nodded.

"All right, hurry up then," she said, extending her hand.

I climbed up the three steps after her into the train compartment. It was so packed we had to stand in a space toward the back. Suddenly, I started to feel strange again. Dizzy. The compartment started to spin. The crowds of people were suffocating. Sweat started pouring off my brow and began trickling down my back. My knees buckled, and I sank to the floor. I closed my eyes, and little black spots started dancing in front of my eyes.

"Will!" I heard my mother say as if she were a long distance away.

Nausea began to well up. Cold chills coursed through my body. I found myself trembling and shaking, and the last thing I remember was mother feeling my forehead before I blacked out.

The next thing I remember, I was waking up sitting on a hardwood bench against the wall of the train, feeling the bumping wheels of the jouncing train beneath me. Slowly I raised myself up from the battered bench and looked out the window at the war-torn landscape rolling by. Raindrops streaked across the window. The locomotive gave a loud, piercing whistle.

My mother sat across from me. She patted me on the knee with a bright smile on her face. "How are you feeling?" she asked.

"Weak." I smiled. "But better."

"Now," she said, "you lie back and get some more rest. You must regain your strength."

As I closed my eyes, I felt like I was floating like a feather. My mother sitting opposite me was moving in circles and her voice was drifting off like a balloon at a funfair. It seemed like she talked in a peculiar singsong voice. She said we were still in Germany and that we had been traveling for several days now. Whenever the train halted people got off to find something to eat, because no food or drink had been provided.

I was still so tired. My eyes began to close, and I fell back asleep to the rhythmic sound of the iron wheels clicking across the railroad tracks.

When I woke up, there was the sound of voices coming through the open window and I noticed that the train had stopped. I slowly sat up and looked around the compartment. It was nearly empty. When we started, it was so packed that there was hardly any room to breathe. Where were all the people? Where was my mother?

I looked out the open window and saw maybe 30 feet away a small group of prisoners standing or squatting on their haunches alongside the railroad tracks under the trees around small fires. My mother and my brothers were out there too. I sat back down. I wanted to go out to join them, but I was too weak.

Slowly, I leaned my head out into the fresh spring air and saw the black painted locomotive sitting on the railroad tracks hissing white steam and emitting a steady sound of a pounding piston: Boom, boom, boom. About a dozen armed SS soldiers were standing near the train or were sitting on the train steps, leisurely smoking cigarettes, watching the prisoners.

I closed the window and sat back down.

Across from me was an elderly Dutchman, another human skeleton with a shaved skull and hollow eyes in a leathery, wrinkled face. He turned to look at me. "Feeling better?"

"A little," I told him. "Where is everyone?"

"Many have died along the way and were buried beside the train tracks. You are one of the lucky ones to survive the typhoid."

"How long was I sick?"

"Days. Your mother nursed you, trying to get you to drink water, one drop at a time."

The old man kept on talking. Old timers like to talk. And that was okay by me. I didn't mind. Let him talk. Yes, he told me, I had been pretty sick. He nodded his head very slowly. There had been a problem, I needed to drink lots of fluid, but there was no water, nothing, and when the train stopped, which it did quite often, mother and other prisoners got off and collected buckets of water from nearby creeks. There was no way to escape. We were under constant watch. Even though we all knew that liberation was at hand, to the Nazis, orders were orders, and they would follow them to their own end if necessary. The almost liberated prisoners on this train were to be brought somewhere, and the guards would by God make sure they got there.

"Where are we going?" I asked the old man.

"At first, we were headed to Czechoslovakia, but so many tracks had been bombed by the Allies that we had to take many detours. Every delay meant more of us died. No food. Water from rivers. While the Nazis ate in local restaurants." He spat on the floor. "And then was the attack."

I looked up at him. "What attack?"

"You slept like a log," he told me. "The Allies shot at the train from the air."

"Why?"

"It's a Nazi train."

"That means the Allies are close."

He nodded.

I slowly stood as he pointed a bony finger at a wooden side panel, where I saw the bullet holes not only in the train wall but also in the window above it. There was an ugly spider-web crack framing the tableau.

I felt a sudden dizziness and quicky sat down.

"It's only a matter of time now," the old man continued, "before the war is over. I hope we can survive until then."

An hour or so later, my mother returned, carrying a roasted potato and small canteen.

"Will," she said, "you're awake!" She hugged me. "How do you feel?"

"Better."

"Are you hungry?"

When I nodded, she gave me the potato and started to eat it slowly. It was warm. "Your brothers are in the next car," she said. "They are okay."

"Are we still going to the new camp?" I asked her.

"I don't know. They don't tell us anything."

"Nobody knows," the old man interjected. "Not even the Nazis. They're on the run from the Allies."

"Rest now, Will," Mom said.

As I grew stronger, I realized how disgusting the train had become. The latrines were overflowing and the stench was so bad it made you wretch. Most people had to wait until we stopped to relieve themselves outside.

Although it was less crowded so we could sit on the long wooden benches throughout the car, the bodies of living skeletons, too weak even to sit up covered the floors. When we stopped, guards would inspect the cars and carry out the dead for burial in shallow graves. It was a living nightmare with no end in sight.

And the train kept rolling.

The train was hurtling northeast toward the Czech border. Outside, spring seemed near. It had turned sunny again. Occasional cumulus drifted slowly across a blue sky. The train lurched and careened. Mother was sleeping.

I got up to go to the bathroom. As I moved down the aisle of the train car, my legs quivered and my head spun round and round. The car screeched as the train went around a curve, and I had to steady myself, propping my hands against the aisle seats to stay upright. Slowly, trying hard not to lose my balance, I made my way down the car toward the rear where the toilet was located. My legs shook, and I felt like I'd just taken a severe bruising in a boxing ring.

As I opened the door and entered the reeking toilet, I found it difficult to breathe. The train toilet lacked a seat. Outside in a corner in the corridor, I had noticed a black-painted iron bucket, which I assumed was put there in case the lavatory was out of order.

Afterwards, I walked shakily like a drunken blind man, holding my arms outstretched, groping my way forward. The train sounded a loud whistle. Flat, brown countryside swept past.

When I got back to my seat, the old man was gone. Mother was still asleep. I stretched out over the two seats opposite her. Three human skeletons sat nearby conversing in low voices while another prisoner sat slumped on the opposite bench, eyes sunk in his head, dozing.

I closed my eyes and went back to sleep.

I must have slept 30 minutes or so when I was awakened by the sound of a plane passing over us with an ear-deafening roar. And then whoosh, another plane. My mother woke up. Everyone ran to the windows.

I saw another plane with the five-pointed star glistening on its wings in the sunlight coming in from the southeast. Whoosh, it flashed over, and seconds later roaring back, it's nose guns spitted fire at our train. It was another attack by the Allies. The bombs exploded on either side of the train. But we kept moving.

"Mom..." I said, turning my head to look at her. I felt a wave of panic and terror sweep over me.

"Get down," she said quickly.

I put my head down and closed my eyes tightly and pressed myself as close to the bench as I could and I lay there motionless, my heart in my throat, afraid to move a muscle as mother shielded me from bullets whistling through the open window. Overhead the metallic clatter of machine-gun fire began. Bullets flew into the car, breaking windows. Down the aisle, a couple of more windows exploded. One man was hit and fell to the floor. Everyone dove for the filthy floor, huddling near the benches.

My mother clung to me more tightly. My heart bounced around in my chest, hearing the nerve-racking clatter in the air getting closer and closer. All I could think about was how long is the attack going to last? It seemed to go on forever.

A few minutes later, the gun fire stopped and I heard the planes soar away. The train stopped. People jumped from the train to escape. The Nazis ran after them, yelling to get back on. Several people were shot and were left in the field.

Mother sat up. "It's over," she said. "Are you okay?"

I nodded.

Just then, Eli and Josef came through the shattered door into our car.

"Mom, Will are you hurt? This was worse than the last attack," Eli said apprehensively.

"We are fine," my mother said.

We all huddled together.

One hour later, we were traveling again.

The rest of the trip is largely a blur to me. All I remember are moments. People moaning from sickness or hunger. Nazis kicking the dead off the train to lay in the fields, not even bothering to stop or bury them anymore. Someone saying Kaddish in hushed tones. To this day, I believe that it was a miracle that we survived such horror.

Most of the time I slept, but there were scenes, dream-like pictures in my mind that stood out sharply, like a group of pistol-packing SS soldiers standing on a passing station platform with a look of relief on their faces that said they were glad the war would soon be over and they could go home, and mother seated on the bench across from me urging me to drink and eat whatever she had been able to collect. Sometimes it would be a small potato or a little piece of bread. I believed at one point I was eating a hard-boiled egg; today I wonder whether that had been a fantasy.

Slowly I came back to myself, and became aware that around me were the same hollow-eyed and apathetic sunken faces of near-dead prisoners now trying to outlive the grueling train ride. But in the end, a large number would die of starvation and disease nevertheless.

The weather kept changing; one day was rainy and chilly, then the next was sunny and warmer. We passed through flat pasture bordered by forest. Cattle were grazing in the fields. The smell of late spring and fresh cut grass was in the air. Far off, we noticed a farming village and could see cars moving along a road in the distance.

As I looked across the grassy lands and saw the little distant farmhouses and cars that moved along a country road, I wondered: *Did these people know what was happening to us? Did they care?*

My answer came quickly as the iron wheels of the train started to screech and we jolted to another stop, pulling up to a gently rising slope just outside of town. My brothers Eli and Josef, who had come over to our car, were convinced we were in Germany. It was very quiet. The only noise was the hissing locomotive and the pounding of the piston. We sat and speculated how long we would be staying this time. We had gotten accustomed to the frequent stops.

Then the noise of the locomotive had stopped and suddenly, maybe 30 yards away from us, at the top of the grassy slope, a middle-aged woman with two small kids appeared, holding a loaf of bread over her head. Soon several more women with their children joined her waving more loaves of bread. They knew. They were trying to help us. My brothers guessed that they were locals from the nearby village. They kept a discreet distance from our guards, who noticed them but didn't say anything.

Prisoners started to jump off the train and started to scramble their way up to these women, desperate for food. The Nazi guards yelled at them to stop, firing warning shots now into the air. They didn't stop.

"William, stay here," my mother said.

"No," I said. I was all right and was beginning to regain my strength. "I am coming with you."

But my mother and my brothers jumped off the train without me, while I waited and watched the survivors as they grabbed the bread. *Bread. Crusty, delicious bread.* I just watched it. My mouth started salivating. I hadn't had food for a lengthy period of time, and the hunger was overwhelming. Outside, I heard loud jabbering as the first prisoners rolled down the grassy slope, fighting each other, trying to get hold of a little piece of bread.

A little voice in the back of my head was saying to me, "Don't just sit there, get up and get something to eat. If you want some food, go and get it. Nothing comes for free. Go, get up!" I got to my feet and shakily descended from the train. I took several steps toward the slope and dodged an inmate who was tumbling down the slope and fell onto the soft ground. I slowly worked my way up, slowly, very slowly. I crawled on my hands and knees, panting for breath. Soon I began to feel my strength fading. I paused a moment. Then doggedly, tenaciously, gritting my teeth, I inched my way forward, thinking to myself I desperately needed the bread. So I crawled on inch by inch, while a stream of savage curses and eager chattering continued to rage around me. The starving survivors fighting each other for a little crumb of that precious bread seemed like a wild pack of hungry, growling wolves circling a carcass.

I didn't see my mother or my two brothers. Maybe, I thought, they were already eating the delicious bread? I kept spurring myself on, trying hard to pick my way up through the crush to get even an itsy-bitsy crumb of bread. When I finally had almost reached the top, my strength spent, I stopped, took a deep breath, and glanced up with pleading eyes at the group of women who were standing there over me. One of them, staring back down at me with compassionate eyes, was about to toss me a piece of bread when another snarling animal swooped in and triumphantly snatched it away in front of my eyes.

In that moment of despair I lost my grip and started sliding back down the slope. *Oh, my God, no, no.* I slid down, but then somehow summoning every ounce of willpower, I managed to dig in my toes and got myself stopped. I glanced up, breathing hard. I was maybe ten yards away from the top. To me, it felt like a hundred. In disbelief, gathering myself up again, heaving and gasping for breath now, digging in toes and fingernails, clenching my teeth, doggedly I started crawling back up the slope again.

When I finally got close to the women, I glanced up. They were surrounded by starving inmates, their hands outstretched in desperation. But it was too late. The bread was gone.

Frightened at the hungry mob, the women took their children and headed back to the village. The guards had caught up with the horde of inmates and forced them back to the train. I stood up and followed behind them, all the while looking for my mother and my brothers.

I found them back in the car. No bread.

Once everyone was aboard, the locomotive sounded a short whistle blast, the train gave a jerk and we were traveling again.

All that night and the following morning, the train continued. My mother was certain we were traveling through East Germany, though how she could guess this from the flattened towns and shell-smashed buildings I'll never know.

On the third day of that week, the train reached a deserted suburb of Berlin.

The sky was a bright, cloudless blue. The train had stopped again. (This moving back and forth of the train had become an endless broken record.)

This time, we stopped at a small, roofed-over open-air railway station in the middle of what looked like a large city. A broken sign in the station read: BERLIN-SPANDAU.

I turned to my brothers. "Where are we now?"

"Someplace in Berlin, I guess," Josef said.

All around us, as far as the eye could see, not a single building had been left standing. There was only rubble. The city lay in ruins. Crumbling buildings, huge holes in the streets. A few people milled around the rumble.

We opened a window and looked out. The air was cool and crisp. There was an eerie silence. The only sound we heard was the hissing and pounding of the locomotive. We sat down and waited. Through the broken windows, we saw a couple of SS guards standing on the platform. The train guards joined them. It looked like they were getting a report about what had happened.

We couldn't hear what they were saying and just sat there for a couple of minutes, listening to the unsettling sound of the locomotive.

Then suddenly, a siren was cutting the air with a shrieking, nerve-wracking undulating wail. We gazed at each other and looked out the window. What was going on? Nothing moved. Nothing stirred.

Two SS guards, rifles slung over their shoulders, hurried past our window along the platform, waving their arms frantically, hollering to the train engineer to get the hell out of the station.

"*Raus! Raus!*" they shouted. "*Los! Los!* Quick! Out!"

The siren kept blaring.

I got up from the bench, leaned my head out an open window and saw three guards swinging up onto the train as it pulled out of the station.

Farther off, another air-raid siren was dying down.

The train let out a long whistle. I pulled my head back inside. "Must be another air raid," we said aloud.

We watched the shot-up buildings slide by as the train, slowly swaying, was pulling out. Seeing all around us the entire city flattened, we wondered what the planes were going to attack, since there was nothing left to attack but ghostly remains.

Impatiently, I stood up again, despite mother and Eli admonishing me to sit back down, and looked out the open window. Suddenly, though we had not heard any planes, as I turned my head, I could see the black stick of bombs tumbling down from the sky onto the railroad station, as though they had materialized out of the ozone.

Just as we had cleared the station, there was an earth-shaking explosion, and a giant fireball shot up in the air. The station went up in dancing flames and smoke, and a geyser of debris rose in the air, followed by multiple explosions. Within seconds the small station we had just left was ablaze with a furious roaring fire. A few more seconds and our train would have been destroyed as well. The train let out another long whistle and sped up.

Mother and my two brothers who stood beside me now stepped back. We closed the window and sat down, silent. Looking outside, we thanked our lucky stars we were still alive and unharmed.

The destruction of Berlin could mean only one thing: the Allies had won the war. The day of our liberation was close at hand.

But we were still prisoners.

After leaving Berlin-Spandau, the train went on and headed southeast. We saw that the trail of devastation stretched for miles. Small cities like Finsterwald and Falkenberg were all but destroyed. It was just a matter of time before the Allies caught up with us. We hoped.

LIBERATION

Railways had been destroyed, and trains were bombed. The SS guards had been trying to find passages to get through.

And now, on the 12th day of the train journey, we came to a halt in the countryside on the German-Polish border.

I can vividly remember that morning. Dawn was coming up. The smells of ripe fields and pines filled the air. Somewhere in the distance were rumbling explosions. The train came to screeching halt. And then silence. We heard the rattle of small-arms fire and men yelling. Then again silence.

What's happening? I thought. I looked out the windows to see the SS guards, hands raised above their heads, being marched off at gunpoint by khaki-uniformed soldiers.

One of these soldiers boarded our car. He shouted something in a foreign language and motioned for us to get off the train. As we gathered near the tracks, what appeared to be a commander on a horse approached our group. He wore a tall, black Cossack fur hat. His machine gun lay across his saddle and his brown leather boots were stuck in metal stirrups.

He stopped in front of us, said something in the same foreign language. "*Nemetskiy?* [German?]" he asked, looking down at us from his horse, knitting his brow suspiciously.

We all looked around not understanding what he was saying.

"*Nyet*," one of the inmates said. "*Gollandia* [Dutch]."

He nodded. "*Dah, dah.*"

Having grown up in Galicia, Poland, my mother recognized the language as Russian. She understood a few phrases and said, "They are Russians. Allies. They have come to liberate us. The war is over."

The commander turned to another officer and barked some orders, then wheeled his horse, spurred it and galloped away toward the pine forest, followed by the Nazi guards marched at gunpoint by Russian military men. A few minutes later, we heard gunshots.

"Nazi swine," one man said. "Serves them right."

With the Cossack's appearance, we suddenly realized we were free. Such a blasé ending to two and a half years living through the horrors of the camps.

The Russian soldiers marched back and led us toward the nearby village of Tröbitz. Most camp survivors remained calm. They were too sick to stand or move and too apathetic to even celebrate their newfound freedom. Later on, we would think a great deal about losing our father, about the friends we knew who had been left behind in the camp, and of course, all those who had died such pointless and horrible deaths.

Not long after that, things started to move fast. The Russian military set up a command office in Tröbitz and moved us into houses of German civilians, some of whom had fled the advancing Russian forces.

We lived in a three-bedroom house with another family. Klara Bertram, a stout German housewife in her forties and her tall, redheaded 18-year-old daughter Margit were our hosts.

Klara's husband had been killed on the Eastern Front. It took a while for them to become comfortable with us because we were Jews. Hitler had told them that we were monsters, responsible for everything bad in Germany. However, when they got to know us, they realized that these were all lies.

We learned from them that Tröbitz had been a village of 700 before the war. With most of the men gone, the women and elders struggled to keep the town going. Our prime concern after the liberation was food. We were like dehydrated itinerants wandering the desert looking for water. And there was never enough food. Since the major roads of Germany had been destroyed, food and other supplies got increasingly scarce. Klara shared whatever edible things were available like canned meat they had kept stocked in the basement or home-made bread and sometimes soup. Fruits and vegetables grew in the little garden in front of the small house. We were grateful for whatever they gave us. It felt good to bathe and wear the clean clothes villagers provided. It felt good to be back in the free world. No guards. No roll calls. No dead bodies piled up outside. No barbed-wire fences surrounding us. It took some getting used to but we did.

However, our German hosts hated the Russians and being occupied. First, they had killed so many of their husbands on the Eastern front. Second, they took advantage of them as the conquered enemy. But to us, they were our liberators and we were grateful.

One pleasant mid-morning, I stepped out of the house and walked down the main street, passing the rows of gray-painted brick homes with well-maintained gardens. As I walked along the street, I stopped to watch a stocky Russian soldier dressed in Russian uniform roping a little pig to a thick tree trunk.

What would he do that for? I wondered. Around me, passersby stopped to stare at him.

One bystander, a fellow survivor who spoke Russian, told us the soldier took pity on the survivors and wanted to give them something good to eat.

After having tied the pig to the tree, the soldier took a couple of steps back, put his arm behind him, removed the service revolver from his holster, leveled it at the animal, and fired two short bursts. The pig gave a high-pitched squeal, went down on its knees, thrashed about wildly for a long minute, and then went over on its side and lay still.

We passersby stood there and gaped at it.

After shooting the animal, the soldier calmly holstered his pistol and without a word to us, turned and walked away. Maybe half a dozen of the survivors stood there perplexed for a moment and then went to their houses and fetched big kitchen knives. They then cut large slices of meat from the animal and brought it back home and cooked it. That was the first taste of a great meal we survivors had savored in a very long time. After the camps, you'll eat whatever you can get.

We figured that sooner or later we would have to leave. But for the time being, we were content to live in this peaceful pleasant village with its old houses, green lawns, and surrounding woodlands.

It had been almost a month. A typhus epidemic raged, and many people became ill. Maybe that was the reason, I figured, not too many people were seen out on the streets, except for Soviet soldiers who several times a week would march in long columns, five abreast, singing Russian songs while female soldiers would join in with brilliant soprano voices.

Sitting with our feet curled up on a stone wall underneath the rows of shady elm trees near the square, my brothers and I would watch this spectacle as they marched in rank and file down the streets. Sometimes there was a Russian dance performance in the main square in front of a rose-brick office building. Many of the people from the camp would sit on stone benches in front of the building and watch female Russian soldiers pertly swinging their hips, dancing round and round and round, singing and clapping hands in a fast rhythm as other soldiers play the balalaika. Then two Soviet male soldiers would squat down, cross their arms, and kick their legs out in a fast tempo as the rest of them stood in a circle playing the accordion and fifes while beating time with their feet. It was fun for us, a nice bit of amusement after the years of cruelty and deprivation. The German villagers did not attend as they were afraid of the Russians. We soon found out why.

As the occupying force, the Russians commandeered food and other supplies, leaving little for the villagers and us. They were abusive and condescending as well. But for us, compared to the Nazis, they were just strict and greedy, not vicious murders.

When night fell in Tröbitz, drunken Russians soldiers would go from door to door, force their way inside and to take local women away. All the women in town, young and old, bolted their doors, pleading for mercy when the Russians pounded, scared out of their wits.

As the days wore on, we were slowly running out of food. My mother was worried we'd starve. Klara appealed to the Russians but they didn't do anything. Then, an idea struck me. I had heard that the neighboring village of Schilda was not occupied by the

Russians. Margit said it was only four kilometers away. I thought they might have some food to share.

One morning, after a meager breakfast of stale bread and milk, I told my mother and my two brothers my idea. I would walk to Schilda and beg for food. Josef stared at me. "Really? You want to go to the village and ask people for food?"

I nodded.

Eli laughed. "What makes you think they'll share their food with us?"

"Why not? They must know what's happening. Margit said the people there were friendly. It's worth a try. It's the least we can do to help Klara and Margit."

"Are you sure you are strong enough to walk there?" Mom asked.

"Sure," I said. "I feel fine. Margit told me it's about 30 minutes."

"It might be dangerous. Eli, go with your brother to help him."

"Mom, it's a crazy idea. I'd rather try to find food here."

Josef agreed.

"There is no more food here," I said.

My mother looked concerned. Then: "Okay. Your brothers will see you to the end of the village. Just be careful and come back as quickly as possible."

Eli shooting me a smile, slapped me on the back. "Hats off to you," he said.

My brothers told me they would have liked to come along, but had already arranged to meet with friends from the camp in town.

"It's okay. I'll manage," I said.

It was a sunny May morning, as we set out for the village. I was carrying an old floor sack. When we got to the outskirts of the village, my brothers stopped.

"Say hi to the farmer's daughters for us," said Eli.

"Yeah, and don't eat all the food on the way back."

"You'll see."

They laughed and went back to the village.

It was pleasant walk in the morning sun along the winding road with the cool early-morning smell of grass, the green pine forests and green farmland surrounding me. Here and there a bicycle rider or an automobile would drive by. A slight summer breeze was blowing. Everything was quiet otherwise.

Soon, ahead, I saw the first lovely white single-family homes nestled under a grove of old trees. It looked like a fairytale setting. All around me was deep silence. Here and there, birds were chirping in the trees or a dog was barking in the distance. A hint of cattle manure scent lingered in the air.

A short while later, I came to a small stone house surrounded by elm trees. The forest-green shades were pulled down over the windows. The place looked deserted.

I took heart, walked up to the front door and knocked. Maybe a caring person would come out and invite me in and serve me all kinds of yummy food?

But nothing happened. Nothing moved. I waited a bit longer, then knocked again. No answer. Okay. I moved on to another identical house a short distance away. Same result. *Where were all these people? Had they fled the Russian Army?* Klara had told us many Germans were afraid of the Russians and fled to other parts of Germany. *Were they just too afraid to open the door to strangers?*

I turned and walked a short distance to the next home, a white-plastered two-story farmhouse with an adjacent old stone barn. I knocked three times on the door. Knock, knock, knock. Tomblike silence. A strong smell of summer and fresh-cut hay swirled through the air. I waited. Cows were cawing nearby. Seconds passed. Then: "*Wer ist da?* [Who is there?]" a woman's voice said.

My heart leapt. Finally, someone was home. "*Bitte, Fräulein,*" I said. "*Lebensmittel?* [Food?]"

Then the front door opened slowly and an elderly woman peered out at me, and then quickly closed the door. I knocked again. She didn't answer. *Terrific*, I thought. I tried three more houses. No answer. I was feeling dejected. Maybe my brothers were right. Why should these people help strangers? They were probably starving themselves. But I kept on and came to a nice yellow brick farmhouse shaded by old willowy oaks. I knocked two times. After a moment, a slight young woman with a friendly face opened the door and stood inside the doorway with two small girls.

"*Guten Tag,*" I said. "*Bitte, Fräulein. Lebensmittel?*"

The woman looked at me. "*Woher kommen Sie?* [Where are you from?]"

"Tröbitz," I said, and briefly explained my circumstances.

She gave me a knowing nod, and after gesturing for me to wait, went back inside with her two girls. A few moments later, she came back with a small box filled with food: Bread rolls, a tin of condensed milk, a jar of homemade jam, and some apples and pears (which must have grown in her garden).

I stood there surprised at her generosity. "*Danke schön,*" I said, thanking her and put all the food in my flour sack.

"*Bitte schön,*" she said. "You're welcome." She pointed a finger at the flour sack and asked, "Will you be able to carry all this back to the village?"

I nodded.

"Good." She smiled warmly, held out her hand, and wished me good luck. "*Viel Glück.*"

I shook it, and I thanked her.

Then the mother with her children stepped back and slowly closed the door.

I stood there and looked down at myself and thought, *you are looking like some fearsome scarecrow, William.* Though in much better shape than before, I still was all bones and skin. Anyway, the warmth and kind-heartedness of this family had been wonderfully invigorating.

After the first kilometer on my way back, I rested on the grass under a grove of trees near the edge of a dense wood that gave way to fields of hay. The sack full of food was heavy. I put it down and took a deep breath. The scent of hay had a wonderful soothing calming effect.

Shortly afterwards a big wide-faced man in his sixties with a dour expression, rode up to me on his bicycle from across the field.

He got off his bike, let it drop to the ground and sat down across from me. He began to speak to me in German.

"*Guten Tag, junger Mann.* [Hello, young man]."

"*Guten Tag.*"

I had picked up enough German in the camp to understand him.

He must also have realized just by my looks that I was one those survivors who had wound up in the village of Tröbitz because he asked if I were one of the refugees in Tröbitz. I nodded.

At one point during our brief conversation, he eyed the bag with food I had set down beside me. He got up, took a peek into one, and smiled. He pointed a beefy finger at it, then sitting back down asked if I would trade the food for his old bicycle. I could tell that he was baiting me.

Sitting there, I listened quietly as he spoke. When he finished, I looked at him and said in broken German, "*Sie wollen ein altes Fahrrad tauschen für gutes Essen?* [You want me to trade old bicycle for good food?]" I shook my head. "You are kidding, right? All this delicious food for that ridiculous bicycle you've got there?" I stared at him for a long moment and asked, "Are you serious?"

He nodded his big head. "*Jawohl.*"

Again, I shook my head disbelievingly. That food was not worth trading for anything in the world, not even gold.

"*Nein,*" I told him. "*Es ist für meine Familie.* [It is for my family.]"

He studied me for a long moment with narrowed eyes. Then got up.

"*Du willst Geld?* [You want money?]" he scowled at me.

"*Nein.*"

He shot me a hard look and snarled viciously, "*Gieriger kleiner Jude.* [Greedy little Jew.]"

I got scared he would just take the food from me. Muttering under his breath, "Money-grabbing kikes!" he bent down to pick up his bike by the handlebars then jumped on it and, still cursing me with a continuous stream of invective, started to pedal furiously away across the grass toward the asphalt road.

I got to my feet and looked after him. A torrent of emotions surged through me. This man, this German had the gall to talk to me like that, so soon after what had happened to us? Well, I learned that not only the Nazis hated us. Regular Germans seemed to dislike us as well. Maybe it was because of the Nazi lies that had poisoned their minds. But maybe it was just the way they were. I was filled with bitter rage and frustration. The world outside the camp might not be as safe for us as I thought after all.

I stood there for a long moment and watched him pedaling down the road until he disappeared from sight. I wanted to do something, anything, but what could I do against that big German ox?

For a brief moment I saw myself hollering and throwing rocks after him (there were plenty of stones lying around in the grassy field to pick up and hurl after him), but what was the point? What did I expect? It wouldn't do any good.

Across from me, a light breeze was moving the branches and leaves in the treetops.

I picked up my bag from the grass and started up the road back to Tröbitz. It seemed like a longer walk this time, and I had to sit down a few times and rest.

Sweat-soaked and tired out I arrived back at the house where I received a joyous reception from my family and Frau Klara Bertram and her daughter Margit. My brothers were shocked but proud of my success.

Grabbing the paper sacks and emptying them on the old table, they gaped with wide eyes as the tin of condensed milk, the bread rolls, fruit, and the rest of the food rolled out. Mother clapped her hands together and then gave me a proud hug. Both my brothers and Klara and Margit joined in.

While we ate well that night, it didn't solve the problem of having enough food for the future. Hunger was a constant in our lives. The feeling, this craving for food, would accompany me for many years to come.

It seemed like a disease. You couldn't get enough food. You were hooked on it. Like an addict to heroin.

RESCUED BY AMERICAN FORCES

About a month after we arrived in the village, Mom took ill. Rose-colored spots appeared on her face and arms. She coughed frequently and suffered severe headaches. She was too weak to get out of bed.

One look at her told me what was wrong. I swallowed hard. I had experienced this awful disease and had seen the suffering all around me.

She became delirious, murmured incoherently and ran a high fever. Klara Bertram appealed to the Russians to call for a doctor. A Russian medical officer showed up. He tried to explain her condition. The only word we could understand were: "typhoid" and "hospital." He left quickly.

One hour later, a bright green truck with a red cross on its sides arrived at the house. Two men took my mother on a stretcher and put her in the back of the truck.

"Where are you taking her?" I asked, gesturing.

"Hospital," one man said shortly.

As we all stood outside in the street, watching the truck turn the corner, I felt a lump in my throat. I hoped she'd be all right.

"Don't worry," Klara said to us. "There is a Russian hospital in Tröbitz Northfeld. They will take good care of her."

We hoped she was right.

After two days without any word of her condition, we tried to visit her, walking the whole way. But when we got there, we were told typhoid patients weren't allowed visitors to avoid spreading the disease any further. All we could do was wait and hope for the best.

Weeks went by. No news of my mother.

All the while, we kept wondering what was going to happen to us. How much longer are we going to have to wait in this quiet village? Waiting for what? To go home? Where was home? Where would we be going? What would the future bring? While we were grateful for being safe and free, it was very frustrating not knowing what was going to happen to us. The Russians told us nothing, keeping their mouths shut.

Then, one day, a large crowd gathered in the middle of the town square. People were talking and gesturing excitedly. I wondered what was going on. I watched the faces of people standing near me. They were smiling. My brothers and I went to see what was happening. When we reached the square, there was a young soldier in a green uniform, his web belt and pistol slung low on the hips, one hand resting on his leather holster flap, standing in an open-top jeep in the middle of the crowd. We pushed our way through to listen to what he had to say. He wasn't Russian, but he spoke in another foreign language.

I asked one of villagers who he was.

"*Amerikane* [American]."

I nodded. The Americans had won the war. They were here to rescue us. I had to know what he was saying, but couldn't understand any of it. After several minutes of talking, the crowd stepped back to make room as the soldier climbed down from the jeep and made his way across the street toward the Russian commandant's office. Luckily, there was a Dutch woman who could speak English fluently who was listening, even asking him questions. We stood there in a circle listening to the young woman who had asked the questions, translating into Dutch what she had learned.

Apparently, the American explained that a couple of days earlier two survivors of the camp had left Tröbitz on bicycles, hoping to get back to Holland. They stopped in Delitzsch, a small town in eastern Germany, then occupied by the American forces. They told them about us. The American army sent this soldier to Tröbitz with specific orders from the US Third Army Command in Leipzig to coordinate with Russian military authorities repatriation of survivors to their home countries.

Hearing this, the crowd broke into loud cheerful applause. I looked around to find my brothers, but I couldn't see them. They were somewhere in the crowd. All of a sudden, I had mixed feelings. Strange, I thought. Why was that? I figured it was the unknown. Yes, probably. But then why would I think that way? Home. Holland. Strange. It's been a long time since we had lived in

Amsterdam. Almost three years. Well, finally, at long last, here it was; the goodbye to Tröbitz. You've gotten used to the lazy-pleasant-not-doing-much-but-loafing and waiting-for-whatever-would come, lifestyle, haven't you? Well now the time has come to bid farewell to Tröbitz.

We had been living in the village for over seven long weeks and now things began to accelerate. Like an express train.

The next day, we were told to prepare for transport to the US military base in Leipzig, in northeastern Germany which was only 90 kilometers away. We would travel by truck, while the sick would make the trip in ambulances, separated from the rest of us. My brothers and I were excited to be heading back to the Netherlands, although we didn't know what would be waiting for us there. But what about Mom? Was she still alive? Did they know she was in a Russian hospital in another town? Would she be among the sick traveling to Leipzig? We could only hope.

When a convoy of US military trucks arrived in the square in the center of the village, we were told to take our belongings and line up. We'd be assigned trucks in order. Housewives and kids had moved out into the street to say goodbye to us. Shopkeepers had filled the sidewalks and wished us good luck.

There was a feeling of hope and freedom in the air.

My brothers and I waited in line for our turn to board the long row of trucks. As we waited, another group of trucks arrived, each one painted with a red cross on a white background. They were coming from the Russian medical facility. They pulled up in the middle of the *Dorfplatz*. I watched as Russian paramedics in olive-green uniforms opened the back doors and started moving patients on stretchers toward the waiting American trucks. I looked at my brothers.

"Mom's got to be on one of those," I said. "I'll check. Wait for me." I got off the line and headed over to them.

The Russian medic who had examined my mother was supervising the transfer of patients to the American trucks. I went up to him. I said one of the few Russian words I knew. "*Mamushka*," pointing at my chest. "Wingort? Typhoid."

He frowned, then nodded and looked at the list he was carrying. He pointed at the third truck.

I ran over to it just as two Russian female medics were unloading a patient onto a stretcher to carry to the American trucks. It was Mom, lying on the gurney, covered by a pastel-blue blanket. I stared at her in shocked silence. Oh, my goodness, I thought. I felt my heart plunge within me. I hardly recognized her. Her eyes had sunk deep into her head. Her cheekbones jutted out alarmingly. She appeared more emaciated – if that were possible – than when I last had seen her. She'd lost so much weight she looked like one of those living skeletons back in the camp.

The Russians waived me away.

I shook my head. "Mamushka," I said, pointing to her.

Their expression changed. They let me close to the stretcher.

"Mom?" I murmured, looking down at her.

She glanced up at me, barely able to talk. "Will? Are you alright?"

"Yes, Mom," I said. "We're going home."

Doors of other trucks clanged shut. There was a rapid exchange in Russian and the medics started to move. I walked alongside the stretcher until we had reached the American trucks marked with the same red cross.

A US medic stood there waiting and opened the back doors.

Mom glanced across at me and said, "Take good care of yourself, Will." Her voice cracked. "You hear?"

I nodded my head.

The Russians carrying the gurney paused a moment.

"Mom," I said. "I'll see you in Leipzig. Hang on until then."

She nodded silently. There were tears in her eyes.

German passersby stopped and watched.

From a radio somewhere, a German song carried faintly across the square, drifting through the balmy summer air to us.

I watched as the medics slid the stretcher into the rear of the truck. As

the doors closed I felt my stomach twist into a knot. *Will I ever see her again?* Moments later, the engine sprang to life and the ambulance drove away.

I picked up the few belongings I had accumulated in Tröbitz and started back to the line to rejoin my brothers.

One of the US soldiers checked off our names from a list and motioned us to board the fourth truck in the convoy. My brothers and I climbed onto the open military truck and as I sat there, I watched a German local speaking to a GI who was lighting up a cigarette. The German held out a hand and the US soldier ignored him, looked away, and quietly kept smoking his cigarette. It was general knowledge in those days that the US military discouraged fraternizing between GIs and German civilians.

A few minutes later, we started off.

We were traveling across the German *Autobahnen* [expressways] at a good pace. There was a refreshing northern wind blowing in our faces. We passed fields of grain and barley and here and there little villages with two-and three-house hamlets and cattle grazing beneath the tall trees in the sun.

When we got to Leipzig, we were put up in former German army barracks in the center of town, a drab two-story building with green-painted walls and polished concrete floors. Being housed in former SS barracks, naturally, triggered bad memories of the camp, but without Nazis it was just another building.

As soon as we got settled, I asked one of the military people about my mother. Luckily, he spoke German and sent me to the UNRRA (United Nations Relief and Rehabilitation Administration office) to find out the whereabouts and condition of my mother. Officials in charge had no information about her. I was worried that might have meant she hadn't made it alive, but I kept checking with them each day.

The days in Leipzig passed swiftly. All around us in the streets, we saw American soldiers walking around the rubble-filled streets, snapping photos and enjoying the bars and cafés when they weren't on duty.

Our barracks was located near a US military base, and at daybreak, we would hear a noncom's hoarse voice coming through the open windows counting a steady cadence: "Left, right, left, right, get in step, left... left..."

The first morning we heard this, my brothers and I got up to look out the window and watched columns of uniformed GIs marching in formation across the asphalt road under rows of elms, singing drill songs.

This sight of someone else having to show up early in the morning while we slept in late finally penetrated the fog I was in, and I knew the feeling of true freedom. After the camp, it was like another world, another universe.

There was a café-bar named Arkada – a favorite of US servicemen – located not far from our barracks. The bar was usually crowded and smoky inside and there was loud laughter while an old radio played American pop songs. GIs sat at little wooden tables, some playing cards, some chatting away while drinking cups of coffee or having rounds of beer or wine. My brothers, being older, loved to go there. Sometimes, I'd go with them and get a soda.

One day as I walked in looking for my brothers, I noticed three uniformed GIs sitting at a corner table. I observed them for a while. They were laughing as they drank wine and smoked and talked about whatever GIs talked about. The men were obviously having a good time. One of the three men seated at the table, a tall, broad-shouldered, uniformed soldier with a military crew cut in his twenties, glanced across at me, said something to his two companions, stood up and made his way to me.

"English?" he asked.

"*Nee. Duits... Nederlands.*"

He smiled at me. "*Ik spreek Nederlands* [I speak Dutch]."

We shook hands. He told me that his name was Pete Hoekstra

and I introduced myself. He invited me to sit at their table to meet his buddies.

As we started toward their table, Hoekstra gave me a curious sideway glance, and said, "Were you in one of those concentration camps?"

I nodded my head. It must have been obvious I had been in the camp. One look at me would have told him.

"I'm sorry. It must have been hell," he said sincerely.

Talking to strangers about the anguish I had just lived through for more than two years was hard. I had only lived among fellow survivors who understood. I just nodded.

When we reached the table, he indicated a chair for me to sit.

He introduced me to his friends, ordered another wine for himself and his two buddies and a soft drink for me and soon he began to ask questions about the camp. I told them all they wanted to know about what we'd gone through as prisoners of the Nazis. He translated to his friends as I described the hours long roll calls during the freezing winters and piles of bodies carried on trolleys to the crematorium. The GIs' brows furrowed. They seemed angry.

"Damn Nazis," one of his friends cursed in English.

I understood that.

After that day, I became friends with Pete and saw him often. He was sort of an uncle to me. My brothers teased me about it but I didn't care.

One day, as we were seated at the corner table in the crowded room, just the two of us, Hoekstra put down his glass – a sign that he was about to say something important. "If your mother doesn't come back, would you like to move to America?"

That was unexpected. I looked at him in surprise. He was aware of my status, that my father had died and so far, there was no word of my mother. I stared back at him. *Move to America?* "How do you mean?"

He told me if things, God forbid, turned out bad for me, his own family would be willing to act as a sponsor and adopt me to live in a place called California.

"What about my two brothers?" I asked. My brothers had

several times stopped at the Arkada café and he had met them. He paused a moment. "No problem," he said. "There are quite a few families, like my family, who want to adopt orphans who survived the camps," he added with a smile. "We'd find them a home as well."

There had been some talk about orphans surviving the Nazi camps who found new homes in the US and had been adopted by GIs stationed in Germany. For a brief moment, it was an exciting thought and suddenly a new future seemed to open up before me.

He looked at me. "Well?"

"I don't know," I told him. "I still don't know about my mother."

"I understand," he said. "Just remember it is something to think about."

After that, Pete got reassigned to another outfit. He promised to stay in touch, but he never did. So the notion of my being adopted and living in America never happened, but his kind offer to me and my brothers, virtual strangers to him, offered a ray of hope. His friendship toward me changed my attitude about people. After all I had been through, seeing him smile warmly and patting me on the shoulder heartily, reassuringly and telling me he wanted to help, was a gesture that showed me that some people cared. It was a gesture of kindness and goodwill after years to cruelty. It was America to me.

GOING HOME

We got word from the UNRRA that the Dutch survivors who had survived the train journey and lived in Tröbitz would be taken back to Holland. We would be leaving in a week. My brothers and I were overjoyed, but we were worried about Mom. We didn't want to leave her alone.

Frantic, I kept trying to get information about her, but it was impossible. There were so many survivors mixed in with war casualties, they couldn't keep up and the records were in a state of confusion. They couldn't help me. All they could say that if she was well, she'd probably be repatriated to Holland at some point. I knew that Mom would want us to be safe and start a new life. We just had to hope she'd rejoin us in the future.

At the end of July 1945, my brothers and I boarded a special passenger train with the other Bergen-Belsen camp survivors bound for Maastricht, in the south of the Netherlands.

Memories of the time we spent on that train remain with me today. The train was comfortable. There was a wonderful smell of delicious food hovering in the air. During the trip, US servicemen were serving us hot coffee and slices of crispy fresh sandwiches that tasted like heaven. They would walk up and down the train aisle, carrying loaded trays, and with warm smiles on their faces would call out: "More coffee? More sandwiches?"

It seemed unreal, like a mirage. It was a far cry from the misery of that death train trip from Bergen-Belsen.

One of the railway station stops was at Erfurt, a small city some 185 miles (300 kilometers) west of Berlin. It had not been destroyed in the war and was a busy station. When the train stopped, we got up and looked out the open window at a long, roofed-over platform. Hundreds of people were milling about on the platform.

There was a roaring noise of trains pulling in and out of the station. The constant sound of metallic German voices barking orders to the crowd was heard over loudspeakers, and as far as our eyes could see, there was a mass of German people standing there, elderly people and young children with mothers. Apparently, they were fleeing westward from the rapidly advancing Red Army that was about to take over the eastern zone of Berlin. Some of them were standing or sitting on backpacks or wooden crates beside the railroad track, glancing at our stationary train with downcast looks.

At one point, when I was about to go to the rear of the train to get some refreshments, a US serviceman standing right behind me was leaning forward to get a closer look at the crowd waiting there on the long platform. Turning toward me, his eyes searching my face curiously, his expression seemed to say, *what do you think about these poor things standing out there on the platform?* The truth was, these Germans left me completely cold. I couldn't have cared less. I watched them again from the train window. Now they were the people on the run, homeless, and scared to death of the Russians as we had been of the Nazis. No, I had no sympathy for their plight. They had supported the Nazis and didn't care about the atrocities they had committed to millions of Jews. And unlike us, they were being helped by the Allies to avoid capture or worse, not corralled like animals in death camps.

We arrived at Maastricht early in the evening where we were housed in a long, gloomy high-ceilinged hall of a former elementary school with windows on both sides and rows of makeshift beds lining the bare inside walls.

A couple of days after our arrival, officials of the Relief and Rehabilitation organization began to interview us for repatriation back to our different hometowns. There were many people from Amsterdam and eventually, we joined that group on a train to the city where it all had started.

I remember the feeling of coming home after years of hellish deprivation at the hands of monsters in the death camps. The language, food and streets were all familiar to us. We were free in our own country once again. However, I couldn't help but feel sad at the same time. We had returned home, but without our parents. We still had no information about our mother. Where had they taken her? Was she alive? Did she survive the illness? Had she died? What was her condition?

We were quartered in *De Joodse Invalide,* a former Jewish hospital for the aged or disabled, located in the center of Amsterdam. In the postwar period, the six-story building served as an asylum and provided aid to a large group of Jews and Gentiles left homeless after the war. As minors and orphans, we were under the supervision of a family who were also refugees from Bergen-Belsen.

Our house was no longer ours, and we had to live in this former hospital that had been transformed into a home for refugees. I was assigned to a separate dormitory room from my brothers, with boys more or less my age on the second floor – the orphans' floor. For the first time in a long time, I was living an ordinary life in a well-kept building, sleeping in my own bed, and sitting at a properly set table and eating as much as I wanted – a glorious feeling!

And now, the feeling of *liberation* we all had repressed for such a long time flooded over all of us. The word had some kind of surreal connotation.

We had lived like on another planet; now, people around us seemed to move about light-heartedly without really seeming to have to carry the albatross of a grievous past.

We felt reborn and wanted to adapt to this new free life quickly. But it took time.

We were greatly appreciative of the Dutch government for giving us not only shelter, but also stipends to live on. Despite the freedom and support I enjoyed, the horrors of my experience in the Nazi camp haunted me. I had recurring nightmares and woke up in the middle of the night screaming, reliving the fiendish memories of the concentration camps. Many of the survivors suffered. It would take time for these deep wounds to heal. For many they never did. For some the pain was too great and they escaped through suicide.

I was lucky I had my brothers to help me cope. They understood and often had the same nightmares as well. The truth was nobody came back without scars.

We had a lot of catching up to do now that we were back; and boy, we sure did.

Like people almost dying of thirst getting their canteen filled, we started to relish life to its fullest; we savored, indulged, and reveled in our newly regained freedom. And without any parents or school or work, my brothers were out nearly every night. I was still too young for carousing in bars, so when night fell, we survivor boys went out with Jewish and non-Jewish girls at De Joodse Invalide. We shared whatever money we received and went to the roaring *kermis*, the local amusement park on the outskirts of town. To us who had lived in filthy barracks behind electrified fences, who had gotten used to piles of corpses and never knew which one of us would die that day, this carnival was like opening the door to another universe.

We gaped wide-eyed in rapt, disbelieving fascination at the breathtaking thrill rides and dazzling glittering lights and listened in speechless awe to the cheery, happy laughter of the crowd that swirled around us and to the tinkling tinny music of the merry-go-rounds and the hollering voices of pitchmen who welcomed us to their booths. With pounding hearts, we rode the whooshing, shrieking roller coasters and simply took delight in our newly regained lifestyle. I loved the games and the delicious *appelflappen* [apple turnovers]. It was like some heavenly fairyland.

Those of us youngsters who had been in camps enrolled in a temporary school for Jewish refugee children to catch up on what we had missed.

I found myself sitting in a classroom of survivors of various ages, none of whom were particularly interested in what was being taught. I remember I was very rebellious and angry during this time. Sometimes we survivor boys had fist fights with Dutch youngsters, particularly when they threw antisemitic insults at us.

Some of us, including me, took up boxing classes (skipping rope, learning how to move, guard, punch, and defend), with the intention of never being humiliated again should we face tough ruffians in dark alleyways. It helped me build my self-confidence against these rough older kids who liked to humiliate survivors; we would be victims no more.

First and foremost, I and other survivors of the Nazi oppression wanted to put the horrors behind us and enjoy life and we sure rejoiced. But there was something, something indefinable, something that seemed to cling to us like a leech. We were filled with a wild, savage hatred, we hated everything German with a cold, fierce hostility. We loathed whatever was Nazi-related. Everything that was clearly discernibly German we considered evil; they were the despised foe, and we solemnly promised to wreak vengeance upon them until the last murdered victim had been avenged.

Many religious leaders both Jewish and Christian promoted

forgiveness of our enemies as the redemption of the soul, but I found it difficult to accept. There are other words, from the Torah, etched on our memory:

Remember what the Amalekites did to you along the way when you came out of Egypt. When you were weary and worn out, they met you on your journey and attacked all who were lagging behind; they had no fear of God. When the Lord your God gives you rest from all the enemies around you in the land he is giving you to possess as an inheritance, you shall blot out the name of Amalek from under heaven. Do not forget! (Deuteronomy 25:17–19)

We shall abhor the tormentor with every fiber of our being and *not* forget and *not* forgive. We will remember our enemy till the very end, because *remembrance* is of the essence here – and that's what we camp survivors, after our liberation, had been thinking...

A NEW NORMAL

World War II in Europe ended officially on May 8, 1945. Over 50 million people had been killed. Six million Jews out of 9.5 million who lived in Europe before the war, had been murdered. The continent was left in shambles, in chaos and despair. Licking its wounds, the population of the European countries was slowly trying to find the way back to normalcy.

Return to normalcy. What did that mean for me and my brothers? Our father was dead. We didn't know where our mother was. We had been imprisoned in Westerbork and Bergen-Belsen and we still had nightmares.

By the time Eli, Joseph and I returned to Amsterdam, four months had passed since our liberation. Eli, 17, and Josef, 16, went to a different school. As older teens, they lived a life independent of mine. We lived together but didn't see too much of each other. They were busy with their own friends. I was pretty much on my own, doing practically whatever came to my mind.

The mornings I spent at school. The long afternoons I had for myself. It didn't take long for me and other survivor youngsters who lived in the same building to band together. Since our government stipend was just enough for living expenses, we couldn't afford some of entertainments the city had to offer, so we formed a gang to steal things that would sell quickly, enabling us to go to the movies, to swimming pools, other amusements. That was my new kind of normalcy; living without any responsibility, accountability and moral code and feeling free as a bird. I ignored all the lessons of honesty and hard work my parents had taught. I did not really care about anything during that time.

Then, a miracle happened.

MOM

In the spring of 1946, the authorities finally gave us news of our mother. She was alive and would be coming in by plane to Amsterdam from Kaiserslautern, Germany, where she had been recuperating since leaving Tröbitz.

My brothers and I were overjoyed.

On the appointed day, we took a bus to Schiphol airport, located southwest of Amsterdam. We stood there in the crowded hall and waited impatiently for the first passengers to enter from the plane on the tarmac outside. At first, we couldn't see through the crowd. Pushing to the front, we finally saw a thin woman come through the door.

"Mom!" I shouted.

Mom saw us, hesitated and then smiled and waved. She was dressed in a light gray coat over a beige two-piece dress. She still looked somewhat frail but healthy. We rushed toward her, hugged and exclaimed with a big smile on our faces, "Welcome back to the free world, Mom."

My mother also lived in De Joodse Invalide building and shared a room with two other women. We three boys stayed in our own rooms, in a separate wing. On the surface, daily life continued as it had before she arrived. However, seeing that we had gotten too free, she resumed her role as head of our family and started making plans for the future. We could no longer do whatever we wanted. We now had to answer to my mother.

The time went by quickly and then came a change. Now the first priority was for Mom to look into our finances. She went with my two brothers to the ING bank in Amsterdam. It was a commercial bank in the center of the town. Dad had been a client of the bank for years. The banker handling the account, Mom told me later, was very polite, very forthcoming. A real gentleman. He was sorry, he told her, what had happened to us. He remembered Dad as an honest businessman and despite the winds of war that swept across the continent and the ravages of the Nazis in Europe, his account had remained intact. It was a joint account, so Mom had no problem withdrawing cash when she needed it.

Her next priority was to find a new home where we could live together again. We bought copies of the *Algemeen Dagblad* newspaper and studied the classified ads. It was hard as apartments were at a premium after the war. However, two months later, we found ourselves living in a tiny apartment on the third floor of an old four-story brick building near a canal. It contained a small living room, two small bedrooms and a tiny bath with a big window that looked out on the tile roofs of houses across the street. The furniture was old, the carpet was somewhat frayed, but we were happy to have our own home again.

My mother didn't want to rely on the government stipend. She planned to open a small retail store, selling jewelry and watches and accessories. Mom knew the ropes; after all, she had helped father with his business. To get started, she applied for a bank loan. The same bank manager trusted her and approved the loan.

From that point on, we settled into the new routine of daily life similar to the time preceding the war. Mom had us attend a better school than the provisional postwar school. They were well-organized, with books, notebooks, watercolor painting – all things I hadn't seen for years. Gone were the afternoons hanging out with friends. Mom saw to it that we attended each day and did our homework at night. There were regular evening meals around the table. Sometimes when I came home from school and entered home there was this delicious smell of my mother's fresh bakes floating through the kitchen. There were the family gatherings on Saturdays and Sundays and there was vacation...

Our days of carousing were over. You could call it a return to normalcy. But there were challenges.

The return to normal turned out not to be easy, not for us and not for anybody else. We had to adapt to the change. We faced people who looked at us differently (and treated us differently). As survivors of the camps, people talked and behaved toward us as if they were walking on eggshells with some sort of guilt written all over their faces. Everybody it seemed was sorry for what we had been through and strangely enough, we seemed to make them feel uncomfortable around us. There was this constant hush-hush atmosphere around us. Maybe it was guilt that they had escaped the worst of the war and we had not.

None of us spoke about our experiences in the camps to each other or to others. We wanted to forget the past. But the hatred we had for those who had caused us all that misery still burned in our hearts.

We all followed the Nuremberg trials on the radio. We rejoiced when evil men including Hermann Goering, Rudolf Hess and the other chief architects of the deaths of millions were brought to trial. It was difficult to listen as the prosecutors described their crimes. We had lived it and the trials brought back bitter memories.

There were newspaper clippings of the opening day of the military trial in the Palace of Justice in Nuremberg. Photos appeared on the front page. In the pictures the Nazi War criminals sat rigidly, staring stoically ahead and behind them stood ten white-helmeted American sentries with their backs against the walls as the indictments on charges of crimes against humanity were read: Charges of committing unlawfully and willfully war crimes against peace and humanity; these crimes included murder, cruelties, tortures, atrocities and other inhuman acts. The defendants encouraged, abetted and took part in the systematic murder of millions of Jews. We were filled with a deep sense of satisfaction when the sentenced were carried out on October 16,

1946 and ten members of the military leadership of Nazi Germany were hanged.

But what about that monster SS officer Lukas Pavlenko? Where was he? There were quite a number of SS, mostly the high brass that were indicted for war crimes and were sentenced to death by hanging, but where were the others, all the other lower-ranking SS henchmen, like the brutal sadist Pavlenko?

Many were tried, but we had heard that hundreds of these criminals had run away like rats on the sinking ship of the Third Reich and were hiding from the justice for their despicable acts...

My mother has started her retail store and was successful. My brothers attended college and the university in Utrecht. I was studying at the Academy of Art. The days slipped into weeks and the weeks into months and months into years. Our lives had gotten back on track and we were happy.

When I was 19, tragedy suddenly struck our family. Eli died at age 26 from an accidental fall down the stairs. The classes had ended and the students headed for the exit when Eli waved to a friend and lost his footing, slipped and crashed down the flight of stairs, hitting his head violently. That same evening, he was admitted to the hospital where he died seven days later from a severe brain injury.

We were devastated. After all we'd gone through, to lose Eli to an accident seemed so unfair. It struck Mom hardest of all. She had lost Dad and now her oldest son. While she bravely went on with her life and helping us with our own, she was never the same. Her health began to fail. One year later, Mom was diagnosed with lymphoma. In those days, there was no effective treatment. As she grew weaker, she was admitted to the University Hospital.

Seated with Josef at mother's bedside at the hospital, my mind flashed back to the agonizing days she had endured in the death camps. Now, seeing her lying there in the hospital bed with all kind of tubes and wires attached to her body, struggling against this dreadful disease, I got all choked up. Grimly she fought the illness and had tried to survive the way she survived against the horrifying ordeals of starvation and terror in the camp but sadly didn't win the fight against this dangerous disease.

I tried to keep the business going, but didn't know how and it went under. My brother went back to Utrecht, started his own business and I took odd jobs to pay the rent, but eventually went back to school and got a degree in business. I got a job selling jewelry, and eventually got a certificate as a gemologist. When I was 20, I decided to emigrate to the United States. It has been the dream of my father to leave the European continent and start a new life there.

AMERICA

During my first year in New York City, I was lucky and got a job as a traveling jewelry sales rep for a large company. When I was in town and was not traveling, I dated and went out with friends.

Then one day, I met Megan Koppel at a friend's wedding. Megan was a tall, long-waisted, attractive, black-haired girl with intelligent blue eyes and a bright cheerful smile. She was five years younger than me. We dated for four months after we met and then got married. Wanting to settle down, I found an opportunity to start my own jewelry business with Megan. It took time but with hard work, great customer service and resolute determination, we made the business successful and managed to put together a comfortable middle-class lifestyle. We lived in a four-bedroom apartment on the Upper West Side of Manhattan. Then we were blessed with our son Matt.

Time flew. Like a bird through the air, so fast. And through all the years of doing business and traveling my past haunted me. But I never shared it with anyone. Even Megan only knew bits and pieces. For many years after the war, I avoided anything German. Germany and German goods were taboo to me. Under no circumstances would I travel to Germany, buy German products, or watch German TV. But as they say, life goes on and things change. And what about people? I am not so sure about that.

I spend a great deal of time with people of different

nationalities in my business. There were also German business people whom I could not ignore. From the beginning, when meeting a pleasant and very courteous German man, I'd immediately ask myself: Where were you during the war? Are you a Nazi in disguise? A member of the SS? My hatred of the German people who supported the Reich still burned in me.

It wasn't a pleasant way to live. But eventually, age and experience did soften me. I learned to deal with it. They say things change and people change. I know that not everything in life is black and white. And I am no longer looking at every German as a potential Nazi. However, for me, everything that has to do with Germany and Germans still gives me the creeps. After all, Germany was the birthplace of Nazism – the source of the worst of all possible evil.

One oasis of peace I found was reading. I was grateful to my father for that. My father would sit in a chair after work in the evenings reading books by the light of a floor lamp. He would glance at me over a book he was reading and say, "These books offer portraits of real people, of *real* life. They'll give you a lot of insight on how the human mind works." I often accompanied our father to the library to check out the books.

With every book I read, I marveled at the skill of writers, how they created stories that would lure me in and transport me to worlds beyond my own experience. I thought that I would like to write something, someday. Maybe not right now you know. I had a business to run, a son to raise. There was no time.

Once a year I would go with Megan to the jewelry trade show in Chicago. We would stay at the Palmer House, a nice, comfortable hotel. We liked it there. The hotel manager, the desk clerks, the bellboys and bartenders remembered us from past years.

During the three days we stayed at the show in Chicago we met new and old customers. We purchased new products and sold past items and frequently – an important factor at trade shows – made contacts with new, prospective clients. There never seemed to be enough time left to do anything else. But whenever possible we took time out for a drink at the hotel's granite-topped oak bar with the other out-of-towners who were there for business. In the evenings, after the trade show, to help us relax, we went out for dinner at Joe's Steak house restaurant.

REVISITING THE PAST

Once, while on a business trip to Europe, my flight had a mandatory three-day stopover in Frankfurt, in Germany. I hadn't been in the city of my birth for many years.

I recall when the cab driver pulled up in front of the Intercontinental hotel and I stepped out of the car, I saw two elderly, well-dressed men being engaged in conversation in front of the hotel. Again, I wondered immediately; where had they been during the war?

In the lobby, when checking in, hearing the German language, struck me forcibly; like an echo of the past, it reverberated through my mind: The *Bitte schön's,* and the *Danke schön's on the lips of the clerks and servers* seems so disgustingly polite, even hypocritical. Were they mocking me, an old Jew? I couldn't help my bitter thoughts.

I decided to walk around the city, looking for my old neighborhood, *Scheidswaldstrasse 11, Frankfurt Ostend.* Being back after so many years, it was astounding. Everything had changed. I recalled seeing the ruins as Germany was flattened by the continuous relentless Allied bombing and people wandering around homeless in the rubble and now everything looked new, rebuilt, no hint of the devastation. Like a different, opulent-looking country altogether. I recognized nothing. Modern buildings lined the three and four lane streets. There were shiny looking BMWs and Mercedes cars parked along the streets. Ritzy-looking hotels and shops were filled with expensive goods and people shopping. Granted, it has been many decades since I even thought about my childhood in Frankfurt, but nothing was recognizable.

As I wandered the streets, I walked past a synagogue. It was near the place where my family had lived. It looked like it might be the same synagogue where my brothers had their bar mitzvahs and we had attended services. But it was a modern building. I noticed that one of its walls had a sign that read in German and Hebrew: NEVER FORGET. The rest of the wall was covered with hundreds of metal plaques, each with a name on it arranged in alphabetical order. I wondered. Could my parents' names be among them?

As I followed the names, toward the end I finally saw it: Victor and Rachel Wingort. And Dad. I stood there a long time, my eyes filled with tears. Memories flooded back of those dark days. They were not forgotten.

On my way back to the hotel, I thought about everything we'd been through. Then a thought crossed my mind. Bergen-Belsen was located up north near the town of Bremen, several hundred kilometers from Frankfurt. I had a few more days. Why not go, why not revisit the place where I had been as a boy? I had not been back since. Now something wanted me to bid farewell to my father and my friends who had died there. Like a magnet, it kept pulling me back to the former concentration camp. Could I stand to see that hideous nightmare camp again? Might take a two-or three-hour train ride, not more... I resolved to try.

I enquired at the front desk about how to get there. The clerk was very helpful. Apparently, many people visited the camp. He suggested taking a train to Hamburg, then rent a car at the railroad station. The drive, the desk clerk said would take about one hour to the camp memorial. What about a hotel, I asked him, as I probably would need to stay overnight. The young desk clerk smiled politely. He said he could book everything: the train, the car and the hotel. I agreed and he made the arrangements for me to leave in the morning.

That night, I found it difficult to sleep. I was anxious about revisiting the horrible memories I had of that place.

The train was comfortable and efficient. It went along the scenic Rhine and the beautiful Lorelei valley. It was surrounded by birch-covered hills. I had a delicious breakfast in the dining car. What a difference, I thought, from the cramped, filthy train we had taken to the camp. After a trip of three and half hours, I arrived at

Hamburg station on time. I picked up a car at a Hertz car rental nearby, got a roadmap and set off for the memorial.

As I rode through the countryside the tall pine woods and the flat grain fields seemed intensely familiar. It brought back the memories of our transport to the camp. The fear and anxiety we felt. Not knowing what to expect. As I pulled up to the front gate of the camp, it was just the way I remembered it. I got a knot in my stomach. I parked the car in the visitor's lot and walked toward the entrance where under a small stand of trees a large brick wall stood with the inscription: GEDENKSTÄTTE BERGEN-BELSEN.

Off to the side, someone had tacked a small, hand-painted wooden sign that read: *Zur Hölle von Bergen-Belsen* [to the hell of Bergen-Belsen]. Below it, some furious graffitist had written: *Willkommen zu der Menschheit* [Welcome to the Human Race]. The graffitist was right. *Welcome to the Human Race.* He was exactly right. Couldn't have said it better.

A middle-aged balding man in overalls came through the gate and got on a bike. He was one of the people who tended the camp grounds. He was about to start down the road, stopped, turned his head and asked me where I came from in accented English.

"New York," I said, looking at him.

"Have I ever been in Germany before?" His eyes were staring back at me curiously.

I nodded yes and told him I was born in Frankfurt before the war. *Damn German.*

"Much," he said, "has changed in Germany. You will find us different. We are different people today."

Yeah, right. A leopard doesn't change its spots.

He wished me well and rode off on his bicycle. I looked after him. Then I turned, took a deep breath, and went through the gate, stopped and stared. And I no longer knew where I was. Where were the rows of barracks, the barbed-wire fence, the hated watch towers, the ovens? As I stared at the large expanse of green, lush fields and the stone walkways and the surrounding woods, I tried to picture how it had been back then, in the years when I had been imprisoned here with my father, mother, and two brothers. Typhus and other diseases had spread through the camp, which caused the British troops shortly after liberating the camp to burn down the barracks and everything around them.

It was bucolic, peaceful. It looked more like a park than the death camp I remembered. There were memorials all around the grounds. I followed a small group of visitors to a brown brick building that housed the memorial museum.

Inside, visitors stood in silence. They talked in hushed voices and gazed wide-eyed at brightly lit pictures displayed behind glass walls. I stood and stared at the photos, images that were all too familiar to me. Many photos were taken by British military amateur photographers at the time of the liberation. There were pictures of the victims' clothes, jewelry, watches, and diaries. I looked at the photos. I carefully studied each one of them and stared at the people in the pictures, people whose faces were memorialized there. I felt as if I knew them. I had lived like them and my heart went out to them painfully, warmly, compassionately. For a moment, tears welled up and I had to fight them back.

There was a now famous US Army photo of a group of German civilians from a nearby town, boys and girls, disbelieving old men, and young women, forced to file past a line of corpses of Jewish women who had died of starvation in a death camp. Some of the civilians had their eyes lowered in shame, others simply had turned their faces away unable to look at the misery they had denied.

Another photo showed a group of the 50 SS guards in custody. I recognized the coarse-faced Josef Kramer, the last commandant at the Birkenau death camp, and the notoriously cruel Irma Grese, a 21-year-old guard who had been a member of the SS staff at Auschwitz. I looked for the young SS Officer Pavlenko and for SS overseer Krumm. But I did not see them in the photos. *Where were they? Had they slipped away, and escaped the Allies before the camp was liberated? They could be anywhere. In South America, in North America, in Germany, you name it.*

Looking at the faces of the Nazis in the photo, the faces of Commandant Kramer and of Irma Grese, these two barbarians (I remember seeing both in the camp) just watching them was deeply frightening and I asked myself *Has today's Germany changed?* as that caretaker had said. These monsters looked like the people I'd seen on the streets of Frankfurt. After all the misery I'd seen back then, the death of my father, the beatings and starvation and disease, these "ordinary" Germans had caused, how can I look up at Germans any differently today. They all were complicit in my mind as were their descendants. How can anyone with common sense even think of these people as having changed into law-abiding citizens? On the other hand, there are both bad and good eggs in a basket. So maybe you'd better not generalize and be careful with any judgement. But my God, if I recall what they did to my family how can I judge objectively? I simply can't. And that's the reality.

And then there's one other thing. I mean, when like now, you stare at these two beastly humans – they are not really humans are they? They are true animals – this Josef Kramer and Irma Grese, just think of what that *SS Aufseherin* Krumm did to us. Extending her arm then pointing her finger at my family and imperiously order us to stay. TO STAY! And we couldn't leave the camp on that train to freedom and had to stay behind in the camp. How can I judge Germans any differently? But hey, once you experienced all that horror and saw what these people could do to you, murder you in cold blood, just remember...

Of course, I thought, listening to my inner voice, I remember. I do. I recall all of it. I can see it before my eyes: the floggings with leather whips. The beatings with rubber pipes. And not to forget other atrocities I learned about later; the cruelest torture the SS had on hand; the lethal injections and drowning in pools. Keep all that clearly in mind, so you won't forget, okay? These inhuman punishments were often meted out in front of the prisoners standing there in freezing weather lined up for roll call. And after listing all these heroic deeds, how on earth can anyone with common sense even think of these people as being law-abiding citizens? How preposterous. And to add fuel to the fire, so to speak, how long could it have lasted before someone somewhere rose up and proclaimed the Holocaust never happened? Nothing was true? It was all fiction? Everything, they say, is an invented lie. I know people. Trust me. I know what they are capable of, so I can't be surprised... And that's what you have to put up with. Like it or not.

I stopped myself and turned and walked out of the building, and once I was outside, moving around the former open camp grounds, the floodgates opened up. For 15 months, this place, this Nazi death camp, had been my home. I looked around the long stretches of green fields, the trees and pinewoods. And that's about it. Everything else was gone. The Brits had made a fine job of burning everything down when they arrived.

I started walking down along the brick walkways. I gazed at the small burial mounds with the little metal plaques that were scattered across the grassy grounds; 5,000 buried here... 10,000 there... 15,000 over there... then 20,000 ... It didn't stop.

Other visitors were wandering through the well-tended grounds. Some stood in solemn silence in front of a tall obelisk erected by the British in the 1950s. I stood there for a while on the grass. I looked at the scene in front of me. It's hard to describe what standing on the grounds of that place meant to me after all these years. Those trees, I thought. Those beautiful trees. I had faced them for 15 months. Now they seemed to talk to me, "Remember," they told me. "We witnessed everything."

After a moment, I pulled myself away. I continued walking around the grounds. I had studied the display case of the former camp inside the museum. So I roughly knew where I was. I stood in the spot where once the roll call square had been. We had stood here in the rain and freezing weather listening to the obscene expletives and hollering voices of the SS men. I stood here looking out at that SS guard savagely beating mother with a wooden club. I was here and zigzagged across the quadrangle as the Allied planes had attacked the camp. Now, the area looked almost like a peaceful picnic park. No human skeletons were visible. No barbed wire fences. Where once the barracks and the watch towers stood were now grain fields and forests. And silence.

All these people, I thought to myself. All these people, Dad, my friends, Uriel and Kees, and countless others – they just wanted to live like everybody else and got mercilessly murdered, had perished, their young lives wasted, shot to hell. They seemed to cry out to tell the world what happened here, and not to forget.

My father was lying here somewhere. In one of the mass graves. Or was he cremated in the furnace? I pictured how my father had died in the hospital ward. How his body was put on a stretcher and was carted off in the middle of the stormy night by two men of the death unit. Standing there, the stillness engulfing me, I felt the tears well up in my eyes and I cried. Cried for what they had done to him, cried for why I couldn't cry for him at the time.

Trying hard to control my emotions, I pressed my lips together, wiped the tears away, and slowly, softly began to recite Kaddish. For my father and for all those who were lying here and elsewhere who had died at the hands of their Nazi tormentors.

Before I left, I visited the documentation center which showed films about Bergen-Belsen and its liberation.

As I left the theater, I noticed that the site started to get busy. Large groups of young people visited the camp. Teachers with busloads of German students arrived talking in hushed voices. The color pamphlet I'd picked up at the museum mentioned that there were guided tours available in German, English, French, Dutch, Spanish and Hungarian.

Watching the German youngsters, I had mixed feelings and wondered: *Will they continue the fight against this evil from ever happening again by every means possible? Will they glorify this wickedness or shrug it off as another boring history lesson, and just shut their eyes and ears as did most Germans at the time?*

On the way out, casting a last glance at the place for several seconds, the song "A Last Goodbye" about the loss of loved ones was much in my mind.

It was getting dark when I pulled the little blue car out onto the road and headed south to Celle, a small picturesque city where the hotel clerk had booked me a room for the night in the hotel Ringhofer Celler Tor. The drive lasted 20 minutes. When I drove past the old, now vacant loading railroad platform outside the camp, for a moment the past rose up in my mind again; it was here that mother, my two brothers and I got evacuated from the camp in trucks and we boarded the train to that had become known as the "Lost Train."

When I checked into the hotel there was a long line-up at the front desk in the lobby. There was a big convention staying in the hotel, the girl told me as she handed me the keys for the room. I was glad I had reserved a room for the night. I took the keys and started to the elevators.

My room was on the second floor. It was large and comfortable. That night I felt strange, lying in a German bed in a German hotel, closeby from the place where I had suffered so much as a boy. My eyes kept staring at the dark ceiling. I kept telling myself that it was the right thing to do, to come back and revisit the camp. In a way I felt – as the only survivor of the family left, as my brother Josef had died several years back – I had come back to Bergen-Belsen to bear witness to the atrocities we had endured, and to never forget what happened.

The next morning the main dining room was filled with convention people. Many people at the tables seemed to know one another. Some of them was standing around, sharing thoughts. There was a self-service buffet and salad bar. White-jacketed waiters were busy getting drinks from the bar for some guests. There was a soft hum of talk and laughter, clinking sound of dishes. I had a grilled vegetarian sandwich and a cup of coffee. I didn't feel at ease. Not at all. I looked around the room. It was filled with German people who were digging into their food, slurping beers, feeling satisfied and prosperous, while a mere 10 kilometers away, my father was lying in a mass grave or had been cremated after having been starved to death by their ancestors. Maybe one of them, a former SS man, was right here, sitting at the table, enjoying the freshly baked bread and made-to-order eggs and omelets?

The mere thought made me lose my appetite. Quietly, I placed my fork and knife beside my plate. Feeling a wave of disgust sweep over me, I stood up and walked out of the dining room.

It took me a few minutes to pack. I went down to the lobby and checked out, and headed back to Hamburg.

My wife Megan told me later, when I got back home that I

wasn't myself. I was in a state of shock. I acted as if I was in a trance. I didn't communicate and kept to myself. She was right. It took me a good couple of days until I managed to come out of it and got back into my daily routine.

I still wonder how an entire nation with a rich history and fine culture such as Germany, could have plummeted the world into the abyss of cruel murder and organized barbarism. I am fully aware not all Germans were killers and as time passed, I have learned to get along well with new generations of German people. But, deep down inside, right or wrong, I will never trust them.

And against all odds, I have survived the Holocaust and, in time, recovered and could provide a good life for my family. Nevertheless, I'll be aware of the evil that lurks.

I am the living proof that evil does not triumph and my son and future generation of survivors will make sure the world will never forget the horrors wrought by Nazi fanaticism.

HEARTBREAK

Then tragedy hit. My beloved wife Megan died in a freak car accident. My world collapsed.

After her funeral, I just wandered around our silent apartment desolately and looked at Megan's dresses that hung in the closet. Dresses I always enjoyed seeing on her. We had built a life and business together. Seeing her bright smile, her being at my side, encouraging me when I was down. All the good memories...

Like a never-ending movie, it kept running through my mind. Without Megan, I lost interest in the business. I sold it and retired. I lost touch with my friends. My son Matt tried to get me to go out, see people, find some joy. But without Megan and the distractions of everyday life, the nightmare of the camps haunted me. When Matt got me a computer to stay in touch with friends, I thought about writing a memoir. Maybe it would stop the painful memories I had harbored all my life. And without telling Matt or anyone else, I began on this memoir.

PART III
RETRIBUTION

10

Matt Wingort turned off the computer screen and sat in silence for a minute. There were no clues as to father's whereabouts in the diary nor in his memoir. He didn't find any useful piece of information, no leads, nothing. He let out a deep breath and sat back in his chair. Reading his father's words felt like a blow to the guts. His father never shared anything about his past. He kept it all to himself. It must have been a heavy burden for him to bear all those years. He wondered if his mother had known all the details. He felt so bad for his father, keeping the painful memories bottled up inside for his entire life. Well, he thought, now you know. It helped him better understand his father in a way.

Trying to digest everything he was reading Matt was deeply shocked. He felt a cold chill ripple through him. Could these horrible memories have finally overcome him and led to his mystifying disappearance? It didn't make sense though. He had lived with them for decades. *Why now, on a vacation, would they suddenly overwhelm him?*

Frustration gnawed at him. He had questions. He mulled them over for a moment. He looked at it from all sides carefully, but he found nothing. *Where is father? Did Stettler have anything to do with it? Why can't they find him?*

Aside from shoulder shrugs and getting negative head shakes, there was nothing concrete he could point a finger at father's sudden disappearance. He had his suspicions though. Leaning back in his seat, Matt closed his eyes. His father's facial features came to the fore of his mind. It demanded questions. It demanded to know what had happened to him in Orlando. Father went to Orlando on vacation. Okay. Fine. *Was it a business trip? Was it a holiday trip? What kind of a trip was it? Did he knew Steller was living there and did he want to confront him?*

Matt sat there looking out the window at the sunny weather. He thought some more. What he had learned so far, was that after his arrival at the Courtyard Marriot, his father had vanished off the face of the planet. He felt he had been abducted. *Who were these two sinister-looking guys that have been following me? Who were they?* He shook his head slowly. *Do I imagine things? No, I don't think so.* Running his four fingertips through his curly hair, he stopped himself, rubbed the side of his jaw, sighed. It was all speculation. Hypothesizing sure does complicate things, doesn't it? His mind started swirling and diving and wheeling like a flock of hungry seagulls in search of food and while sitting there trying to unravel the baffling entanglement, it was to no avail. The threads of the mystery kept slipping through his hands like grains of sand.

Back home in New York Matt felt frustrated. The police would be of no help in investigating his father's apparent abduction. That was clear as daylight. He knew his father must have tried to contact Stettler, the man he felt was the hated SS officer Pavlenko, and most likely got kidnapped. But how could he prove any of it? He wasn't even sure Pavlenko was alive. All he had was his father's memoir, his diary, a photo of a scarred face from his cell phone and his instincts as a journalist. He had to find more conclusive evidence. He resolved to take Sam Kluger's advice and travel to Germany to get the answers.

He googled Arolsen, Germany. It was north of Frankfurt. He booked a flight to Frankfurt and packed.

That evening, after checking out, he drove out the parking lot and headed for Orlando International Airport.

Two men in a dark SUV followed him.

When Matt dropped his car at the rental place airport and boarded the shuttle, one of the men spoke into his cellphone. "He's at the airport," he said, "on his way to a terminal."

"Follow him," the other said. "Find out where here's going."

"Follow the bus," he said to his partner, then got out and boarded the shuttle.

The Orlando airport terminal was crowded with international travelers. At the Lufthansa ticket counter, Matt Wingort waited on the long line to check in.

A man in a dark suit stood behind him.

Matt moved towards the counter.

"Matt Wingort," he said to the clerk. "I've got a ticket to Frankfurt." He pushed it towards her. The girl looked up smiling.

"Passport." She checked it and nodded. "Any luggage?"

Matt nodded. "Yes, one bag."

The clerk checked it in and handed him the boarding pass. "Gate 12."

The man standing inside the terminal, said into his cell phone, "He's on the two o'clock Lufthansa flight to Frankfurt."

"Okay," his companion said. "I'll take it from here." He turned and headed towards the gate.

11

Matt disembarked the plane at Frankfurt International airport, went through customs, then walked outside toward a line of taxis. A man was standing near the exit. "Subject has just arrived," he said into his cell phone.

"Follow him," the voice said, "and keep me posted."

Matt entered a cab. He gave the driver the address of the hotel and the car pulled away. A second cab was right behind him.

Thirty minutes later, Matt pulled up in front of the hotel Westin on Adenauerstrasse, in the Innenstadt district of Frankfurt.

The second cab also pulled up at the entrance and a man got out and took out his cell phone. "He's at the Westin on Adenauerstrasse."

"Stay with him. I want to know his every move."

The man hung up, entered the ornate lobby and went into the bar, with a clear view of the front door.

Matt went up to the reception desk. "My name is Wingort. I have a reservation."

The clerk nodded. "Let me check our computer for a moment." There was a brief pause. "Ah, yes. Sign here, please."

Matt picked up the pen and signed in.

"Here we go," the clerk said after a moment and handed Matt

some keys. "Room 320. I'll get someone to take your luggage to the room."

The blue-clad bellboy escorted him to the second floor to a pleasant, comfortable room.

The following morning after breakfast, Matt dug into his pocket and found the address and phone number of the International Center on Nazi Persecution Kluger had given him. Matt punched in the phone number. A woman answered.

"I'd like make an appointment to look through the Arolsen Archives."

"Yes, sir," she answered in accented English. "Is this in relation to a family member?"

"Yes."

"Well," she said, and paused a moment, "we have an opening at one tomorrow afternoon."

"Yes, that would work."

"Your name?'

"Matt Wingort."

"We see you tomorrow, Mr. Wingort. Have a good day."

He called the front desk to have them arrange for a rental car to be waiting tomorrow morning and decided to explore the city where his father had spent much of his youth before the camps.

It was a nice, cloudless, spring day.

As Matt left the hotel a man was standing across the street. "He's on the move," he said into his cell phone. "Let's go."

Matt roamed around Sachsenhausen. It was a popular beer garden and music bar neighborhood. A refreshing breeze blew in from the river. He started down Zeil and then explored the elegant Goethestrasse. Looking around at the fancy stores, cafés, restaurants and modern buildings, he thought about his father's memoir. How happy his family had been here before the Nazis.

As he walked the streets, he couldn't get the images his father described of the Nazi takeover out of his head. Matt pictured brownshirts carrying burning torches, marching with pounding drums through the German streets. SS trucks would screech to a sudden halt and SS would jump out, guns drawn, ready to arrest Jews. He thought grimly, *Well, that's the way it goes.*

The images kept following him the way a dog is following a side of beef. Get a grip, he told himself. Better keep your head on straight.

Continuing along Brückenstrasse, he crossed an old bridge. Off to the left, he could see the rising skyline of modern buildings. Looking up ahead at the broad boulevard busy with expensive cars and with people going for a walk and others sitting at restaurants and cafés at tables outside on the brick pavements, Matt stopped walking. His brows furrowed for a moment. He remembered something. His father had mentioned a memorial wall in his old neighborhood when he revisited Frankfurt on business years later. Something like *Scheids-something. Where could that be?*

He saw a policeman across the street and went over to ask him if he knew the place. He didn't speak much English. "Scheidswaldstrasse?"

"Yes, that's it."

He nodded and directed Matt to it, using hand signals and some broken English. It wasn't far away. Matt thanked him and set off.

When he arrived, Matt glanced around him. He reminded himself that this had been another world when his father had lived here. He started to walk along the streets until he came to a synagogue with a Star-of David above the entrance and a yellow-gray granite wall along one side. It had hundreds of metal plaques, commemorating the Jews that were deported to the camps and died there.

This must be the place Dad found, he thought.

Matt walked down the street along the wall checking the

names. After five minutes he stopped and found himself staring at the plaque: *Victor and Rachel Wingort.*

Matt stood in silence another minute. What must it have been like to watch your own father die in a concentration camp? A shiver shot down his back. He didn't want to imagine it. His father was so brave to visit the camp after seeing this plaque.

As Matt turned away from the wall, he noticed two men leaning against a building, smoking. They didn't look like occasional tourists. As he walked toward a large street to hail a cab to take him back to the hotel, the men seemed to follow him.

The men were watching Matt as he entered a cab. "The subject is in a taxi heading east."

12

My instinct gut tells me, Matt Wingort thought to himself, that these two men are following me. They are Stettler's minions for sure. Who else would it be? Who else would cling to me like a leech? He was certain that a dark grey Mercedes with two men in it kept following him. Then suddenly, the car was nowhere in sight. Another time he could have sworn the gray Mercedes-Benz car was moving slowly behind him. A short time later, the car was parked in a hotel parking lot a block away. Waiting. It could be a warning: *Watch out. These people are dangerous. Be careful.*

Sometimes it seems like I am surrounded by an unseen enemy; hard-faced men seem to lurk on corners or loiter in dark doorways. I'm not kidding, the city seems to have become a ticking time bomb, a hostile jungle full of killers trying to capture me.

I mean, he thought, what choice do you have? You are an investigative journalist and you are investigating a former SS guard who is charged with accessory to commit murder. Stettler must surely have figured out about you by now. Figured out that you are investigating him. You've got no choice but to find out what happened to your father. Sooner rather than later you'll have to look him in the face and tell him that he is the kidnapper. That he kidnapped your father. And if it comes to that, he told himself, you'd better be prepared and take the proper precautions.

You cannot pay a visit to his office anymore. Not after he has threatened you with legal action. Can you believe this? You just do what you need to do. If you've got to deal with it, okay, then you do it, deal with it. There is no other way around it. The man's hunting you up you know, he wants to do away with you, the way he did with your father. So you'd better be careful and watch your back.

Putting himself in Stettler's shoes, Matt thought, the man is in it up to his ass. And he knows it. For sure.

A vivid mental picture of Pavlenko aka Stettler jumped to Matt's mind; holding a shot gun in his hand, Stettler, was shooting him down. Like a wild animal. The picture shot chills up his spine. You have to fight back, Matt, he told himself, you have to defend yourself. You know that. Of course, you know that. He pictured himself standing there, arms crossed, staring Stettler in the eye (like that movie actor John Wayne or Hop Cassidy did in those Westerns), stare him down till he blinks and then reach for the gun and cock the thing and then bang, bang. The mental pictures flashed through his mind like a series of close-ups on a movie screen. The problem is though that you don't wear a firearm. You are a journalist, not a cop. Owning a handgun is a good thing though. He had to admit that and it irked him that he hadn't thought of that before. It was stupid. He had seen a gun shop about half an hour drive away from the Marriott. You could apply, he figured, for a firearm license and drive down there, purchase a 9-millimeter Glock pistol or Smith &Wesson short barrel, 38 caliber. It could help you plenty and you'll feel saver to have it in your pocket when confronting Stettler. Just in case, you know. As a precautionary measure. What other choice do you have but to carry a weapon? You'll have to defend yourself from that man and his confederates. Sooner or later, you've got to confront them. So you better get ready and do something about it.

But I need someone by my side, he thought. It would be much better when I got somebody I can depend on. Detective Debra Garfield and the Feds can help me checkmate him. They sure as hell can help me figure out what I should be doing. I've got to think straight and figure how to do it right. I can't make any mistakes. No, not one. Maybe, he thought, there's time enough left me to get things organized. Get my firearms license and make a stop at the gun shop, choose the right one and apply for the first available gun training course at a local range. Before the big day arrives. Better safe than sorry, he said. You better play it safe.

13

Early the next morning, Matt set out for the city of Bad Arolsen two and a half hours from Frankfurt in his rental car, a green Audi. The black SUV followed.

When he arrived, he drove for ten minutes through quiet streets with baroque-style buildings on both sides, pulled up in the front of the three-story, gray-painted brick building of International Center on Nazi Persecution and parked at the curb outside.

When he entered the glass entrance of this place where an archive of millions of documents on the Nazi persecution were housed, he felt his heart constrict thinking of the horrible things that had been done to human beings that he would find in the records.

Outside the Tracing Center, a man was pulling into the parking lot across the street. His mobile was vibrating inside his pants pocket. He put it to his ear.

"Urgent message," the voice said.

He recognized the voice immediately. "What's up?"

"The subject entered the Tracing Center."

The man frowned. "The Tracing Center Archive?"

"Right."

"What do you want us to do?" he said after a short pause.

"Wait until he comes out the door back into the street" the voice said. "Then stay on him. And keep me posted."

Click. End of conversation.

Inside the Tracing Center, the long reading room was quiet. Matt looked out a large floor-to-ceiling window at a flower garden filled with rows of elm trees.

A young man sat in an office at a small wooden desk with a computer. The man looked up and asked for Matt's name.

"You are early, Mr. Wingort. My name is Karl Friedenberg. I will be able to assist you. What is it you are looking for?"

Matt explained that he was seeking information about his grandfather, Victor Wingort and a particular SS Officer at Bergen-Belsen in 1943.

The young man led Matt to a small, windowless, fluorescent-lit room at the end of a narrow hallway and told him to wait a few minutes. He would bring the documents connected to the concentration camp Bergen-Belsen Matt had requested.

About 15 minutes later, the door opened again and the young man returned with two yellow folders labeled, *Bergen-Belsen,* and laid it down on the table before Matt.

"These documents should have the information you need. We have many more in case they do not."

Matt turned his attention to the two folders. He picked one up and found inside a brown pouch marked WINGORT–BELSEN. He opened it and found a gold wedding ring, an old blackened pocket watch and a photo of a young couple. He turned over the photo and read the names: Rachel and Victor, 1936.

Matt carefully picked up the picture and stared at his father's mother Rachel, stern-faced and slim-waisted in a dark dress with a high neck and his father's father Victor in a striped suit, crisp looking white shirt and pocket watch with a chain, round-faced and earnest, distinguished-looking. He stared at them for a long moment. Matt tried hard to control his emotions.

These were the personnel effects his grandparents had with them in the camp. Then there were brittle documents, sheets of paper all in very meticulous bureaucratic typescript stating the names of the entire family, their last residence in Amsterdam, exact dates of arrest, the deportation and dates they arrived at Westerbork, and ultimately Bergen-Belsen. His grandfather's death was reported as from "natural causes." The translation of the German was handwritten in a separate document.

Matt set the documents aside and reached for the second folder. The words BERGEN-BELSEN/ MILITARY STAFF were written in ink across the front. Inside was a page that listed in alphabetical order SS guards by name and rank, a brief personal history when available, and the role they played in the camp along with what looked like official photograph next to each name and their status. Captured, tried, and their sentence or still at large.

He scanned the page and found SS Officer Lukas Pavlenko and read the guard's story:

Nazi guard, officer Lukas Pavlenko had volunteered for the Waffen SS at 18. He served as an SS guard at the Belsen camp until the British troops liberated the camp on April 15, 1945.

Apparently, he escaped capture and disappeared. He was still wanted by German authorities and Interpol for war crimes to this day. Pavlenko's file was marked: whereabouts unknown.

The Nazis documented everything, and took photos of themselves, proud of their service to the Third Reich. In one of the photos in front of the camp's infamous barbed-wire fence where his grandmother was tortured, two SS guards, one male and one female stood next to an officer. The caption identified them as Lukas Pavlenko, Irma Grese and Josef Kramer.

Matt pulled the photo his father had taken of Stettler from his pocket and placed it side by side with the photo. The scar on the faces of both men were identical. Just as he suspected. Bruno Stettler indeed was Lukas Pavlenko, only older. His father was right. The cruel Nazi was still alive.

Had his father discovered Stettler's identity and confronted him? Was that the unfinished business he mentioned in his text? To expose this hated Nazi war criminal and finally see justice done for his crimes? Had he met with Stettler? If so, was he somehow involved in his kidnapping and disappearance to prevent him from going to the authorities? So many questions needed to be answered. But at least, he had established beyond a shadow of doubt that Pavlenko was alive as Bruno Stettler.

Matt took a deep breath and selected the photo of his grandparents, the camp photo and the short profile of Pavlenko, and returned the other items to their envelopes and asked the young man to photocopy the photos and profile.

Ten minutes later, the man handed Matt the copies officially stamped as true copies of archive documents and a large manilla envelope.

Matt took the papers, put them in the envelope, thanked the man and left.

Matt stepped outside into the freshening cool breeze and got into his car and headed back to the highway. *Whew! By God, that was worth coming here.*

But now that he finally had Stettler, how was he going to catch the criminal bastard and prove— after all, he had solid evidence now – who he really was?

The black SUV was parked across the street.

The man spoke into his cell. "Subject has left the Tracing Center, carrying an envelope," he said. "In pursuit."

14

Inside a locked back room in a two-story wooden farmhouse, William Wingort, trying desperately to free his bound hands, was asking himself over and over, *What has happened to me? How did I end up here? How long have I been here?* Like a theater curtain that had been lowered at the end of a play in front of his eyes, what has been going on before or afterward, William Wingort couldn't remember anymore... His hands were tied and his legs were bound at the ankles with a cord of ropes against a straight back wooden chair. He could barely move without the ropes cutting into his skin, cutting off the circulation.

A tall, middle-aged man with a blond stubble on his chin brought him his daily meals and would escort William down a marble-floored corridor to the bathroom.

William felt foggy. His throat was dry. Like he had swallowed an entire bottle of whiskey. He tried to see through it, clear his mind. One of the men had pistol-whipped him. No wonder he felt woozy, very foggy. Again, the image of that hooligan and the hypodermic plunging into his flesh, flooded in. Awful. He felt drowsy. That damn needle must have caused it.

William shifted uncomfortably in his chair. Daggers of stabbing pain shot up through his chest. A wave of dizzying nausea swept over him. The room began to spin, went round and round. Forcing his eyes shut, William broke into an instant sweat and threw up bile.

He sat back and took a deep breath. He closed his eyes and the wheeling feeling stopped. In the distance the sound of dance music playing softly on a speaker system carried up to him in the quiet room. After a while he dozed off.

He awoke to the sound of the door opening behind him. He turned to see the middle-aged Mexican man with the blond stubble and brown face enter the room. He carried a tray with a cup of coffee and egg salad sandwiches. The man set it on the table, nodded at William, turned and left the room.

Feels like you are in a bank vault, he thought, and you wait for the smooth-spoken banker to give you the key for the safe deposit box. You open it and take out whatever you came to take out and then ring the bell for the bank clerk. When you are finished the clerk enters the subdued atmosphere of bank richness and dutifully bows his head, asking you if you are through. You nod your head and he locks the two-key locks, while smiling politely, and you say goodbye and leave the bank. Just like in a bank, he thought. *Very irreverent.* But then he amended, don't compare it to a place like this.

William watched the tray, smelled the cup of coffee and suddenly he remembered... An image flashed into his head, the picture of him having coffee with the two agents of the Homeland Security Department in the lobby of the Marriott and memory pictures of what happened to him flipped through his mind... He had recognized Pavlenko back at the Marriott.

Feeling a chill, William had snapped with his built-in camera a picture of him and wondered what he was doing here? Shortly afterwards, William met the two agents of Homeland Security Department in the lobby of the Courtyard Marriott.

He remembered that he was needed at the station for further questioning. They stepped outside, climbed into a black Chevrolet with tinted windows and drove off. After a couple of freeway interchanges and a 40-minute drive, they turned onto a lonely road.

There had been almost no traffic. A few moments later, just as they had arrived at the one-story red brick house, one of the men pulled out a hypodermic needle. Grinning sardonically at William, he snarled harshly, "Relax old man, it's harmless. It will just put you to sleep for a couple of hours." Struggling to get free, the other one seated next to William pistol-whipped him, grabbed his hand and he felt the sting in his arm. Seconds later, everything plunged into darkness. After that, he found himself in a small room with attached bathroom.

He stayed at the house for a couple of days. Then, they moved him to a second place near the ocean, a secluded two-story farmhouse with green shades which was surrounded by rural landscape near the water's edge. Adjacent to the south side of the house grew an orange orchard. He was locked in another back room with white-washed walls that had been barely furnished. It contained a bed, a wood table, and two chairs.

So now I am in captivity again, William thought. Suddenly he was back in Bergen-Belsen and he could see it all in his mind, just the way it was; the same crowd of prisoners with SS overseer Krumm standing there with the clipboard in her hand, her face set and relentless, her index finger pointing and her voice saying authoritatively, "No, no! You stay, you can't go. *You must stay!*"

The image of that SS warden standing there with her outstretched arm, her middle finger pointing, ordering William's family to stay and the picture of his mother's anguished face as she begged and pleaded with the SS overseer, to let them go, kept flashing in a series of close-ups across the front of his mind.

William Wingort thought that his past was done and over with, thought that he had come to terms with his past. He couldn't have been more wrong.

Waking up in the middle of the night, soaked in sweat, his mind going in circles, without forewarning, images popped up out of his subconscious. Images like movie shots passed through his mind, pictures of women and men being forced to dig their own graves in front of German soldiers who stood ready to mow them down with tripod-mounted machine guns... The images of people standing there lined up, collapsing in the hail of bullets kept coming.

William was unable to shut out the past. How could he ever forget? Those monsters! Visions of German soldiers aiming their rifles at terrified inmates kept running through his head like a song's refrain; night after night. And now, this monster from the past has reappeared and has opened a Pandora box. It was like someone rubbing salt into the wound.

Inside the back room, filled with anxiety, William was thinking about the small pill box organizers, the medication for his heart condition he had left in his hotel room. *I need these pills badly.* The doctor's cautionary words were still ringing in his ears: *"You want to make sure not to miss the medication."*

Alarming thoughts flashed through his mind: *What if I die here?*

William had given Stettler the exact description of the medication he needed. But Stettler didn't listen. Instead, he had cold-heartedly disregarded him and had refused to give him the drugs.

Now sitting here in this miserable tiny room – like being in a prison cell –and not knowing what was going to happen next, filled him with cold fear and bitter rage. The fear was because of the unknown and the rage for being powerless. *What am I going to do now?* William thought. He felt like a stray person lost in the scorching desert searching for water. *How long will I be able to keep this up? Stettler is a stone-cold killer. I know what he's capable of doing.. How long is this going to go on? And where's the police? And where are the feds? Do they know about these two rogue agents who set me up, double-crossed and abducted me? Did Matt go to the police? Maybe he found some incriminating material and informed the police?*

William shut his eyes. *Will I survive this captivity again and get out of here in one piece?* Tied to the straight back wood chair, he watched as the door opened again and the man entered the room. He was in his late seventies, tall, long-necked and broad-hipped with a prominent chin, white hair and cold steely-blue eyes. He stood there and watched William curiously as though he was some weird creature from another planet. He closed the door behind him then pulled up the thick wooden stool and sat down across from William.

Bruno Stettler alias Lukas Pavlenko was dressed in an open-necked golf shirt, khaki shorts and loafers. He sat there silent and studied Wingort for a long moment. His eyes bored into Wingort's. "I understand that you have been checking up on me, yes?"

William did not answer. *That thug looks good for his age,* he thought. *Fit and trim. And that scar of his is still very visible. Watching him stalk into the room like a predatory animal, listening to his snarling voice and watching his dead eyes, he remembered the brutal, sadistic SS guard Pavlenko from the Nazi camp. Just look at him,* he thought. *Just look at those ice-cold hawk eyes and the way he sits there thinking he has gotten the better of me.*

Watching Stettler studying him, recalling how that monster beat his mother mercilessly, it took all of William's willpower to stay calm. A searing rage surged in him and bitter hatred filled his eyes. *If I just could attack this monster,* William thought, *and beat the crap out of him, slug him in his arrogant face and break his jaw, give back what he has done to us. But being held captive here, leaving him practically incapacitated,* William felt helpless in the power of this evil man.

After a pause Stettler took a folded sheet of paper out of his pocket and opened it. He held up the paper, shook it in front of William. "The moment," he snapped, having an evil look on his face, "I got your message and you started your little investigative job we kept a close watch on you."

William's lips curled in sick disgust. He remained silent.

Stettler fixed his cold eyes on William's face. "Your reason was what?" He waited expectantly. "There must be a reason for doing what you did."

"I remember you," William said evenly. "I remember you very well." He paused a moment. "We've met before."

"Oh?" Stettler raised his eyebrows. "We've met? And where was that?"

Looking into his eyes, William said slowly, "How about Germany?"

"Germany?" Stettler said, his eyes locking on William. "Germany? I don't quite understand. Could you be a bit more specific? Where in Germany?"

William said, "Does the name Bergen-Belsen ring any bells?"

Stettler's brow furrowed. "And when exactly was that?"

"In the 1940s," William dead-panned. "During the war."

"During the war?" Stettler said, smiling a benign smile. "In the 1940s? That must have been what?" He started ticking it off on his finger. "Let's see now, 60 years ago?" Looking at William, his smile slowly faded from his face and his eyes narrowed. "And that's why you have been snooping on me?"

"Yes," William said. He sat there in silence for a moment and glanced across at him. Something began flashing furiously in the back of William's brain. Like a green Go signal telling him to go ahead. He should tell Stettler and *who the hell cares? Expose him for all you give a good damn. Let him have it. Give it to him cold turkey.*

William looked at him steadily and said, "You were an SS guard at the camp."

"I was *what?*" Stettler blurted in mock surprise.

William gave him a look.

Stettler's face expressed a total phony, made-up disbelief.

"An SS guard," William said. "In Bergen-Belsen."

"If this is some kind of joke…" There was no shame, no moral guilt, there was nothing on his face, it was closed and stayed emotionless. Exactly like in the camps, he recalled. Exactly the same. William looked at him, at the former SS guard as he sat there, relishing his new found fiefdom.

William barely could believe it. This criminal, this murderer was sitting here on the stool right across from him in all his glory and he was not able to do anything. Could not get him arrested, could not do a thing, nothing at all. Just sit there and look at him.

And his hands were tied. A wave of disgust and rage (actually, more disgust than rage) rushed over him.

"No," Wingort shot at him. "It isn't a joke. And you know it isn't, or you wouldn't have kidnapped me and held me here all this time."

A sudden memory picture of Pavlenko standing over his mother beating her viciously with a wooden truncheon flashed into William's mind.

"I was there," William said savagely. "I know you. I saw you. Every day. I've lived it. I recall every little thing you did. And it's stored," – he tapped his temple with his second finger – "right up here." He paused again. "I wasn't looking for you. But now I've found you. Right here. In Orlando."

Stettler didn't say anything, just sat there and stared at him, his eyes shooting daggers at William. The frown on his face deepened. After a moment of silence, he said slowly, "Sixty-five years ago?" He gave his head a disconsolate shake. "*Sixty-five years ago?* And you sit here and you maintain that I was an SS guard? Ha, ha!" Stettler scoffed out loud. "Don't make me laugh!"

"*I know*," William said doggedly, "it was you."

"You *know* it was *me*?" Stettler said, eyeing him scornfully. "Well let me assure you, it definitely wasn't me you saw."

William watched the former SS man changing his roles like an actor getting on stage. From an evil, murderous, callously calculating, cold-blooded killer, he became a cheerful, uncaring, confident man, trying to hide his feelings and guilt behind a flat poker face. Stettler sat there very still for a long moment before he leaned forward. "Did you ever hear of the phrase, 'A case of mistaken Identity'?"

Matt nodded.

"Well then," Stettler said triumphantly, forcing a gleeful smile. "Your story is without any proof."

Stettler was pleased with himself, William thought. Little wonder, he thought, the man was convinced he got the drop on him.

William was persistent. "*I am the proof,*" he said stubbornly. "And," he said bluntly, "I'll talk and testify against you."

"Well," Stettler countered, raising his eyebrows at him maliciously, "it won't do you any good. It will be your word against mine." *A witness is the last thing I need right now, a survivor bringing charges against me,* he thought.

His cold blue eyes watched William closely. "Tell me, what more do you know about me that I don't know?"

William looked at him curiously. *What the heck is he talking about? His Nazi past isn't enough? What else is he hiding? Maybe he has got some other little dirty secrets that I do not know? Well, I won't say anything. Better let him guess. Better be very careful. Who knows what's going on behind the man's flat poker face? Remember the old saying: Talk is silver, silence is golden.* And William kept his mouth shut.

As Stettler sat there, the wheels in his brain started to whirl and click. And then stopped. He rose to his feet, scowled at Wingort, turned and walked out of the door.

Looking after him, panic rose in William's throat and a wave of cold terror rolled down his spine. What is it that that Nazi monster is planning to do? *I know what he's planning to do. They set me up and kidnapped me because I know too much. And they know it. They know everything that I know. Don't kid yourself, he told himself, they are a dangerous gang and they are smart as a whip and they have their eyes on you. You better watch it. That damn Lithuanian,* he thought.

It was after 11 a.m. the following morning when the four of them, Bruno Stettler, William and the two FBI men, started out the door. They headed towards a sun faded blue Pontiac Sunfire parked across the street. A northern wind was blowing hard and dark clouds streaked overhead, presaging a stormy summer day. The men climbed into the car. They closed the doors. The car went into gear. It started to move in East direction. Twenty minutes went by. Then the dark sky opened up and it began to pour, cascading down like a waterfall, beating against the windshield of the car. Taylor reached out his arm and turned on the windscreen wipers. Ten minutes later, it started to let up a little.

After driving for 50 minutes through rainy stretches of flat grasslands and pine forests, the car got off the highway and into the swamp area. Taylor continued driving down a narrow concrete road until they reached an empty parking space amongst a row of cypress trees. He pulled into a parking lot and cut the engine.

The four men got out of the car.

A steady rain began to fall again.

Stettler and agent Taylor were the last ones to exit the car.

A deep silence surrounded them, occasionally broken by a screaming bird in the trees. The former SS guard stepped forward and took Taylor back to the car where nobody could overhear them. "I want Wingort's death to look like an accident or suicide." He paused. "Okay?"

Taylor nodded. "Sure thing, boss."

Another bird, circling overhead in wide arcs, screamed.

Stettler's brows furrowed. "On second thought," he continued, "we could dispose of him in another way."

"Oh?" Taylor looked up. "How do you mean?"

"We could arrange that he disappears without a trace." Stettler let a beat pass. "At the swamps."

Then he added, "I don't want anybody to be able to identify his body."

Taylor nodded. Without saying a word, he walked over to the car, took out a cellophane bag with something white inside and held it up.

"You mean," he said, grinning viciously, "like a racket, something like a dope deal that went wrong and led to an accident."

Stettler nodded. "Yes," he said. "Exactly right. I'll handle it myself.'"

Taylor nodded his head obediently. "Okay. Whatever you say, boss."

"This will stop," Stettler reasoned, "any further police investigation." He stuck his jaw out grimly. "I don't want any cops to get involved. No Feds, and no cops." He pressed his lips together. "Under no circumstances." Then his eyes narrowing: "Understood?"

"Yes, sir."

"It's t too damn risky."

Yes, sir."

"Okay. Great."

Nodding to himself, Stettler motioned with his hand for the others to follow him. "Let's move!" he called. And to Taylor, "Let's get this over with." With the bag and a Ruger pistol in his hands, Stettler started off toward the swamps. He was followed by William and the two FBI agents. Taylor was at William's side and agent Martinez, holding a gun in front of him, was bringing up the rear. Overhead, a roaring thunder rolled through the dark sky very loudly, echoing deeply back and forth across the countryside.

William sensed that his moment of death had come. (Actually, the writing had been on the wall from the moment that he had confronted Stettler and indicated t he would testify against him. Sure as God made little green apples).

He had no fear. He was filled with an impotent rage that this former Nazi SS guard who had murdered innocent people, would continue to live and keep murdering and destroying other people's lives.

Hopefully, Matt would track this man down and exact retribution for what this former SS officer had done to so many people in the concentration camp.

Yes, he thought confidently to himself, Matt will get the man to expose himself. Matt and the feds are going to catch him and they will get even with this evil man. And take revenge. They will avenge me.

They arrived.

There was a deep and deadly silence for a long moment. Then a lightning bolt shot through the sky, followed by a loud thunderclap.

Matt drove back to Frankfurt, eager to get back to Orlando to share the information he found with Detective Garfield. Perhaps now she would believe him that his father vanished in some kind of cover up.

When Matt got back to his Frankfurt hotel, he ate an early dinner, and headed up to his room to pack. He stepped into the elevator and pressed the button for the second floor. Just as the elevator door started to close, two big, men pushed their way in.

"*Verzeihung Bitte* [excuse me please]," one man said gruffly.

Matt just nodded. He studied the faces of the two men in the half light of the elevator. One of the man was heavy-set with broad shoulders, prominent cheekbones, a grim mouth and narrow eyes. The other fellow was tall and big-shouldered with an eagle's nose and chin thrust forward murderously. Matt's pulse quickened. *I have seen them before. They must have been following me.* His gut instinct had been accurate. I didn't imagine it, he thought. Yes, they have been following me. When I went to visit the synagogue's memorial wall where names of the victims are engraved on memorial metal blocks against the wall, I became aware that I had company. When I left the building of the Arolsen Archive, I noticed these two menacing-looking characters standing there, one holding a cellphone. Later when I returned to Frankfurt, I spotted two different men loitering in the background. Apparently, Stettler had assigned a team to follow me. Yeah, that must be it.

The tall man and his heavy-set companion got off with Matt. Heading for his room, Matt sensed the two men following him. As Matt opened the door, the men behind him pushed him inside, entered the room and shut the door.

"Hey," Matt said, stopping and turning around, his heart quickening, "what the hell do you think you are doing?"

Between the two men the tall one looked the youngest.

"Shut up," the tall one said in heavily German-accented English. "Sit."

Matt clenched his jaw and stared back at the men. They are

Stettler's gang, he figured. An organization of killers. Run by Stettler. No doubt about it. He recalled seeing these two characters, the tall one and his companion leaning loafing against the wall of the building across from the synagogue smoking cigarettes. What, he wondered, should I have done? Calling them out? Challenge them without having a gun in my pocket? He was bitter and angry of having missed an opportunity. It was stupid. Stupid and foolish.

"Where is it?" the heavy-set one said.

Matt frowned at him. "What?"

"The envelope!"

Matt shrugged. "I don't know what you're talking about."

A dangerous smile was playing at the corner of the man's mouth. He pulled out a Ruger pistol. "We don't have time for this," he snapped. "Where is it?"

Matt shook his head. "You've got the wrong..."

The heavy-set one hit Matt across the face hard. "Tell us!"

Then it went *whack* and the man's fist blow to the side of Matt's head, knocking him back. A second blow sent Matt to the deep-carpeted floor, making his head ring while colored lights dance and explode in front of him like fireworks on the Fourth of July. Automatically, Matt's fist flashed out savagely, landing on the heavy-set man's knee but apparently it didn't upset him much because a vicious kick caught Matt across the ribs sending a jolt of pain through his body.

"You heard him," the man snarled.

The other one snapped, "Tell us!" and hit Matt again in the face. Then his companion kicked him in the body, a wicked, brutal kick, making him want to throw up. He got a glimpse of the one who kicked him. It was the tall, the big shouldered one. Then another vicious kick. Higher this time. Matt sat down on the floor beside the chair, blood running down his nose.

"Who are you?" mumbled Matt. They outsmarted him. Now they've got him. Should have been more careful.

"Keep him covered," the tall man said, and started to search the room. He turned Matt's suitcase upside down, scattering his clothes on the floor. He opened his laptop case, looked under the bed and in all the closets.

"Stand up!" he said harshly.

Matt stood. The man patted him down, checking his pockets. Matt watched both of them. Killers, he thought. As sure as I am standing here. They are stone-cold killers. He watched the big-shouldered man who stood beside the tall one pointing the Ruger pistol on him. Heartless killers. It was written all over their faces and everything points to that villain Stettler. Matt had no doubt about that at all. He could bet his bottom dollar on it. It was our friend Stettler who was behind everything.

"I told you," Matt said. "You got it wrong."

The man punched him in the stomach.

Matt doubled over.

"Look, Jew boy," he snarled, "give it up or you're coming with us."

Matt stood up. "Go to hell."

The big-shouldered man gripped Matt by the arm, while his partner, gun still drawn, opened the door. They pushed him out into the hall. "Walk," the man ordered harshly. "To the elevator."

Matt glanced down the hall. He realized it was a foolish thought to fight back because muscle boy here had a 9mm Ruger pointed to his head and the corridor was deserted, completely empty, just the three of them. Nothing was moving. No one stuck his head out the doorway. No cameras in sight. Nobody appeared to call for hotel security. Nothing but a stony silence.

Matt saw the sign for the elevator. He walked that way down the long hallway, looking for a way to escape. Then he saw it. A fire alarm. He stumbled toward it, as if he were still injured. Then he hit the wall and pulled the switch. Alarms went off immediately.

"Bastard," the man growled and hit Matt on the head with his pistol.

Matt fell to the ground as the men ran to the staircase and disappeared. He stood up slowly, staggered back to his room and collapsed. Moments later, he spoke to EMT Medical Services on his cell phone and gave them the address. And lay on the floor until the EMT worker found him. He bandaged Matt's face and his side, then called the hotel staff. A person came in and opened Matt's room.

I've got to get out here before they come back, he thought. Can't wait. Might be back any minute now. Better hurry up. He packed quickly and took the elevator down to the garage and went to his rental car. He retrieved the envelope from the trunk. He stuffed it in his laptop case. Then he left the keys in the glove compartment and walked out down the sunlit street to get a cab to the airport.

Avoiding the Lufthansa terminal for fear the men would turn up there, he went to Delta. He booked the first flight back to Orlando leaving the following morning. He slept in the terminal that night.

15

The flight to Orlando got in the following evening. Deciding not to go back to the same hotel, Matt took a cab to a Hilton instead. He checked in and collapsed on the bed, exhausted.

The next morning, he was in detective Garfield's office.

"Matt," she said, "are you okay?"

"Yeah, " Matt said. "Only a little jet lagged. I just got back from Germany."

She looked at him. "If you're here about your father, there's no news I'm afraid."

"Well," he said, looking back at her, "I've got some. I found information that could tie Stettler to my father's death."

She looked puzzled. "Proof of what?"

He took out the envelope. "I got this from the Holocaust archives in Germany. It proves that Stettler is in fact SS Officer Pavlenko who worked at the death camp my father was imprisoned in during World War II. He swore revenge against him and I believe that he recognized Stettler, tried to expose him. Stettler had him kidnapped and possibly killed to prevent it." He slid the envelope across her desk.

She opened it and looked at the photo of Pavlenko at the camp and his father's photo of Stettler, then read the profile. "Very impressive." She sounded excited. "Now we have justification to involve the FBI. This could blow the whole case wide open."

Matt nodded. "What's the next step?"

"I'll tell my chief and we'll contact the Orlando FBI office. They'll want to interview you."

"Good. I'm staying at the Hilton Orlando for now."

"Got it. I'll be in touch."

The next day, Matt received a call from an agent Kelly in the Orlando FBI office asking him to come down for an interview the next morning.

The office was a large, glass building set next to a small man-made lake, right off the highway. Matt drove up to the main gate. A guard stopped him.

Matt rolled down the window and said to the guard. "I've got an appointment with Agent Kelly." Matt handed him his driver's license.

The guard checked his computer. "Okay, Mr. Wingort," he said. He waved Matt in. "Front entrance is straight ahead."

After the car dropped him off, Matt entered the large lobby and checked in with the receptionist. He was issued a visitor's badge and told to wait.

After a minute a young woman came out. "Mr. Wingort?

Matt got up.

"Please follow me," she said and smiled.

Matt was ushered into a large, bright conference room and was greeted by the two FBI agents. One man was short and stocky with a strong chin and sardonic smile. The other of medium height was curly haired with a friendly and polite manner. Both were wearing dark suits, white shirts and dark ties.

The stocky one put out his hand, introducing them. "Special agent Frank Kelly. And this is Agent Harry Clark."

Matt shook hands.

They took chairs and sat down.

"We're part of a federal team investigating Hulot & Associates," Frank Kelly said. "We understand from the Orlando police that you might have some information regarding Bruno Stettler, its CEO."

Matt raised his eyebrows at them. *Investigation? Regarding Bruno Stettler?*

"What is the nature," he said, "of your investigation?"

"I'm afraid that's classified," Kelly said.

Investigation? Matt thought. Classified? Sounds intriguing. Interesting things, he thought, keeps turning up. "My information," he said, "is related to the disappearance of my father, William Wingort several months ago. He vanished under suspicious circumstances and I suspect that Mr. Stettler was connected."

The agents looked at one another.

"Please explain," Harry Clark said.

Matt told the agents about his father's kidnapping by two men, days before he disappeared. He took out the envelope with the information from the archives and the photo his father had taken. He explained about his father's memoir and the notes he'd made in his diary before he disappeared.

"We are sorry to hear that your father has disappeared," Clark said.

Frank Kelly looked at him across the table. "We received the report from the Orlando coroner's office. There seems to have been some sort of mix-up."

"Yes," said Matt, "there was. I have never seen the man before."

"He had a similar build as your father," Clark said. "He had no police record, no ID on him." He paused. "The report states that he died of natural causes."

"Well," Matt shrugged indifferently, glancing at each of them in turn, "it was not my father." He shook his head and frowned. "Anyway, why would he wander in the swamps alone? Miles away from his hotel? I believe that my father tried to see Mr. Stettler at his offices to expose his true identity and Stettler had him kidnapped and" – he looked from one to the other – "may have murdered him, after all."

"Whoa!" Kelly frowned at that. "That's a strong accusation you are throwing around."

Harry Clark turned to him. "Do you have any evidence that your father made contact with Stettler?"

Matt hesitated. "Uh... no, not exactly."

"So how do you know he was kidnapped?"

"Detective Garfield interviewed a hotel clerk who remembered my father being escorted out of the building by two men. He never returned."

Kelly made a note. Then looked up. "Is there any other evidence," he said, "of his past as a SS officer? These photos are pretty fuzzy."

Matt shook his head. "No. But it seems obvious if you look closely."

"In the course of our investigation," Clark told him, "we have checked his immigration history." Leisurely leaning back in his chair, the agent placed one foot on the other knee and said, "Mr. Stettler came to the US in the 1950s. From England. He became a citizen in 1960. We don't have any record of his birth place or life during the war."

Matt's brow furrowed. "Doesn't that seem odd, given his position as CEO of a major international company?"

Clark was thoughtful for a moment. "Yes, to some extent but records after the war are often chaotic at best. Millions of people were displaced."

Matt was getting frustrated. *Looks like I am knocking on closed doors.* He paused a moment. "I tried to see him personally but was stonewalled. Following a lead, I visited the Holocaust archives in Germany for this information. I was followed on the trip. Two thugs beat me up, looking for this information. I escaped with my life. Stettler has to be behind it."

Matt turned his head at them. The agents didn't seem to look particularly impressed. Their faces expressed total indifference and impatience.

He guessed that the FBI's priority was its own investigations and therefore quite likely he couldn't count on them. He just sat there and waited.

Harry Clark cleared his throat. "Again, we need conclusive evidence of his connection. Unless we can get the identity of these men, either in Orlando or Germany, the connection seems weak. We need to continue our investigation. We'll make copies of the photos and document. Thank you for your cooperation."

Matt looked from one to the other. "So, you're just letting him go?"

"As I said, he and his company are under federal investigation."

There was a momentary pause.

"What about my father's disappearance?"

"We will follow up with the local police," Kelly informed him. "Right now, we assume he's holding your father captive at a place somewhere. We'll get on it. Don't worry. Sooner or later, he'll screw up. Then we've got him and he'll pay for what he has done."

"Will you keep me informed?" asked Matt.

The two FBI men exchanged a silent glance. "In so far as we can." The agents stood. "If you think of anything else, Mr. Wingort, please give us a call." Kelly handed him his card. "Thanks again for coming in. Ms. Stephens will see you out."

Matt got up from his chair. *Well, there's a beaut of a problem for you there, buddy,* he thought. *Hard as a nut to crack.*

He left the building angry and without any faith in the government's efforts to take down Stettler. Matt clenched his jaw. He wasn't leaving Florida until he found out the truth.

16

After booking a one-bedroom airbnb in a quiet apartment complex for the next month, Matt checked out of the hotel, and took an Uber to this new place, deciding a car rental was too dangerous in case he was being followed.

The next day he called Detective Garfield.

She picked up on the third ring. "Garfield."

"Hi Debra, it's Matt."

"How did your meeting with the FBI go?"

"Frustrating to say the least. They didn't feel the documents were enough to expose Stettler or follow up on my father's disappearance. Apparently, they are engaged in their own investigation."

"Into what?"

"The company," Matt said. "It's classified."

"Typical."

"Yeah. I'm here for the month, staying in an airbnb in the Clement complex. I'm thinking about trying to see Stettler again."

There was a short silence on the line. "Why?"

"Maybe I can get him to show his hand."

"You're already on his radar," Debra told him. "You'll never get close. It's too dangerous."

"Maybe, but I've got to try something." He paused. "Can I ask you a favor?"

"What?"

"Could I give the documents to you for safekeeping? Just in case?"

Debra paused. "Sure. No problem. I can put them in the case file."

"Thanks. I appreciate you're trying to help. How about dinner tonight? I'll give them to you then."

"Uh… sure. I'm off at 7. Juan's is a nice, little sea food place near the station."

"It's a date. Thanks. See you then."

Matt walked into the Hulot offices. This time, when he gave his name, he was told to wait. The tall attractive woman in his father's photo of Stettler came out to greet him.

"Mr. Wingort, I'm Carol Best, vice president of communications and chief counsel. What can I do for you?"

"I'm trying to see Mr. Stettler on urgent personal business."

She nodded. "He has authorized me to deal with whatever business you need to discuss."

Matt shook his head. "Sorry," he said, "but this matter is for him only."

Best stared at him. "Mr. Wingort," she said emphatically, "this is the second time you have tried to reach Mr. Stettler. I have to warn you that it borders on harassment and if you don't disclose your business, we will take legal action."

Matt stared back at her disbelieving. Of all the gall! The temerity to threaten me with legal action. Can you believe this? Well, to tell the truth, that was good news. "I look forward to it," Matt said easily. "I'm sure my contact at the *Orlando Sentinel* would be interested what I have to say."

She looked at him evenly. "Is that a threat?"

Matt gave a dismissive shrug. "Take it as you like." *The hell with it.*

"You've been warned," said the woman. "Good day, Mr. Wingort."

At least now they know I mean business, Matt thought. *This wasn't over.*

He went outside in the sunny air and called an Uber to take him back to his place and waited.

Suddenly, a light-blue Pontiac Sunfire swerved up to the curb and screeched to a stop. A tall, lean and wiry man in a Hawaiian shirt and jeans got out of the passenger side.

"Matt Wingort?"

Matt turned. "Yeah."

The man moved closer, reached his arm behind his back and pulled out a gun. "Get in," he snarled. "Now!"

Matt started to back away.

The man grabbed Matt's arm. His other hand pointed the Glock against his neck.

"Get your hands off me!"

Matt looked around the street. No one. Nothing moved. Nothing stirred. Not a living soul was in sight.

"In the car," the man barked, "or I'll blow your head off." He put the snub-nosed .38 in his belt under his shirt and shoved Matt into the backseat and jumped in beside him. The rear door closed and the car sped away.

Moments later, special agents Clark and Kelly pulled out of a parking lot in an unmarked black SUV. They followed the Pontiac at a discreet distance.

"Finally," Clark said, "this stake paid off."

Kelly picked up the handset. The radio crackled to life. "This is unit one. Over."

"Roger," the voice came back. "Unit one."

"Possible kidnapping at the Hulot offices. The subjects are

heading east past Hillcrest Street. We'll keep the light-blue Pontiac Sunfire under surveillance. Over."

"Plate?" came back the flat, placid voice.

"8-1-6-Papa-Delta-Apple."

"Got it." A few minutes went by. "Registered to an Ida Gold for 206 Jetta. Reported stolen."

"Shit," Clark muttered. "Okay. Out." He switched off the radio and floored the accelerator.

The light-blue Pontiac Sunfire passed through the western residential part of Orlando. It moved into open country through pine forests and swampy land. Twenty minutes later, the Pontiac arrived at a small two-story, gray-painted wooden house with green shutters beside an orange orchard. It was sweltering. Some guys were guarding the house.

"Get out," the thin man said and pushed the car door open.

Matt got out.

"Move," the man said and shoved him forward.

Another man opened the front door of the farmhouse. Hawaiian shirt pushed Matt roughly inside.

Matt felt cool air. At least it's air conditioned, he thought.

"Stand still," the man said. He frisked Matt, taking his cell phone and wallet. Then nodded his head at a closed door across the hallway. "Back room."

A muscular young man took his arm and walked him down the long dim lit corridor to the door that led to a back room.

The barely furnished little room contained a bunk against the outside wall, a straight back wooden chair stationed in the center of the room, a coil of rope lying loosely on the bare board floor and wooden stool in the corner.

"Sit."

The man pulled out his cell phone and picked up the coil of rope off the floor. He started running 18 yards around Matt's neck, torso, waist and legs and bound him to the straight chair with police knots.

"He's secure," he said and walked out of the room.

Matt watched as the sun slowly went down. When I don't show

up, he thought, Debra will do something. She has to, or I'm dead. No, he told himself reassuringly, she will do something. She will find me.

At seven, detective Debra Garfield walked into Juan's. She was seated by the head waiter at a corner table. She looked around the modern art décor, glanced at the two dozen people sitting at elegant oak tables – most of them well-dressed business people – and watched the white-jacketed waiters move through tables putting down drinks.

The waitress approached her table with the menu. "Can I get you something?"

"No, thanks. I'll wait until my friend arrives."

"Very well," the waitress said and left.

Debra glanced at her watch. Nearly 7:45. She frowned. The minutes went by. The restaurant was slowly filling up.

The waitress came back to the table. "May I bring you anything, ma'am?"

Debra shook her head. "No, not yet. I am awaiting my guest here any minute now."

The place was getting crowded. Debra's frown deepened. Where was Matt? Where could he be? Was he being held up by traffic? She bit on her lower lip and thought, what could have happened? It wouldn't be the first time she was stood up by a guy. But this wasn't a date. It was work. He'd been so serious about getting the file to her. Maybe something happened at Stettler's office. Filled with a sense of unease, she reached in her pocket, took out her phone and called Matt's cell. She listened to the phone ring a dozen times before she turned it off. A few minutes later, she called Matt's cell once more. Straight to voice mail. Nothing. At eight Matt still had not appeared. Her frown deepened. She was worried. She left the restaurant and headed back to her office. She dialed her contact at traffic control.

"Traffic."

"Hi Freda. It's Debbie."

"Hey, girl. It's late. You on a case?"

"Kinda. Just got stood up by a CI."

"A guy?"

"Yep."

"Figures."

"Listen," said Debra. "I need you to pull up the footage around 2 pm on Hillcrest and Grand, in front the Hulot & Associates building."

"Okay. Give me a sec." A minute or so later. "I'm up. What are you looking for?"

"A 30-something white guy," Debra said. "Shaggy hair, not too tall, exiting or entering the building."

"Yeah. Got him. He's standing outside. Looks like he's waiting for something. Wait," Freda said quickly. "A car pulled up fast. Some guy's getting out, grabbing the young guy, pulling him into the car. Then it takes off."

Debra gasped. "What direction?"

"Looks like east."

"Plate? Model?"

"Can't see the plate. Light color. Looks like an old Ford or Pontiac sedan."

"Anything else?"

Freda paused. "A black SUV pulled away right behind. Looks like government, unmarked."

FBI, Debra thought. "Thanks, Freda. I owe you."

"I'll take lunch at Taqueria. Good luck."

"You're on." Debra hung up.

Matt was in trouble.

17

Matt desperately pulled at the cord of ropes that bound his hands and ankles. The more he pulled, the tighter the ropes got. These ropes were killing him. That guy knew his stuff. *How the hell*, he wondered, *do I get out of this hole?* He tried to move his arms and to sit up. The position was killing him. The cord between his hands and feet was causing cramps in his legs. He took a deep breath and tried to relax. The way he figured it, sooner or later, they are likely to make mistakes. Then he would beat it out of here. But tied up with ropes like a convict in in a prison cell, how could he get out of this rathole? Trust yourself. Be confident. Believe and don't give up hope. Hope is a motivation to keep going. That's the important thing. You'll get out of here. Don't worry. Just remember the psychologist's moto: Positive thinking, is half done.

And he was thinking some more... How did you actually end up here? What kind of a situation has his father gotten himself into?

He figured Stettler being involved in shady activities had complicated the investigation. Money laundering was a serious federal crime. It was a financial crime. Stettler didn't know Matt and his father had been checking him out. Had no idea. Stettler got a team of cops and federal officers right on his heels now.

Those bandits were not to be trifled with, by God. None of

them. They were a pack of ruthless, cold-blooded predators, ready to shoot and kill you. At the flip of a coin. Heads or tails. Live or die, you know. A steely look came over Matt's face. But nothing held Matt back from achieving his goal. To get his father's kidnappers behind bars. Nothing. Come hell or high water.

Well, it didn't turn out the way you thought it would; no shootout scene from some Western and no Wyatt Earp and no Doc Holliday. Just you and that former SS guard Stettler. The man had let his wild dogs out of the cage. Let them roam freely in the open country and with their heightened sense of smell easily found you. Now he turns up with his confederates, who obey whatever he tells them to do. And you don't own a firearm. Not to purchase a gun was stupid. Yes, that was definitely stupid. Now you figure it out. Things didn't turn out the way you expected. Well, he told himself, at least you spared yourself a trip to that gun shop. Now you find yourself waiting for him to show up here in this room. You didn't figure it out, did you? You didn't foresee it. No, you didn't. Not like that. It was impossible to predict what their next move will be.

Seeing in his mind a picture of Debra waiting for him in Juan's restaurant he figured she was getting pretty worried when he didn't show up, and maybe, he thought, she alerted the police chief and his men and was looking for him right now. Thinking about it made him feel good, made him feel content and at ease. It truly did.

Matt's ears perked up. He heard the sound of footsteps on the floor in the corridor outside. A moment later, the door opened. The man in Hawaiian shirt walked into the room. "Who's the chick?" he asked.

Matt frowned. "What chick?"

"Debra. She's hot for you. Called a few times in an hour. Then texted."

Matt gave a careless shrug. "Just some girl," he said dismissively, "I was supposed to have dinner with."

He laughed. "Looks that's not gonna happen."

Matt looked at him. "Why the hell am I here?"

"Damn if I know." The man shrugged.

Special agents Clark and Kelly were parked down the road from the house, keeping it in view. The two-story wooden house was set off by itself. It looked deserted. The green shades were pulled down over most windows. No other homes were visible nearby. A light breeze with the soft scent of flowers and freshly cut grass carried to them through the open window. Birds chirped in the tall oaks. Then silence all around. They sat back and waited.

Kelly moved his head. "Think he'll show?"

"Who?" Clark said. "Stettler? Maybe. He's got a lot to lose. Forensics approved the German files as authentic. The photos are a match."

"Unit one," the radio squawked. "Report in. Over."

"We're outside a house outside of Apoka." Kelly said. "Over."

"Any activity?" the voice said. "Over."

"Nothing yet," Kelly said. "Over."

"Okay. Out."

An hour or so later, a black metallic Mercedes pulled up in front of the house.

"Bingo," Clark said as two men got out followed by Stettler. The agent raised a pair of binoculars up to his eyes and trained the glasses on the three men as they walked across grassland under two rows of trees to the house and then he lowered the glasses on the leather strap.

"Unit one requests backup, asap," he said. "Over."

"On its way. Out."

"Where is he," Stettler, dressed in open-necked blue golf shirt and khaki pants, barked as he entered the house.

"Back room," one of his men said.

Matt heard footsteps approaching. Here it comes, buddy, he told himself. Here it comes. He looked up as the door opened.

Stettler walked into the room. "Mr. Wingort. I'm– "

"I know you are," Matt shot back. "You'll pay for this."

Stettler laughed. "It looks like you're the one who's going to pay – just like your father."

"You bastard," Matt shouted, struggling against his ropes. He stared across at Stettler. There was a look of sudden comprehension and impotent rage coming onto his face. Well, he thought, I'm damned. I knew it, yes, I knew it. He had known it, he had known it all along. As a matter of fact, I've known it all along. Stettler killed my father. He openly confessed it now. That SS criminal. Look at him. Look at his face. Look at that scar. He is the monster father wrote about in his journal. He is the former SS guard who caused Dad so much pain, grief and suffering. Look at those dead eyes. Holy mackerel. The man has the deadest eyes I have ever seen in a human being. And look at the sneering mouth below the broad cheek bones. A brutal face that expresses ruthless, cold contempt. He killed my father. Most likely dumped his body alongside a swamp canal, making it look like an accident.

A searing fury surged in Matt and bitter hatred filled his eyes. It took all of his willpower to stay calm. If he just could attack that monster, slug him in his arrogant face and break his jaw and give back what he did to Dad, but being held captive he felt helpless in the power of this evil man.

The door burst open and Hawaiian shirt ran in, gun drawn.

Stettler put up his hand. "I'll handle it, Frederick."

"The FBI has the files," Matt told him. "It's just a matter of time."

Stettler's eyes shot daggers at Matt, and slapped him hard across the face. "That is unfortunate," he snarled. "My lawyers will deal with it. After 60 years, even all those Jew hunters couldn't find me. There's nothing conclusive."

"Then why kill my father?" Matt's question hung in the air. Like a floating balloon.

"To avoid the unpleasant inquiries and bad press. It's not good for business."

That was all it meant to him. It's not good for business. Obviously, that was the point. A bad press mattered to the criminal more than murdering people in the camps. It was more important to him than his past. You could laugh at it, if it wasn't so unbelievable and so tragic.

Matt gave him a long, hard look. "Oh yeah? Well," he said. He felt his lips tighten. "They're looking for me right now. You can't escape."

"You mean," Stettler said, "your little girlfriend at the Orlando police?"

Matt was shocked. "How do you know– "

An evil grin danced across Stettler's coarse face. "Otto," he said coldly.

A big man came in followed by the Hawaiian shirt. He carried a cellophane bag filled with white powder.

"Untie him," Stettler ordered curtly.

The man stopped to watch Stettler. "Sir?"

"Do it!" Stettler roared.

Hawaiian shirt untied Matt and kept the gun on him.

Stettler moved closer to Matt. "You'll be found several miles from here, dead as a result of drug deal gone bad." He gave him a wicked grin. "Your little game is over."

Outside on the pavement, car doors opened. FBI men in raid jackets with FBI printed on the front and back, weapons held out in front of them, leaped out of cars. One of the agents opened fire, hitting one of the gang members who was guarding the house near the entrance. The man gasped, staggered and crumpled to the ground.

Matt heard the shouting outside. Then there was the rapid-fire noise of gunshots, going pop-pop. Then more gunshots.

He lurched forward, knocking Stettler off guard.

Hawaiian shirt raised his pistol, fired and shot Matt in the arm.

Matt fell forward on his knees.

"Dirty Kike bastard!" Stettler shouted. "Get him out of here."

"FBI!" an agent's voice shouted from the other room. "Weapons down. And on your knees."

"Idiots!" Stettler yelled. "You were followed." He moved toward the window, looking to escape.

"Stop!" agent Kelly said, bursting into the room. "Get down. On the floor."

"You're making a mistake," said Stettler. He got down on the floor. "These men lured me here."

The agent ignored him. "Cuff them all," he said. And to another agent, "Read him his rights."

The agent, charging Stettler with kidnapping and conspiracy to commit murder, impassively reeled off the routine statement: *You have the right to remain silent. Anything you say can and will be used against you in a court of law, you have the right to speak to an attorney and to have an attorney present...*"

Clark turned to Matt. "Are you okay?"

"I'm shot," Matt mumbled. Blood trickled down his arm, to the ground.

Clark nodded. He moved his head at a younger agent. "Call the EMT."

"Yes, sir," the agent said. He turned to Clark. He was a tall and heavy-shouldered man. "Already on their way, sir."

Matt was leaning his back against the wall. He was suddenly dead beat and dog tired. Just to be able, he thought, to rest a little bit. That would be nice.

As the agents led Stettler and his men to the waiting SUVs, an Orlando police car pulled up. Detective Garfield got out and walked to the house. She was wearing a black tailored suit with a white blouse underneath and her auburn hair fell loosely down on her shoulders.

"Detective Garfield," she said to the agents at the door, flashing her badge.

They let her inside.

Matt sat in the living room, a towel on his wound.

"Matt!" Debra said. Her face was white. She knelt down next to him. She gave him a long, worried look. "What happened?"

Sitting back, Matt said calmly, "Stettler kidnapped me. He confessed to my father's murder and was about to get me when the FBI showed up." He paused. "How did you…"

She reached over and patted his hand gently. "Don't worry about that now," she said. "The EMT is on the way."

Just then, the EMTs showed up.

"You'll be fine," Debra smiled. She looked across at him. "I'll see you later." She stood up then, smoothed her skirt, and left. He watched her go out. He felt a strong sense of gratitude towards her. Debra said to him she'd do whatever she can do to find out about his father. And she did.

They wheeled him out on a stretcher to the ambulance.

18

Recovering in his apartment the next day, Matt turned on the TV. The news about Stettler was the lead story.

> *Prominent CEO Bruno Stettler of Hulot & Associates was taken into custody by the FBI and local police in association with an alleged kidnapping and conspiracy to commit murder. He's been arraigned on these and a variety of other charges including fraud and money laundering. His lawyers have no comment. Currently, he is under house arrest on a one-million-dollar bail.*

"Nazi son of a bitch," Matt said out loud. He almost burst with anger. What about his father's murder and his war crimes? They need to be the part of the trial. He'd have to..." then he winced in pain. His arm was in a sling and the pain killers were wearing off. "Damn."

His phone rang.

"Matt, it's Debra. How do you feel?"

"Like shit, honestly."

"I'm sorry. I just heard that Chief Anderson and the FBI guys are holding a press conference at noon." There was a pause on the line. "I thought you'd probably want to be there. If you're feeling up to it."

"Okay. Where?"

"The municipal building 4000 South Orange in downtown Orlando. I can swing by if you need a ride?"

"That would be great. Thanks."

"See you at 11."

At noon in the conference room in the municipal building, Matt sat in the audience among the dozens of TV, newspaper and wire service reporters. This was big news.

On a stage, Chief John Anderson of the Orlando Police and Special Agent Kelly stood at the podium on the stage. Detective Garfield, Agent Clark and several other officers stood behind them.

Chief Anderson tapped the microphone to quiet the crowd. "In a joint operation between the Orlando police and the Federal Bureau of Investigation, Bruno Stettler, CEO of Hulot & Associates was arrested yesterday evening and arraigned on several criminal charges including fraud, kidnapping and conspiracy to commit murder. At present, he is under house arrest on a one-million-dollar bail. His passport has been confiscated."

"Chief, had he been under investigation?" one of the reporters asked.

Special Agent Kelly took the mike. "The FBI has had him and his business activities under surveillance for some time."

"For what?"

"A variety of alleged financial crimes."

"We understand that the arrest took place in a deserted farmhouse in the swamp outside Apoka," a reporter from the *Orlando Sentinel* said.

"Yes," Chief Anderson confirmed, "that is correct."

"Was anyone injured?"

"Yes, Mr. Matthew Wingort sustained a gunshot wound to the arm by one of Stettler's men who is also in custody."

"Was he part of the ongoing investigation?" the reporter asked.

"No. He was allegedly kidnapped by Mr. Stettler."

"Why?"

"The reason for his capture is unclear at this point in the investigation."

Wait, that's bullshit. They know the reason. Matt stood up. "What about Stettler's history as a Nazi war criminal and his role in the death of my father, William Wingort?"

There was a buzz among the reporters.

Chief Anderson took charge of the mike. "Mr. Stettler's past history is not part of this investigation and has no bearing on this case. There is no evidence of his connection to the unfortunate death of Mr. Wingort."

"Isn't it true," Matt continued, "that evidence of Stettler's past was given to the FBI?"

"Law enforcement and the District Attorney's office remained focused on the current charges. That's all."

Chief Anderson, Agent Kelly and the other officers walked off the stage.

The reporters turned to Matt. "Hey, what was that all about?" one reporter from UP asked.

"I'm Matt Wingort. Stettler kidnapped me to hide his true identity as Nazi SS officer Lukas Pavlenko in Bergen-Belsen. He had my father killed for the same reason."

"What's your proof?"

"His file is in the Arolsen Archives in the International Center on Nazi Persecution in Germany. I copied them and handed them over to the FBI."

The reporter looked at him. "What happened?"

Matt shrugged. "Nothing. They were too involved in their ongoing investigation."

Another reporter rose. "How did your father know about his true identity?"

"He was in the camp as child. He watched as Pavlenko killed and tortured dozens of Jews. His father died there."

"What happened to your father?"

"It's a long story."

A woman pushed through the crowd with her film crew. "Mr. Wingort, I'm Sally Heid from *CNN*." Would you be open to giving an in-depth interview?"

Matt nodded. "Sure. The true story needs to be told."

They exchanged cards.

"Thanks. I'll be in touch."

After a few more questions, the reporters left to file their stories. Matt walked toward the entrance.

Detective Garfield met him there. "The honchos are pissed."

"Screw them," Matt said. "Stettler's identity needs to be exposed. If they won't do it, I will."

"It will complicate their case, for sure. Especially if FBI are ignoring key evidence related to the death of your father."

"Yeah, well," Matt said, "let them deal with it. I'll do what I can to get the word out here, then head back to New York." He paused and looked at her. "But I still owe you that dinner."

She smiled. "You bet."

After Matt's interview on *CNN*, the news about Stettler's identity exploded in the news, almost eclipsing his arrest and other indictments. The archival information was published along with additional information about Bergen-Belsen and other victims. Representatives from the International Center on Nazi Persecution gave interviews. Jewish groups including the Simon Wiesenthal Center, famous for exposing escaped Nazis, petitioned for the extradition of Stettler after his trial to be tried in the International Criminal Court in the Hague for his war crimes.

Matt told the story about his father's memoir, his recognition of Pavlenko posing as Stettler and demanding clarity about the whereabouts of his father. His editor at *Vanity Fair* commissioned him to write an investigative piece. His agent arranged for the publication of his father's memoir. His father's life and legacy would finally be heard.

Matt was back in New York, frustrated that he had no evidence of his father's death. He was at his computer, putting the finishing touches on his article. He was struggling with a title. He had dozens of notes, suggestions from his editor and friends, but nothing seemed right.

One morning, his cell phone rang. It was Detective Garfield.

"Debra," Matt said. "How are *you*?"

"How are you? How's the arm?'

"It's almost healed," Matt said. "Thanks."

"Matt, have you seen today's news?"

"No, I've been busy."

"Stettler is dead."

"What?!"

There was a pause at her end.

"His lawyer found him in his home, hanging from a rafter in his bedroom. He killed himself."

Matt was silent.

"Matt, I know it's shock."

"Did he leave a note or anything?'

"Nope."

Matt took a breath and exhaled through pursed lips. "That bastard. He escaped punishment to the end."

"Maybe not. I hear that he may be tried in absentia in the Hague."

"Good. At least he won't get away with his war crimes."

"Hopefully," she said. "At least that's some semblance of justice."

"You may be right," Matt said. "Thanks for that. I appreciate the call."

"Take care of yourself." She hung up.

Matt thought about his father. His grandparents. The devastating torture in the camp. The years of personal torment lived in silence, not sharing his story with anyone. Finally, his truth could be told. The world would know now.

He thought about what Debra had said. Stettler's disgrace and cowardly suicide was not the punishment he had hoped for, but indeed was as close a semblance of justice as there could be for the misery he had caused. A bittersweet ending to the story to be sure.

A Semblance of Justice. It was the perfect title.

MEMOIR BY WOLF HOLLES

You can read the memoir written by Wolf Holles in: **Witness to the Dark. A Testimony of Survival (Gefen Publishing, 2022)**

AMSTERDAM PUBLISHERS HOLOCAUST LIBRARY

The series **Holocaust Survivor Memoirs World War II** consists of the following autobiographies of survivors:

Outcry. Holocaust Memoirs, by Manny Steinberg

Hank Brodt Holocaust Memoirs. A Candle and a Promise, by Deborah Donnelly

The Dead Years. Holocaust Memoirs, by Joseph Schupack

Rescued from the Ashes. The Diary of Leokadia Schmidt, Survivor of the Warsaw Ghetto, by Leokadia Schmidt

My Lvov. Holocaust Memoir of a twelve-year-old Girl, by Janina Hescheles

Remembering Ravensbrück. From Holocaust to Healing, by Natalie Hess

Wolf. A Story of Hate, by Zeev Scheinwald with Ella Scheinwald

Save my Children. An Astonishing Tale of Survival and its Unlikely Hero, by Leon Kleiner with Edwin Stepp

Holocaust Memoirs of a Bergen-Belsen Survivor & Classmate of Anne Frank, by Nanette Blitz Konig

Defiant German - Defiant Jew. A Holocaust Memoir from inside the Third Reich, by Walter Leopold with Les Leopold

In a Land of Forest and Darkness. The Holocaust Story of two Jewish Partisans, by Sara Lustigman Omelinski

Holocaust Memories. Annihilation and Survival in Slovakia, by Paul Davidovits

From Auschwitz with Love. The Inspiring Memoir of Two Sisters' Survival, Devotion and Triumph Told by Manci Grunberger Beran & Ruth Grunberger Mermelstein, by Daniel Seymour

Remetz. Resistance Fighter and Survivor of the Warsaw Ghetto, by Jan Yohay Remetz

My March Through Hell. A Young Girl's Terrifying Journey to Survival, by Halina Kleiner with Edwin Stepp

Roman's Journey, by Roman Halter

Beyond Borders. Escaping the Holocaust and Fighting the Nazis. 1938-1948, by Rudi Haymann

The Engineers. A memoir of survival through World War II in Poland and Hungary, by Henry Reiss

A Spark of Hope. An Autobiography, by Luba Wrobel Goldberg

The series **Holocaust Survivor True Stories** consists of the following biographies:

Among the Reeds. The true story of how a family survived the Holocaust, by Tammy Bottner

A Holocaust Memoir of Love & Resilience. Mama's Survival from Lithuania to America, by Ettie Zilber

Living among the Dead. My Grandmother's Holocaust Survival Story of Love and Strength, by Adena Bernstein Astrowsky

Heart Songs. A Holocaust Memoir, by Barbara Gilford

Shoes of the Shoah. The Tomorrow of Yesterday, by Dorothy Pierce

Hidden in Berlin. A Holocaust Memoir, by Evelyn Joseph Grossman

Separated Together. The Incredible True WWII Story of Soulmates Stranded an Ocean Apart, by Kenneth P. Price, Ph.D.

The Man Across the River. The incredible story of one man's will to survive the Holocaust, by Zvi Wiesenfeld

If Anyone Calls, Tell Them I Died. A Memoir, by Emanuel (Manu) Rosen

The House on Thrömerstrasse. A Story of Rebirth and Renewal in the Wake of the Holocaust, by Ron Vincent

Dancing with my Father. His hidden past. Her quest for truth. How Nazi Vienna shaped a family's identity, by Jo Sorochinsky

The Story Keeper. Weaving the Threads of Time and Memory - A Memoir, by Fred Feldman

Krisia's Silence. The Girl who was not on Schindler's List, by Ronny Hein

Defying Death on the Danube. A Holocaust Survival Story, by Debbie J. Callahan with Henry Stern

A Doorway to Heroism. A decorated German-Jewish Soldier who became an American Hero, by Rabbi W. Jack Romberg

The Shoemaker's Son. The Life of a Holocaust Resister, by Laura Beth Bakst

The Redhead of Auschwitz. A True Story, by Nechama Birnbaum

Land of Many Bridges. My Father's Story, by Bela Ruth Samuel Tenenholtz

Creating Beauty from the Abyss. The Amazing Story of Sam Herciger, Auschwitz Survivor and Artist, by Lesley Ann Richardson

On Sunny Days We Sang. A Holocaust Story of Survival and Resilience, by Jeannette Grunhaus de Gelman

Painful Joy. A Holocaust Family Memoir, by Max J. Friedman

I Give You My Heart. A True Story of Courage and Survival, by Wendy Holden

In the Time of Madmen, by Mark A. Prelas

Monsters and Miracles. Horror, Heroes and the Holocaust, by Ira Wesley Kitmacher

Flower of Vlora. Growing up Jewish in Communist Albania, by Anna Kohen

Aftermath: Coming of Age on Three Continents. A Memoir, by Annette Libeskind Berkovits

Not a real Enemy. The True Story of a Hungarian Jewish Man's Fight for Freedom, by Robert Wolf

Zaidy's War. Four Armies, Three Continents, Two Brothers. One Man's Impossible Story of Endurance, by Martin Bodek

The Glassmaker's Son. Looking for the World my Father left behind in Nazi Germany, by Peter Kupfer

The Apprentice of Buchenwald. The True Story of the Teenage Boy Who Sabotaged Hitler's War Machine, by Oren Schneider

Good for a Single Journey, by Helen Joyce

Burying the Ghosts. She escaped Nazi Germany only to have her life torn apart by the woman she saved from the camps: her mother, by Sonia Case

American Wolf. From Nazi Refugee to American Spy. A True Story, by Audrey Birnbaum

Bipolar Refugee. A Saga of Survival and Resilience, by Peter Wiesner

In the Wake of Madness. My Family's Escape from the Nazis, by Bettie Lennett Denny

Before the Beginning and After the End, by Hymie Anisman

I Will Give Them an Everlasting Name. Jacksonville's Stories of the Holocaust, by Samuel Cox

The series **Jewish Children in the Holocaust** consists of the following
autobiographies of Jewish children
hidden during WWII in the Netherlands:

Searching for Home. The Impact of WWII on a Hidden Child,
by Joseph Gosler

Sounds from Silence. Reflections of a Child Holocaust Survivor,
Psychiatrist and Teacher, by Robert Krell

Sabine's Odyssey. A Hidden Child and her Dutch Rescuers,
by Agnes Schipper

The Journey of a Hidden Child, by Harry Pila and Robin Black

The series **New Jewish Fiction** consists of the following novels, written by Jewish authors. All novels are set in the time during or after the Holocaust.

The Corset Maker. A Novel, by Annette Libeskind Berkovits

Escaping the Whale. The Holocaust is over. But is it ever over for the next generation? by Ruth Rotkowitz

When the Music Stopped. Willy Rosen's Holocaust, by Casey Hayes

Hands of Gold. One Man's Quest to Find the Silver Lining in Misfortune, by Roni Robbins

The Girl Who Counted Numbers. A Novel, by Roslyn Bernstein

There was a garden in Nuremberg. A Novel, by Navina Michal Clemerson

The Butterfly and the Axe, by Omer Bartov

To Live Another Day. A Novel, by Elizabeth Rosenberg

A Worthy Life. Based on a True Story, by Dahlia Moore

The Right to Happiness. After all they went through. Stories, by Helen Schary Motro

The series **Holocaust Heritage** consists of the following memoirs by 2G:

The Cello Still Sings. A Generational Story of the Holocaust and of the Transformative Power of Music, by Janet Horvath

The Fire and the Bonfire. A Journey into Memory, by Ardyn Halter

The Silk Factory: Finding Threads of My Family's True Holocaust Story, by Michael Hickins

Winter Light. The Memoir of a Child of Holocaust Survivors, by Grace Feuerverger

Hiding in Holland. A Resistance Memoir, by Shulamit Reinharz

Stumbling Stones, by Joanna Rosenthall

The Unspeakable, by Nicola Hanefeld

Hidden in Plain Sight. A Journey into Memory and Place, by Julie Brill

The series **Holocaust Books for Young Adults** consists of the following novels, based on true stories:

The Boy behind the Door. How Salomon Kool Escaped the Nazis. Inspired by a True Story, by David Tabatsky

Running for Shelter. A True Story, by Suzette Sheft

The Precious Few. An Inspirational Saga of Courage based on True Stories, by David Twain with Art Twain

The Sun will Shine on You again one Day, by Cynthia Monsour

The series **WWII Historical Fiction** consists of the following novels, some of which are based on true stories:

Mendelevski's Box. A Heartwarming and Heartbreaking Jewish Survivor's Story, by Roger Swindells

A Quiet Genocide. The Untold Holocaust of Disabled Children in WWII Germany, by Glenn Bryant

The Knife-Edge Path, by Patrick T. Leahy

Brave Face. The Inspiring WWII Memoir of a Dutch/German Child, by I. Caroline Crocker and Meta A. Evenbly

When We Had Wings. The Gripping Story of an Orphan in Janusz Korczak's Orphanage. A Historical Novel, by Tami Shem-Tov

Jacob's Courage. Romance and Survival amidst the Horrors of War, by Charles S. Weinblatt

A Semblance of Justice. Based on true Holocaust experiences, by Wolf Holles

Dark Shadows Hover, by Jordan Steven Sher

Amsterdam Publishers Newsletter

Subscribe to our Newsletter by selecting the menu at the top (right) of **amsterdampublishers.com** or scan the QR-code below.

Receive a variety of content such as:

- A welcome message by the founder
- Free Holocaust memoirs
- Book recommendations
- News about upcoming releases
- Chance to become an AP Reviewer.

www.ingramcontent.com/pod-product-compliance
Lightning Source LLC
LaVergne TN
LVHW041914070526
838199LV00051BA/2609